OVERLORD

Volume 16: The Half-Elf Demigod PART II

Kugane Maruyama | Illustration by so-bin

NEW YORK

OVERLORD

VOLUME 16

KUGANE MARUYAMA

Translation by Andrew Cunningham
Cover art by so-bin

OVERLORD Vol.16 HALF ELF NO SHINJIN GE
©Kugane Maruyama 2022
First published in Japan in 2022 by KADOKAWA CORPORATION, Tokyo.
English translation rights arranged with KADOKAWA CORPORATION, Tokyo,
through Tuttle-Mori Agency, Inc., Tokyo.

Yen On
150 West 30th Street, 19th Floor
New York, NY 10001

Visit us at yenpress.com
facebook.com/yenpress
twitter.com/yenpress
yenpress.tumblr.com
instagram.com/yenpress

First Yen On Edition: July 2023
Edited by Yen On Editorial: Ivan Liang
Designed by Yen Press Design: Liz Parlett, Wendy Chan

Yen On is an imprint of Yen Press, LLC.
The Yen On name and logo are trademarks of Yen Press, LLC.

Library of Congress Cataloging-in-Publication Data
Names: Maruyama, Kugane, author. | So-bin, illustrator. | Balistrieri, Emily, translator. |
Cunningham, Andrew, translator.
Title: Overlord / Kugane Maruyama ; illustration by So-bin ; translation by Emily Balistrieri ; translation
by Andrew Cunningham.
Other titles: Ōbārōdo. English
Description: First Yen On edition. | New York, NY : Yen On, 2016–
Identifiers: LCCN 2016000142 | ISBN 9780316272247 (v. 1 : hardback) |
ISBN 9780316363914 (v. 2 : hardback) | ISBN 9780316363938 (v. 3 : hardback) |
ISBN 9780316397599 (v. 4 : hardback) | ISBN 9780316397612 (v. 5 : hardback) |
ISBN 9780316398794 (v. 6 : hardback) | ISBN 9780316398817 (v. 7 : hardback) |
ISBN 9780316398848 (v. 8 : hardback) | ISBN 9780316398862 (v. 9 : hardback) |
ISBN 9780316444989 (v. 10 : hardback) | ISBN 9780316445016 (v. 11 : hardback) |
ISBN 9780316445016 (v. 12 : hardback) | ISBN 9781975311537 (v. 13 : hardback) |
ISBN 9781975323806 (v. 14 : hardback) | ISBN 9781975360566 (v. 15 : hardback) |
ISBN 9781975367800 (v. 16 : hardback)
Subjects: LCSH: Alternate reality games—Fiction. | Internet games—Fiction. | Science fiction. |
BISAC: FICTION / Science Fiction / Adventure.
Classification: LCC PL873.A37 O2313 2016 | DDC 895.63/6—dc23
LC record available at http://lccn.loc.gov/2016000142

ISBNs: 978-1-9753-6780-0 (hardcover)
978-1-9753-6781-7 (ebook)

10 9 8 7 6 5 4 3 2 1

LSC-C

Contents

OVERLORD

Chapter 4   **Life in the Village**

Chapter 4 | Life in the Village

1

Ainz and Mare were heading toward the dark elf village on foot.

Instead of his usual gear, Mare was wearing clothes Ainz had provided that made him look like a boy. These matched the set that Aura was currently wearing, and there were no data crystals in them—so no magical properties. They were just for looks.

In this world, equipment sizes auto-adjusted only if the equipment itself was magical. Still, this outfit was from *Yggdrasil* and fit Mare to a T. At the same time, it provided far less defense than he was accustomed to, and he would have to be careful in combat.

Initially, Ainz had planned for the twins to wear something else.

They'd told him BubblingTeapot had prepared all kinds of gear for them besides what they typically wore.

But when he'd asked if any of these outfits were suited for this place and purpose—in other words, if they could disguise their true identities and abilities—both were forced to shake their heads. Almost all their alternate costumes, like Aura's mascot armor or Mare's dress armor, seemed excessively decorative to Ainz, so he dug up something more ordinary for them.

Ultimately, this was his operation, so it was only natural he provided the necessary supplies.

But the three of them weren't dressed exactly alike. Ainz and Mare differed from Aura in one noticeable way.

Specifically, the lower half of their faces were covered in cloth, like a mask. Their heads were covered as well, down to the brows, leaving only their eyes exposed.

This might have been a little warm for Mare, but he'd have to put up with it—the mask was a necessary part of Ainz's disguise.

Aura was waiting for them at the village entrance...or at least that's what it seemed like. There was no clear demarcation. She hadn't spotted them on the approach or been in the area by chance—he'd sent a Message and asked her to meet them here.

She was accompanied by her devotees. Elves spent most of their lives in the trees, so it was rare for them to descend to the ground like this. Even close to the village, the surface was dangerous. The fact that they had come anyway was a clear sign they trusted her strength, or simply wanted to be with the object of their faith.

The rest of the dark elves were watching from above, on a bridge among the trees. Though the whispers were audible, it was too far for him to hear. Still, it was safe to assume the newcomers were the topic on everyone's lips.

"U-Uncle! Mare!" Aura called. She acted a bit embarrassed but made sure her voice was loud enough for everyone to hear.

She waved, and Ainz responded with a smile.

Ainz thought the stutter was unnecessary, but Aura might take it to heart if he cracked a joke about it.

"Oh, Aura! We made it!"

Ainz made his voice sound cheery. He unshouldered his baggage and set it down, waving her over. Then he patted the back of the boy next to him.

"R-right!" Mare said, waving. He whispered Aura's name, too, but not loud enough for anyone to hear.

Of course, volume was not a major concern. The primary goal was to ensure everyone knew Aura's uncle and brother had arrived. They looked like family even without all the waving, but it didn't hurt to drive the point home.

The dark elves watched over them in silence as Ainz approached her.

"Um, so. Let me show you around, U-Uncle."

Aura's smile was a bit strained. Half at a loss, half nervous. Ainz smiled, feeling like this new side of her was extra cute. He fought off the urge to rub her head—but that emotion quickly ebbed away.

"I... Mm."

His voice had sounded a mite too indifferent, so he cleared his throat and tried again.

"I must thank the villagers for their hospitality. Tell me, Aura, have they provided you a place to stay?"

Aura nodded.

"Then why don't you take Mare there? I'll be along shortly."

"Yes, si— Sorry, I mean, um. Sure?"

They were playing it like she was his niece.

There had actually been a long conversation about whether he was BubblingTeapot's older or younger brother, and if the latter, whether he was older or younger than Peroroncino. They'd concluded he was younger than both.

This required a bit of a performance on Aura's part, but she still seemed unsure how to act around him. Since he'd sent her in ahead, she hadn't had time to adjust to the role. It must have been a challenge figuring out how her character talked.

"Ha-ha-ha! Go, Aura, take Mare with you. It wasn't an especially long journey, but he could use the rest."

"R-right! Understood!"

Aura must have come to some sort of resolution, because she responded with enthusiasm. Perhaps a bit forced still.

The twins took their leave, and Ainz watched them go for a moment before turning to the dark elves nearby.

There were quite a few of them.

The elders were not among them, but a good half of the village was present. A few children stood among them. Aura's good deeds helped ensure there was no hostility or suspicion. But they were certainly studying him quite intently, trying to determine what kind of man this stranger was.

Especially Aura's devotees.

That was unexpected.

Though he ostensibly had the duty of escorting Mare, he was still the sort of uncle who'd send a child out ahead. That would certainly make anyone with common sense give him a good hard look.

So if these looks of suspicion had come from ordinary elves rather than Aura's followers, Ainz wouldn't have given it a second thought.

But these people were different.

Aura's followers believed skill trumped age and experience. They seemed more likely to agree with the logic of sending a supremely talented ranger out ahead.

Which meant…

There must be another reason.

Ainz pondered this for a moment and found a likely explanation. *Oh, perhaps they're worrying some idiot grown-up is exploiting her exceptional abilities. That would explain it. Hmm. They're not entirely wrong, which is galling. Oh, I'd better get started.*

There were many eyes on him now. It would be a bad idea to waste more of their time. He couldn't afford to let their curiosity fade.

It's been a while.

Ainz felt a bit tense. He wondered if lecturing professors or stage actors ever got used to this sea of stares. He had his remarks prepared and sold that with a cheery tone, speaking to the audience in the trees above.

"First——"

Ainz removed the cloth covering his mouth, showing them the features beneath.

He smiled, then covered himself up again.

"——I'm afraid my tribe's beliefs require males to keep their faces hidden. Even if this village—or your people—find that rude, I ask that you keep an open mind."

No one sounded particularly offended. His attire had been deemed acceptable.

This was all a lie, of course.

Ainz was wearing a rubber mask and had cast an illusion on top of that to fabricate a face, much like he did as Momon. However, the illusion was not a particularly good one, and under close observation, a ranger's heightened perception might see through it. To avoid that, he was minimizing facial exposure.

He hoped his eyes alone would not be enough to reveal the deception.

"A pleasure to meet you all. You've already met my niece, Aura—and you may have heard my name from her. I'm Ain Bell Fior."

The three of them had put their heads together to come up with this pseudonym. The final product was almost entirely the twins' creation.

"I have brought a few small gifts. Is there a table I can borrow?"

A tree nearby began to writhe, and a plank wide enough to unpack his things grew out. Someone in the crowd had cast a spell.

"Thank you," Ainz said, moving his baggage from the ground to the table. "I can't guarantee you'll like these, but I do hope you'll accept them."

Ainz had spent quite a lot of time thinking about what gifts to bring.

Remembering how much the elves in Nazarick had enjoyed the food, he'd initially considered seasonings—perhaps salt. Even Ainz knew salt was vital to good cooking.

His initial plan was to bring a lump of rock salt. Then he realized that just because humans needed salt didn't mean dark elves necessarily did.

Even if they did, perhaps they could get by with a lot less salt than humans. In which case, the gift might not be appreciated.

From what Ainz had seen during his stealthy observations, no one in this village was using anything resembling salt when they cooked. He'd also never seen them making anything resembling preserved meats. Likely because they had magic that could prevent rotting.

He had wondered if it was simply a rare resource and used sparingly, but that didn't appear to be the case.

Even with Perfect Unknowable, he couldn't exactly rifle through the larder looking for stores of salt.

Given how the hunters didn't like to waste their kill's blood, perhaps they were like carnivores that obtained their sodium from blood.

Incidentally, the E-Rantel area had no significant salt deposits or salt water, so their supply was generated by casters specializing in daily-life magic. This was supplemented with imports from the neighboring kingdom or Empire. For that reason, salt prices had briefly soared after Ainz's occupation, but they'd long since gone back to normal.

Ainz had only a vague recollection of this; perhaps he'd read some paperwork on the subject. Albedo had likely taken care of things.

Either way, he'd decided against the salt strategy.

Instead, he'd brought—

"Metal blades made by dwarves. Impressive, aren't they? I've heard you use wood dramatically hardened with magic, but I doubt that makes them harder than metal. These were crafted by an especially skilled blacksmith. Top-class wares."

First out of his rucksack was a long, thin wooden box that held a carving knife inside. It was followed by more containing arrowheads and steak knives.

These were samples. The hope was this display would help bring outside currency to the dwarves, as part of the Nation of Darkness economic bloc.

Naturally, even if this village became customers, their economy was self-sufficient and they had no coin to spend. He would need to devise some means for the village to generate cash to spend, but Ainz believed with the Nation as an intermediary, they'd be able to incorporate villages like these into a cohesive financial ecosystem.

The only potential issue was that he'd yet to consult with Albedo on the idea.

I'm an idiot, so I doubt my plans will go off without a hitch, but we don't really stand to lose anything…I don't think?

If his plan failed, no one would ever have to find out. If it succeeded, well, he hoped that might impress a few people. Ainz was trying to not dwell on the results. The worst-case scenario was him getting his hopes up and then blowing it. That would really hurt.

If they're not interested, that's fine. This is simply me being generous, so if they don't care for them, then we can just say that's a shame and be done with it. But it looks like I don't need to worry.

The eyes around him were gleaming. The dark elf serving as hunt master stepped forward.

"May I take a closer look?"

"By all means. Handle them yourself."

He moved over to Ainz, reaching first for the arrowheads. That was the expected choice. If a hunter had reached for a carving knife instead, that would have been far more surprising.

"Very impressive. I've heard the dwarves live in mountains, but I had no idea they were such fine craftsmen. This must be supremely valuable. How would one trade for something like this?"

Ah, just what I expected.

Pro salesman Satoru Suzuki was starting to smirk.

He'd successfully anticipated his client's needs.

Prior to the rise of tensions between the elf capital and the Theocracy, they *had* traded with humans; some of them still regularly used coins. Of course, that economic activity had not extended to this remote village. Non-elf traders would never pay them a visit. For that reason, everything was done via bartering. And just as predicted, high-quality unusual wares were more than welcome.

"These are meant to be gifts, so there's no need to trade anything for them. You may distribute them as you see fit."

The hunt master had been testing the edge of the arrowhead, and he made a face.

"Your niece, Fiora, has already done so much for us. Accepting these without giving anything in return..."

"No, no, they're but a trifle, a symbol of friendship and gratitude. But if we were to trade...I also have some magic items made using a fantastic dwarven craft they call *runes*."

The gleam in the man's eyes grew even stronger.

"Runes, you say? Magic items?"

"Yes, rune crafts. I use them myself, but if you're interested, I could trade them for the right offer. Some claim these are but the most basic items, but I'm still disinclined to offer anything magical for free. They didn't exactly come cheap."

Low prices drew crowds, but going too far would just create a consumer base that refused to pay more.

If the dwarves themselves chose to do that, it was one thing, but it was hardly Ainz's place to decide that on his own. The ideal would be to sell quality goods for a high price. Unfortunately, this village had nothing Ainz himself desired—or at least, not that he was aware of.

Honestly, the whole rune business hasn't produced much of worth. We're not seeing much demand for them. But it seems too soon to shut them down just because they aren't profitable right away. Better give these things a century or two to develop.

"Still, with as many druids as you have, they may not be necessary."

Ainz pulled a metal rod from his coat. He'd planned to show it off like this and had practiced taking it out smoothly.

"This simply produces a small flame at the tip. It's more useful for starting fires than as a light source. Let go of it and the flame goes out, like so."

He was relieved this did not immediately generate disappointment.

"I have a few other items, but those can wait till later. For now, I'd rather join the children in their lodgings and recover from my journey."

The dark elves around all nodded.

They rarely left the village but were well aware of the local dangers and knew anyone who had braved them would need rest.

"I'm sure you're tired, but may we ask two more things before you retire?"

"Yes, go ahead."

These questions came from a man named Plum, one of Aura's true believers.

Ainz straightened his collar. If he said the wrong thing here, this man might turn against him. But if he got it right, he'd make a powerful ally.

"First, do you maybe have elf blood in you?"

"Hey, don't—" The hunt master tried to cut in, but Ainz waved him off.

"It's fine. I've heard nothing of the sort. Do I look like I do?"

"Uh, no, if that's not the case, forget I said anything. It was just a vague impression."

"I see."

Perceptive.

Exceedingly so.

Ainz had modeled this face on an elf he'd seen in the capital but adjusted the skin tone to match the dark elves. He'd thought the result perfect, and Mare hadn't noticed anything amiss, but to the eyes of a pure-bred dark elf, the facial features must have appeared slightly off.

"Well, my parents never mentioned anything, but if you got that impression, perhaps there's an elf somewhere a few generations back. What else?"

"Lady Fiora's ranger abilities are truly remarkable. Does that run in the family?"

Calling her Lady even when talking to her uncle? That's certainly dedicated.

Weirdly impressed, Ainz briefly debated calling him out on it. Or was it best left unmentioned?

He couldn't figure out which approach to take, so he decided to answer the question first.

"No, I never had her knack for ranger skills. But I'm confident in my abilities as a first-class wizard."

"...A wiz...ard?"

"Yes, a wizard."

Plum's eyes got real shifty.

Oh, he doesn't know what that is. Is that a thing? I suppose wizards are technically people who control magic through acquired knowledge. In a place with no formal education system, their very existence might be unknown. In which case, I suppose it's not that surprising?

He wasn't convinced, but the evidence stood before him.

"Um, an arcane caster."

"Arcane... Ah. Okay. That's really something! You're not Lady Fiora's uncle for nothing."

Clearly he still didn't understand, but since it sounded impressive, he'd settled for general compliments. Good enough. Ainz got a lot of effusive praise back in Nazarick, so this sort of lukewarm lip service was rather refreshing.

"Uh, I guess that wasn't explanation enough. Wizards are a class that can use magic, like druids."

"Oh! I see. So you make food and things?"

"Huh? Uh, no, sorry. I…believe there *are* wizards who do that, but sadly, I'm unable to. I suppose you could say my magic is focused on defeating enemies."

He'd heard of people using daily-life magic to make spices or seasonings, and perhaps higher levels of that could make primary foodstuffs.

Fundamentally, Ainz didn't mind if people decided he was useless. He didn't think he was particularly noteworthy to begin with, and if people underestimated or looked down on him, that could be taken advantage of. Ordinarily, he would accept that label with a smile.

But here, he was Aura's uncle and had to avoid a bad reputation at all costs. He was here in BubblingTeapot's stead.

"Enemies…interesting. Does that mean you can work as a hunter? That settles it. Definitely Lady Fiora's relative!"

Ainz wasn't sure what to make of that. This man was an actual hunter by trade, after all.

Perhaps in this village, the hunters were the ones who handled external threats, but that was hardly all they did. Their primary role was to bring food back from excursions into the dangerous forest. If the mere act of felling enemies justified the hunter label, this village would be filled with warriors trampling around in full plate.

But Ainz wasn't a hunter, and he wasn't well versed in the village's culture. Arguing the point would be seen as odd and possibly ruffle feathers.

Aura and Mare would be spending some time here, so Ainz had to be careful not to rock the boat. If his presence soured things, he didn't know how he would ever make it up to them. Aura would almost certainly say she didn't mind and mean it, but still.

Explaining properly and getting verbal confirmation was the ideal. He didn't want it coming back to haunt him later. Plus, Aura and Mare were listening closely to everything he said here. If he made a stupid mistake, Nazarick's top minds would read too deeply into it and say, *Brilliant!* but the children had a tendency to innocently ask, *Why'd you do that? Can you explain it to us?* which was a terrifying thought. The last thing he wanted to do was bust out the "figure it out yourself" card on them.

While he silently worried about these things, Plum seemed to have arrived at some private conclusion and nodded.

"Very impressive. As expected!"

Ainz was once again unsure what this man was impressed by but decided that all's well that ends well. After all, things certainly seemed to be going his way. And on that note...

"I've never worked as a hunter, so I can't say for sure. But if this village's hunters think I can handle it, then that's a relief." He shifted all responsibility onto them. "Aura's been helping with the hunts, I assume? But I'd be glad to take over for her. That would give the two of them some time to play."

Plum looked genuinely stunned. Ainz didn't think he'd said anything particularly outlandish. Even after reviewing what he'd said, he still couldn't figure it out.

"These kids grew up in the city, so I brought them out here to let them see what village life is like. I thought they'd enjoy seeing how children play in a place like this. Give them a chance to try their hand at the sorts of things they can't do in the city."

"Aha. I suppose city and village life are pretty different." The hunt master nodded.

It was a mystery what the man was picturing, but Ainz couldn't possibly be expected to keep up with every leap of imagination. He might be stretching the truth a bit, but nothing he said had been a total fabrication. Whatever issues that cropped up later could be handled then.

"Can I ask a question, too?"

This speaker was a ranger on the bridge above. Handsome features—like basically all elves—but this one definitely seemed *cool*.

"Certainly, certainly."

Ainz was less than thrilled and would've preferred not to entertain more queries, but he couldn't exactly openly say that.

The man dithered a long moment, then said, "Is Fiora engaged?"

Ainz came incredibly close to making a weird noise but managed to stop himself. This was the last question he'd expected.

What's this dude thinking? What possessed him to ask that? Ainz looked around and found everyone else looking equally aghast.

…Okay, I'm not the only one who thought he just blurted out something weird, then. But why would he care if Aura was engaged? Does he want to know if she's got someone waiting for her back in the city? Heh. Guess that explains it.

Ainz was sure he'd figured out the purpose of that strange question. Nothing else made sense.

They must want to bring her blood into the village.

A glance at the village kids confirmed there were several boys.

Maybe one of them is his kid? It's so hard to tell how old dark elves are by looking at them. But, man, marriage? That wasn't part of the plan… If Aura finds someone she likes, I suppose I'm fine with it? I'm BubblingTeapot's proxy, so I'll have to give any suitors a thorough vetting. Uh-oh, too much thinking. Do I lie here? Tell the truth? Make up your mind, man.

This wasn't really worth thinking about. There was no downside to revealing the truth, but if he did lie, that would likely force him into more deception down the line.

"…No, not at the moment."

"Aha."

The dark elf looked relieved.

If he's playing matchmaker for his kid, that's some serious hands-on parenting. Not ideal. She's here to make friends. If this guy gets pushy with his own kid and scares off the others, that'll be a real hassle. I need to know more.

"…Um…what's your name?"

The man snapped back to attention.

"Blueberry Egnia."

Ainz couldn't help but notice a pattern. Like this Plum fellow, perhaps it was a hallmark of dark elf culture to name people after foods. If that was true, perhaps he should have come up with a fake name for Aura. He'd initially avoided that because he thought it would be weird to have a friend not even know your real name. Adding murk to the mire was another question: Were they naming these fruits according to cadences of this world's language and that was reaching Ainz's ears via auto-translation, or were they simply calling themselves these things, unaware of what any of it meant? In other words, might this be the sign of a player in the past? It was impossible to tell.

"I'll remember that. Blueberry Egnia, yes?"

"That's right. Thank you for remembering it."

Why thank someone for that?

Ainz opened his mouth to ask, but a stir ran through the dark elves.

The cause was clear. Following their gaze, he spotted the approaching elders.

"About time," he heard someone whisper.

Ainz sighed internally. Tensions had clearly not eased.

Have I been to any business that would let an outsider hear them complaining? Even if they grumbled, no one would openly bash a colleague, I don't think. Should I really be leaving Aura in a place like this? Or is it safe to assume kids won't be involved? Still…they hear what their parents say, and there's no telling what the kids will take away from that or what it'll make them do. I guess I've just gotta handle my own side of things and make sure it doesn't cause trouble for Aura and Mare.

He could see where this might lead, but Ainz didn't want to get mixed up in local disputes. His goal was to maintain a degree of independence and freedom.

He'd have to handle this well. In other words…

Just hope my simulations pay off!

As Ainz steeled himself, the elders drew near, ignoring the sharp looks they earned. One began to speak.

"You hail from the same flow as the sapling Fiora. Well met, voyager from afar."

Sapling? Right, just as I expected.

Ainz suppressed a smirk.

Dark elf idioms. In this new world, the languages of all species were automatically translated into words Ainz could understand. If the word *sapling* remained as is, then it had no real meaning. If it meant anything specific—boy or girl, for example—then Ainz would hear that word instead. In other words, the dark elves simply had a custom of placing the word *sapling* before a child's name.

They'd brought out these phrases to test how much an adult city dark elf knew.

Here in the village, the elders' faction placed great stock in tradition, while the younger crowd was trying to break away from their way of life. Aura had reported on this, and Ainz himself had eavesdropped on conversations about it. The elders were here to figure out where Ainz—and by extension, the city dark elves—stood on matters of tradition.

I'd prefer to play both sides. But a careless word here will force me onto one side or the other. If I'm gonna join a faction, it'd be easier for Aura and Mare to make friends if the kids' parents like me. That means the younger faction is probably a better choice. Still, we don't have solid evidence to support that. We need to know more. I'll just say something that sounds decent and act like that's how we greet people. Smoke and mirrors.

He'd prepared some lines for just this eventuality.

"The earth may be the same, but we hail from separate forests. I am grateful those who live here were willing to accept us."

Ainz hadn't put much thought into these phrases. He was just going with the flow. But this seemed to make a positive impression.

"The sawtooth and evergreen oaks are equally hard, and each grow with equal might. I am pleased. The more trees grow, the more the forest changes."

Ainz let the words flow freely, then nodded emphatically.

He had no clue what this all was supposed to mean. There wasn't any attempt to make it cohesive or logical.

If Ainz himself didn't know what his words meant, there was no way anyone else could, either. But the elders all nodded in return.

As if they followed every word.

Satoru Suzuki had been in the workforce long enough to know exactly what that meant. He'd seen this happen before. Or more accurately, he'd been the one nodding.

That's what this is. It's how a boss acts when a subordinate is rattling off a bunch of jargon or abbreviations they've never heard before.

With the conclusion of Ainz's greeting, there was a brief silence.

"......Glad to hear it," an elder said. "We shall take our leave of you now. Lengthy salutations after a long journey are like overgrown vines."

"Vines?" Ainz asked without thinking.

Perhaps dark elves simply said that when they didn't want to linger. In that case, he should have heard it as words that conveyed that intent instead of a literal translation.

They must have heard his question, but the elders turned and walked off anyway.

......Huh.

That wasn't how he'd planned it.

He looked down at the gifts he'd brought.

He'd expected the elders to insist they be in charge of passing them out.

Um? They came just to say hello? Why? Did I mess up?

The meeting ended so quickly, it made him nervous. It was like being asked if he had any questions two minutes into a job interview.

If they'd grown visibly irked by his performance and made it clear he'd screwed up, he would've at least learned something, even if it ultimately meant Ainz would have to try a different village.

But they'd betrayed no response at all, so he had no clue if this was good or bad. This couldn't even be called a learning experience.

A cursory glance at the onlookers confirmed that no one seemed particularly disgruntled or hostile. They all seemed pretty baffled, too.

I seriously don't get it. But no use pondering. Maybe I'd be better off using Perfect Unknowable to sneak into a meeting of the elders and see what they made of me.

Ainz glanced once more at their retreating backs, then turned to the villagers nearby.

"Apparently I've been welcomed. I did have more to discuss with the elders, but…are they busy?"

"Huh? Uh, yeah…sure."

The villagers were being a bit evasive. To Ainz, it looked like they were racking their brains for an explanation.

"The elders gather at a specific tree. I'll show you the way later," the hunt master said. He certainly possessed a certain dignity. Ainz got why Aura had mistaken him for someone much older.

"Sounds good. I'll have to stop by when they have more time. For now, I'll join the children. I'd appreciate a guide…"

"Allow me!"

A loud voice suddenly cut in. The unexpected shout almost made the heart Ainz didn't have leap from his chest.

It was Blueberry.

He must have quietly moved off the bridge while the hunt master was talking.

"Sudden yelling is bad for the heart. I don't recommend it."

"S-sorry about that. I'll make every effort to ensure it doesn't happen again."

Blueberry acted like he'd done something awful, so Ainz couldn't exactly press the issue. Partly he felt it was best to be magnanimous and partly he wanted this dude to settle down before he did anything else wild.

"I'm pleased you understand. Well, then, Blueberry, if you could show me the way?"

"It would be an honor. While you're in this village, if you need anything—anything at all—just come to me, and I'll help in any way I can."

"Good to know," Ainz said.

He followed Blueberry's lead, but he wasn't quite done yet. The most important thing was still to come.

On the way, he paused, his eyes on the children. He smiled at them—though it was hidden beneath the cloth.

There were six kids here, four boys and two girls.

Two of them were smaller than Aura and Mare. One boy and one girl. One boy looked about their age, the other three a little older.

"Hey there," Ainz said, moving over to them.

The adults around didn't brace themselves or try to stop him. Likely because Ainz had made a good impression so far.

"I hope you have fun with Aura and Mare."

The kids all looked surprised. He couldn't let this end here. He needed one more push. Quite frankly, this exact moment was the whole reason he had embarked on this trip.

"I'd like you to include them in your games. I'm sure they'd easily win anything athletic, so I'm hoping you can find something else to play, something we don't have in the city."

Mare had helped him rehearse for his planned exchange with the elders. However, Ainz had been on his own while getting ready for his conversation with the children. That practice had been entirely inside his mind. He was sure it must've had all kinds of problems.

Screwing up while the grown-ups were watching could certainly be counterproductive. That was also the last thing Ainz wanted to do in front of the kids. But he had his doubts they'd let an outsider talk to their kids without anyone watching. He had to make the most of this opportunity.

He pulled a leather pouch out of his pocket.

From it, he produced an orange lump, the size of the tip of his thumb.

"Hold out your hand," he said, addressing the boy in front. Ainz reckoned he was the leader of the village children.

Careful not to make direct contact with the boy's hands, he dropped the lump into the waiting palm.

This wasn't like a cashier returning change with zero physical contact.

Ainz would've chosen to pass out things normally if he could, but his hands were illusions. If the kid actually touched them, he might notice something was wrong.

That had to be avoided at all costs.

Hmm, what if I cut off a criminal's hand and used that flesh and skin to make a glove? I bet someone in Nazarick is good at that sort of thing. But they might object to it being human… Neuronist would probably be into it, though.

"Errrr…what is this?"

This kid was staring at the lump in his hand, not sure what to make of it.

"It's candy," Ainz said, smiling. "Sweeter than fruit. Don't bite it, though. Just let it sit in your mouth. Though…I suppose really good fruit might be sweeter…"

He wasn't too sure about that part.

In this body, Ainz couldn't confirm the flavor himself. At best, he could tell how it felt against his teeth. He wasn't sure how good these sweets really were. He did have candy before in the world he came from. That said, he'd never tried Yggdrasil candy, so even if those became real, he couldn't be sure they actually tasted good.

And in this world, fruit with magic properties existed, so Ainz had to entertain the possibility that there could be fruit sweeter than the candy he'd brought with him. There was even a chance that the dark elves ate that fruit all the time.

Still, he was fairly confident this candy would outdo ordinary fruit.

This world didn't have much in the way of selective breeding, so fruits were not always diner friendly. There were some in Nazarick who were actively researching this field—the sous-chef, for example.

The boy hesitated but put the candy in his mouth.

The kids around him—as well as Ainz and the grown-ups watching—all waited for this poor brave soul's reaction.

"——Whoa! Wow! It's so sweet—how?!"

The boy's eyes nearly popped out of his head. Ainz grinned. The kid spit out the wet candy and looked it over, stunned.

I'm glad he liked it. And no allergic reaction, either… The odds of that were low, but still.

"I have some for all of you."

Ainz proceeded to dole out candy to the kids.

Some of the adults looked like they wanted to try, but he ignored them.

This bribe was meant for the kids, and there was no use giving it to anyone older. It had meaning only when offered up seconds after asking them to play with Aura and Mare.

And once he'd finished passing the candy out, he pressed that point home, keeping his voice nice and friendly so it wouldn't sound like a threat.

"Have fun with the twins!"

Ainz walked away, confident he had done his bit. He was sure nobody would stop him.

Yeehaw!

——A triumphant cry from the heart.

This presentation had been a smashing success. No—he let his smile fade. Not that he'd actually been smiling in the first place.

He'd only know if this was a success when those children came to invite Aura and Mare. Still—

I've done everything I can. But why didn't Blueberry say anything? I gave his kid some candy. Wouldn't any normal parent thank me? Or is Blueberry's kid not part of that group? Are there more kids somewhere? Hngg, guess I've gotta keep my wits about me.

2

There were three dark elves in the room.

The eldest of them: Raspberry Navarre.

The next eldest male: Peach Orbea.

The eldest female: Strawberry Pishcha.

Only one topic on their lips: the new arrival, uncle to Aura—that incredibly skilled ranger.

They were all clutching their heads.

The reason—

"What in the world is a sawtooth oak? What possible meaning could there be in dropping that name?" Peach asked, wincing the moment the meeting began.

"No clue," Raspberry said, shaking his head. "But we can't exactly just *ask*. If it's a sacred tree that's part of their clan's ancestor worship or sacred rites, then our ignorance could be considered an insult."

Strawberry let out a long sigh. "He clearly assumed we would know. The worst thing we could do was admit we don't."

"If we were different races, that would be one thing, but we're all dark elves. And given the direction he came from, odds are high he dwells in the land our ancestors left behind. Our languages should not be all that different. It's safe to assume that was a formal greeting based on well-established customs," said Peach.

"All I could see was his eyes, so I can't be sure, but those features suggest he may have some elf blood in him. Maybe that greeting comes from their influence?" asked Raspberry.

This was not their only basis for assuming the visitor's relationship with regular elves. There was also his name.

Dark elves put their family names first, while other elves put their given names first. His name seemed to follow the latter style.

"…How am I supposed to know elf customs and manners?! I mean, do you?"

No one answered Raspberry's question.

Frankly, they weren't even all that familiar with dark elf practices. Many oral traditions had been lost when they came to this forest, to the point where they weren't even sure *what* had been lost. That was why this got under their skin.

"At the very least, his people seem to refer to us as the evergreen oak tribe. Or perhaps it has some related meaning? For instance, if those oaks are propagated via cutting, I'm sure you both could see why our people splitting off might be referred to that way."

"From what he said, I can imagine no other meaning. But I know nothing about either tree. Are they simply different names for trees we *are* familiar with? And what is the significance of choosing those specific species?"

Common sense dictated the selection must have some deeper meaning to it.

He would have to be a lunatic to bring up two oaks for no reason. Thus, determining the identity of those trees would enable them to decipher the meaning of his message. They knew many a tree and shrub but couldn't think of any trees with those names. Especially not an evergreen oak.

Even assuming his people must have different names for the species got them nowhere.

"Hmm, if only we could ask him directly..."

"We would have if we could. But if he's appalled that we don't know, what then? He might mention it to those youths."

The elders were perfectly aware the younger villagers had it in for them. But they believed that as that crowd got older, they would begin to respect the knowledge their elders had. Traditions—and the old ways—might seem meaningless at first glance, but the elders knew there was always a reason for them, and it would be foolish to thoughtlessly discard that. In time, those tenderfoots would also come to understand that knowledge was power.

But if those same villagers learned their elders were ignorant of even formal greetings—that the traditions they prized were lost—then what? That could widen the rift between them and the elders permanently.

That was why they were clutching their heads.

"I couldn't see any emotion in his eyes at all, so maybe it was nothing more than a simple greeting... Eyes that blank are downright unsettling."

"...So...what *do* we do? As much as I'd love to pick his brain on dark elf traditions..."

"......Too risky. Even if we swallow our pride and ask to speak in private, there's no telling if he'd really keep it to himself. Which means... Yes, no use treading the path of thorns unless we have to."

"Agreed. Best we maintain our distance."

"Then...what about his gifts? They come from lands where neither elf nor dark elf dwell. They must be rare indeed."

There were obvious advantages to deciding how those were doled out. Of course, their decisions might sow discord, which might offset those advantages. But most of the time, anyone who grumbled about such things would never be pleased no matter what they did. Some of the younger hotheads would gripe simply because the elders had been the ones who made the call. As long as their choices were reasonable, the rest of the village would simply think less of the grumblers.

If the elders did handle the distribution, they would take none for themselves.

Acting the part of a selfless elder was more valuable than pocketing some precious gifts. Still—

"——Like I said, let's avoid the thorny path. If we're distributing his gifts, we'll have to thank him in person. And that means using the proper phrases that etiquette demands."

"And if he takes what we say at face value, he might think we're rude or, worse, think we don't appreciate his gifts."

Fiora's uncle likely assumed the village elders were well versed in etiquette. Who could tell how he'd respond to any social faux pas? The higher the fall, the greater the damage.

Gifts this grand could not be received the ordinary way. The thanks would have to be enthusiastic.

"Then leave it to the young. Fortunately, they were there first. They should have a good idea what they're dealing with, and we can just let them handle it."

"Yes, that's for the best."

Raspberry and Strawberry were in agreement, but Peach looked less sure.

"That's all fine and well, but should we offer any advice? They spurn tradition and might inadvertently insult his people."

"Hmm."

The others frowned.

"Perhaps we should have forced them to learn. Too late for that, I suppose. Fiora drove off that ursus lord so easily, and this is her uncle—his strength is likely considerable. We do not want to turn him against us."

"But even if we say anything, I can't see those blockheads actually listening. I suppose we should just issue a general warning, and if they mess up somehow, let it…be mud on our faces. I'd rather stay above it, but we *are* the elders."

"Yes, we must take responsibility if it comes to that. There's no other way."

"Still…what exactly are we planning to do? Directly ask why this uncle of Fiora's sought us out?"

"What if he came to learn the customs of our village? I really don't want to engage him on that."

"At the very least, we need to hold a banquet to welcome him. When Fiora arrived, we agreed to wait until her uncle caught up, and given how much she's done as a ranger, if we don't throw a proper feast, it'll be a disgrace. And if we don't make an appearance at the banquet, it won't just be considered bad manners. That's basically asking for a fight."

"*Sigh…* Then we'll attend the banquet but do our best not to approach him. Fiora's uncle seems young. The village youths will keep him busy."

"Yes. Thankfully, we can be sure they'll try to pull him to their side."

Their main discussion concluded, Raspberry turned to Peach. He'd been wondering something the whole time.

"What was that line about the vine? I've never heard the phrase."

Strawberry's eyes turned his way, too. She'd been just as lost. Neither had dared ask in the moment, but it was safe here.

Peach shifted uncomfortably.

"Sorry, I, uh…was just trying to match him. I made it up."

"Ugh," Raspberry said.

"The man had clearly never heard it before."

"What now…? What if he asks about it the next time we meet?"

"I don't know. I guess we should concoct some plausible explanation ahead of time. I can't exactly say I was just trying to sound impressive. That would convince the youngsters the traditions we prize are all pretend."

"Yeah, I suppose we have no choice. Don't ever do that again."

"Mm, sorry. I promise I won't."

"Then…*overgrown vines*, was it? Let's decide what that means. We have to keep our answers straight if anyone does ask."

Their meeting clearly far from done, the elders readied themselves for the work that lay before them.

•

While they racked their brains for a suitable rationale, another group was equally at a loss.

Specifically, the younger villagers who opposed the elders.

This youth faction often clashed with the elders over a fundamental conflict of beliefs.

Given the dangers inherent to forest life, they considered it natural to heed those with superior abilities because that benefited everyone; in their eyes, those who'd merely been alive a long time should step aside if their skills were inadequate.

In other words, where the elders prized tradition and oral history, the young faction favored meritocracy above all.

If the elders had real talent—specifically, tangible combat or magic abilities—then the younger generations would happily follow them. Unfortunately, none of them did. And having these mediocre old folks breathing down their backs was incredibly galling.

This conflict had yet to cause outright hostility because the four most respected village leaders—the hunt master, Blueberry Egnia, the apothecary master, and the ritual master—did not want them going to war with the elders.

But now a stone had been thrown.

Aura's arrival.

Though she was an outsider, her words carried weight with them because she was an incredibly skilled ranger. They respected her as much as they did the four leaders they'd long admired. Perhaps more, even.

They were keen to know her thoughts.

And her devotees were the most extreme members of the youth faction.

"So now what?" one of the devotees asked, his eyes never moving.

His gaze was glued to the gifts Aura's uncle had brought. No one had volunteered to handle distribution, so they'd been carried to the elf tree used as a communal storage space.

"Who's gonna take charge here? The elders?"

That was the expected answer. Sticking their nose in this kind of business was what the elders always did. Normally, the youths would maneuver to parcel everything out before the elders showed up, but this time, nobody made a move. Instead—

"——That might be for the best."

They were more than happy to leave it to someone else.

Once again, their respect for Aura was a factor here.

Ever since she had arrived, they noticed Aura didn't possess any particularly fancy manners. This suggested such customs had died off outside the village, or those with real skill simply didn't bother with such things. That gave the youth faction confidence they had been right all along.

But then came her uncle, Ain Bell Fior. Meeting him had given them doubts.

He was a dark elf—possibly with some elf blood mixed in—but they'd understood only half his greeting. It was hard to imagine he'd say anything meaningless at such a significant moment, so his greeting must have been following the etiquette the elders always went on about.

Aura may have shown no signs of it, but her uncle clearly did value those things.

What was the difference?

No one said it aloud, but everyone knew.

She was a child, and he was an adult.

And their uncle specifically asked that the children be allowed to play. Despite her raw talent, in his eyes, she was just a kid.

That seemed unfathomable.

Certainly, in a place as harsh as the forest, children's first lessons were anything but *manners*. There were far more vital survival skills to impart.

So it made sense that a kid wouldn't know any finer etiquette, and even their own village elders had never gone so far as to drill manners into the children.

The real problem here was that Aura's uncle had made no effort to demonstrate any of his etiquette until the elders showed up.

Had he viewed the gathered crowd as children, merely a tad more mature than Aura? No one there, youth faction or not, had attempted to show good manners. And how would a grown-up act around children who lacked that knowledge?

There wasn't much reason to pull out any formal greetings with that kind of audience. Adults would just meet kids at their level.

Turned out the manners they'd dismissed as meaningless had meaning after all. They were a sign of respect, and this visitor had offered that exclusively to the elders.

No one had missed the significance of that.

"If her uncle thinks we're a bunch of overgrown kids and we pass out his gifts—he'll assume the village is run by children. Otherwise, he'll consider us a bunch of barbarians who don't even know basic manners."

"Maybe he won't go so far as to deem us children based purely on our ignorance, but...maybe he will. And if he does, when he goes back to the city, he'll tell everyone the dark elf village had a bunch of kids acting like they were big shots."

"...That'd be the worst."

"I agree. Turning our village into a laughingstock...wouldn't feel great."

"...Does that mean the reason he wasn't super formal from the start was because he wanted to test us?"

"Yeah, and if we'd shown that we know proper manners, Fior would have changed his tune."

That sure felt like they'd fallen into a trap. But perhaps it hadn't been a malicious one. What benefit would he have from engaging them on that level? Unless he was just an asshole. They couldn't rule that out.

"...It don't sit right, but we're gonna have to leave all that proper crap to the fossils."

The elders had demonstrated impeccable etiquette, so Aura's uncle had naturally responded in kind. They could assume he planned to treat them with respect. If the elders were the ones who passed out the gifts, he wouldn't think anything of it.

"Yeah, if we just wait, the elders will step in soon enough. The only other option is to ask someone who wasn't there. That'd leave the apothecary or the ritual master. Thoughts?"

"They'll scoff at the idea. Especially the apothecary master."

The apothecary master did his best to stay out of these conundrums, and if they went to the ritual master, he'd just point them toward the elders.

"Right, I guess that settles it. We'll just handle the tasks we've been given. Let's get moving."

"Yeah, sounds like a plan. Then later…should we get the elders to teach us basic manners?"

Everyone winced.

They'd spent ages insisting those were a waste of effort. But the next time outside talent arrived expecting a formal greeting, they'd need to change if they didn't want to be treated like children.

Still, bowing to the elders sucked.

Caught between a rock and a hard place, all sighed.

"Also, we were supposed to throw a banquet once Fior and his nephew arrived, but what's up with that? I'm sure that involves a ton of etiquette stuff. And we'd just disgrace ourselves."

"The feast itself is one thing, but we can't have him thinking the whole village is just rude children. We'd better let the elders run the banquet prep."

"Good idea. Knowing them…much as I hate to admit it, they know their way around that sort of thing."

•

While the elders and youngsters were dealing with their own headaches, a third group was trying to sort themselves out.

The six children.

They'd formed a circle, at the center of which was the first boy Ainz had given candy to—the one he'd specifically asked to include Aura in their games. He was thinking the hardest here.

The kids had naturally been curious about the girl from the unknown outside world. They still were and would have loved to get to know her and play together. But there was a good reason they'd never tried and kept their distance.

She wasn't like them.

This girl was a better hunter than anyone in the village. Even if they were the same age, she stood leagues above them. You couldn't just walk up to someone like that and start chatting.

Running into a beloved celebrity on the street was enough to make anyone think twice.

But now they *had* to.

"What do we do? What do we play? Games that aren't athletic…that means no running around or climbing. That *is* how we play, though."

The candy had certainly helped convince the dark elf kids to spend more time with Aura, but that was something they already wanted to do. Ainz had just given them the encouragement they needed to act.

"In the leaves?"

This game was what other races called hide-and-seek.

"I dunno about the new boy, but that girl's a super-good ranger. She'd spot us instantly. It wouldn't even be a contest."

"That's fine. I mean, that's how the game works."

"But that'd be her playing games with us, not us playing a game together."

One of the other kids whistled.

"You said it, Ku."

"Nice one."

"You're just pointing out the obvious!"

Ku's proper name was Orange Kunas. The first boy to get the candy. He flashed a cocky grin, then waved them over.

"We all know I'm cool, but never mind that. Can anyone think of a game that doesn't involve moving?"

"How about climb…no, that's still moving."

The kids fell silent. Finally, the oldest girl suggested, "Maybe we could just ask them to teach us a city game?"

Kunas sighed, shaking his head. "Don't be dumb," he said.

"What's so dumb about that?"

"Why are you mad? Didn't you hear what he said? He wants us to show them games they don't have in the city. Stuff you can only do here. Did you forget already?"

"…He said that?"

"He did. So we've gotta find a game…they don't have where they're from. I mean, I dunno what they do in the city! Maybe we should ask that first?"

"Something we can only do in the village…like go into the woods?"

"No!" Kunas yelped, scowling at the suggestion. "You know what happened to Ah, right?"

Everyone got real quiet. The boy who'd made the suggestion looked sick to his stomach.

Inside the village, it was comparatively safe, but the forest was different. If the kids went out there alone, they'd be in trouble. Maybe they'd come back okay once or twice, but their luck was bound to run out eventually. And sometimes kids didn't make it back. The adults took no real measures against this.

They didn't even have someone watch over them or put them on leashes.

If they broke the rules, ran into trouble, and didn't come back, then that was a necessary sacrifice.

If one child's death taught the other kids how dangerous the forest was, then that was no great loss.

It was far worse to grow up never knowing how scary the forest could be.

Every single adult in this village had lost at least one childhood friend to the perils of the woods. That was why they all had a healthy fear of it and went about their lives with ample caution. That was what life here meant.

"That girl's a super-good ranger, so I get why you'd think we're safer with her than we are with the grown-ups. But we'd still be in big trouble. You know how Ailes"—he pointed at the smallest boy—"and me can do totally different things, right? You gotta at least be able to climb a tree quickly."

"Then what *do* we do?"

They were back where they had started.

"I guess we've gotta ask about city games first."

"But what even is a city? Are there more trees than here? Lots of prey for her to train on?"

They looked at one another, then back at Kunas.

He grinned triumphantly.

"I heard the grown-ups who went hunting with her talking."

"Whoa, Ku! Nice work!"

"You're the best, Ku."

"Heh-heh-heh. The city doesn't just have elves and dark elves—they got all kinds of races. And no trees at all! Instead, they got houses made of brick and tar and dirt."

"Dirt…like the glieak?"

That was a race that lived in the forest.

They were omnivorous but didn't eat intelligent life, so if dark elves ran into one, both sides would just sneak off the other way.

And the kids had heard the glieak lived in square homes of hardened soil.

They imagined a bunch of boxes in a field, but it was obvious they didn't really get it.

"Wow. That place sounds nuts."

"I kinda wanna know more…"

"Uh, but if we ask and find out they've done this stuff in the city before, then that's just one less game we can actually play with them. We'll have to think of even *more* ideas."

"Argh."

Once again, the children all stopped to think.

This was a tall order.

"Um, we could play house?" the youngest girl ventured.

The three older boys made faces. They clearly thought they were too old for that. But—Kunas quickly saw the light.

"You wouldn't need any athletics for that. It might be our only option!"

"But that isn't something special you can play in the village. You can play that anywhere!"

"We'll just play *village* house."

Village house.

Kunas seemed to be the only kid who knew what that meant.

"And the boy who showed up second didn't look like he was all that athletic, so house might be right for him. At his age, we still played that, right?"

"No," said the one boy Aura's age.

"Whaaaat?" The kids around jeered. "I saw you playing house all by yourself."

"That wasn't house! I was playing dark elf hero!"

Then the children began arguing about what the difference between the two was.

•

Blueberry led Ainz to an elf tree. Ainz was well aware Aura had been staying here, so he hadn't really needed a guide. But as this was officially his first visit, he'd been forced to pretend he didn't know his way around.

There was no sign of the twins waiting outside, so they must have gone inside.

"Thanks for your help."

Blueberry was looking around, like he was searching for something— and seemed disappointed by the results.

"A pleasure to be of assistance," he said. "If you need anything else, just say the word. Should I have your things brought here?"

"Th-that won't be necessary. No need to trouble yourself."

"You're sure? Don't hesitate to ask!"

This man was being strangely pushy.

Everyone had different concepts of personal space. Did dark elves set that boundary closer than most humans?

Thinking about it, living in a place like this—surrounded by monsters—meant you had to work closely together to survive. Maybe it was a side effect of that environment. Still, Ainz had no need for the man at the moment.

"No, I'm fine. Leading me here is more than enough."

"I see… Then tell Fi—Aura I said hi."

Why only her? Oh, I see. Ainz figured it out. *My blunder. I failed to introduce Mare at all. Aura did say his name, but that was all we did.*

But there was little upside to introducing Mare to the grown-ups. Only the children really needed to know him, and Aura would likely take care of that.

"Yes, I will."

Blueberry turned back several times as he left, and Ainz made sure he was gone before stepping into the elf tree. As expected, the twins were waiting for him.

"Good wor—" Ainz broke off, deciding that was the wrong greeting. "Sorry to keep you waiting."

"Sir, if we could ask—"

"—Stop. Don't be too formal. I'm well aware that Aura's ranger skills ensure her ears will detect any dark elves that come near. Here, we are safe and can speak freely if we choose. But assumed identities are less likely to slip if you maintain them at all times. As long as we are in this village, I am your uncle, Aura. There is no need to be deferential."

"Unh," Aura moaned. She glanced briefly at Mare, then at the ground, then up at Ainz through her lashes. "Um, Uncle Ain, what do we do next?"

Mare was nodding. He had the same question on his mind.

"Now we're cooking— No, if I really was your uncle, I probably wouldn't talk like that. Let's just stick to what I was doing earlier. Not bad, Aura. How's that sound?"

Aura managed a half smile, half embarrassed, half uncertain. Didn't seem like she'd objected—even if she did, he was still going to act more familiar than he usually did.

"Very well— Er, I mean, okay?" Ainz said, looking them both over. "Like our initial plan, we shall be—hmm, is saying *gonna* better? We're gonna be staying in this village for about a week. Can't say for sure, since not much has been decided yet, but let's kick back and relax and learn whatever we can."

"Oh, er, um, Uncle Ain, what sort of information are we looking for?"

"Nice work, Mare. Keep it up!"

He felt like this wasn't actually all that different from how Mare usually spoke but decided to praise it anyway. Mare looked bashful, and Ainz launched into a further explanation. Mare had asked similar questions on the way here, but he'd bought himself time by saying he'd explain once they'd regrouped with Aura.

This had allowed him to concoct a rationale.

"Everything and anything. All information related to this dark elf village. There may come a time when we need the two of you to pose as normal dark elves. Of course, there might not. But in case it does, if you don't know how dark elves think, they might suspect something. So considering what the future might bring, I thought a stay in this village might help you gain some experience."

Ainz thought this was a solid excuse. But the next bit was key.

"And the two of you might have to act like normal dark elf children. Why not try joining in the children's games? Of course, that's not an order. If you can think of anything better, go right ahead."

Given his true objective of finding the twins some friends, these instructions were toeing the line. If he pushed it any further, it would become an order, but if he didn't push them at all, they might never look at the other kids twice.

He had not expected them to appear so puzzled.

Um, what? I did a bunch of rehearsals and thought I nailed it just now. Did I miss something?

"So…not information on the Theocracy?" Aura asked.

That made Ainz look puzzled. Not that his illusionary face moved.

Why were they bringing up the Theocracy all of a sudden? He didn't understand.

Back at Nazarick, he'd said they were here for a paid vacation. If memory served, he'd also called it a test to see if Nazarick would still function with three members of the upper echelon out of the picture. But...

I never once mentioned the Theocracy, did I? I know they suggested we ask that charmed elf about them...but why? Oh...the former slaves in Nazarick are a similar race, so that made them worry? Their karma isn't nearly as low as Albedo's or Demiurge's.

He chose to ignore what they'd done in the kingdom when he drew that conclusion.

It's possible they only felt sympathy for elves and dark elves and cared nothing for humans.

"Uh, sure. If you hear anything about the Theocracy, that's worth knowing."

"Okay! Understood, sir— Er, got it...?"

Aura was still struggling with how to interact with her supposed uncle, but Ainz just shot her a grin and opened up his rucksack.

"Good. Now, if we're staying for a week, we should sort out our things."

He'd brought a bunch of stuff with him, starting with some dwarven dishes. It was quite a pile, but he hoped some of it would interest the dark elves, the way the gifts had. For that reason, he wasn't just putting them anywhere—he was attempting to place them where they'd catch the eye.

In other words, this was a showroom.

Ainz had no real confidence in his aesthetic sensibilities, so he had the twins help him decorate the tree. At one point, Aura paused.

"Uncle Ain, footsteps headed our way. Six pairs are coming. They don't seem to be trying to hide their approach. From the weight, likely children."

Ah. Ainz stopped working and turned toward the door. He hadn't imagined they'd show up today but was grateful for it. The boy he'd first given candy to popped his head in the door.

Most people would think it rude to just poke your head into someone else's home, but in this village, that was normal.

"Hey there. You here to invite Aura and Mare out to play?"

"Uh, um, yes. We are," the boy stammered, gaping at the room.

"I see, I see." Ainz grinned. "I was waiting for you. Kids, go on out and play."

"Huh? Uh, um, b-but, Uncle Ain, we're not done unpacking…?"

"No problem, Mare. I'll handle the rest. Let me take care of things here! Although I'm not sure I have an eye for these things, so if you see anything worth fixing later, I'll do as you say! Ha-ha-ha!"

Ainz let out a laugh, and the twins looked surprised.

Certainly, he was not ordinarily prone to hearty laugher. He realized how strange it might seem. Perhaps his behavior was a bit awkward, but if they asked about it, he could claim it was all part of the act.

"Well, if you say so…gotcha! We'll be right out. Mare, come on."

"O-okay…"

The twins left, and Ainz practically beamed.

I'll have to give those kids more candy to thank them for this! No, wait… What would Aura and Mare think if they knew these kids only invited them because they wanted candy? That might be devastating.

He didn't think either twin was really *that* sensitive, though.

Then again, I'm not Teapot. I don't know everything about them. So I should assume there's a chance it would hurt their feelings and act accordingly. No need to risk it. If the shock of it blows their chances at making friends, how would I ever face Teapot again? Also, I'm curious how they'll play…

Ainz smiled, remembering the past.

Satoru Suzuki's best years. Forty people—plus one more—gathered in the game called *Yggdrasil.*

His comrades who had gathered there all led very different lives.

Some lived inside the megacorp arcologies. Others hailed from the far-inferior domed cities. People like Satoru Suzuki scraped by in the harsh environment beyond. And then there were those enduring worse conditions.

They were all total strangers with nothing in common—until the game brought them together.

"Games tear down barriers. They bring us together. Games alone make that possible. No matter how distant your origins, you can become friends. As I…as we did."

Guardians were overwhelmingly powerful. By comparison, these dark elf children were terribly fragile. Away from this village, they were worlds apart. Even so—

"——Friendship is a wonderful thing. I'd love for them to discover that."

His eyes were not on the twins.

But he could see them in his mind's eye.

If they played together and still found no common ground, so be it.

That had happened to Ainz, as well. He'd lost count of how many players he'd encountered within *Yggdrasil*. There had been so many. But only forty-one of them had become his friends.

Friendships were not made with everyone you met.

He need simply create opportunities for them to find someone they deemed worthy. As long as they learned that making friends was a good thing, then this whole exercise was a success.

Ainz glanced down at his right ring finger—currently bare—and a slight smile crossed his lips.

I wondered this before, but perhaps I should take steps to help Demiurge, Albedo, and Shalltear find friends, too? …………We'll see.

There was little merit in overthinking it now. Even that momentary question had made his spirits sink.

Still, why is no one coming to visit me? From what I overheard using Perfect Unknowable, they should be readying a welcome banquet. When are they planning to tell me about that? Or is it supposed to be a surprise?

He had plans of his own, so an abrupt invitation wouldn't be very welcome.

For one thing, Ainz couldn't actually eat. He wasn't sure what sort of banquet they had in mind, but ordinarily it would involve the village bigwigs and food spread out on the table before him. What would they think if he never took a single bite?

He couldn't imagine that going over well.

If they were different races, then he might have some excuse and it would be the host's responsibility for serving food he couldn't eat. But Ainz was using an illusion to pass as a dark elf.

Allergies might rule out eating specific foods, but no ordinary excuse would allow you to skip over *everything*.

Ainz had to strike first and provide an appropriate reason.

Or are they not planning to come today to avoid interrupting my rest? I certainly don't mind if the banquet itself takes place on a later date. I just don't want them coming to fetch me once it's all ready. Should I go to them? Ainz considered this, then shook his head. *No, let's not. In which case…once someone does arrive, I'll ask them to pass word along.*

He remembered what he'd seen while lurking around.

They generally deliver enough food for the morning and evening meals together. Right about now, actually. I'll have to speak to whomever brings that along. Or was that a service provided to rangers who bring in food, not travelers? I haven't done any work for them yet, so maybe they won't bring me anything to eat. No, I doubt that. Aura worked hard enough, and I brought those gifts—I imagine they'd keep us fed at least a week even if we don't lift a finger.

Ainz fully intended to do his part, of course. He'd told them he was a caster for a reason. Depending on what the situation called for, he was fully prepared to use spells as high as fourth tier. And bring back food in Aura's stead.

He wasn't sure how things would play out and wasn't about to accept charity.

Maybe it's just early. If they come, they come. If they don't, I'll go to them. Then…I'll ask what I want to know.

•

Aura had been racking her brain ever since their master sent them out.

He'd suggested playing with the dark elf children to learn about dark elf culture. But she had her doubts about that.

It wasn't like children knew nothing of their culture or were completely ignorant creatures, but learning through them seemed inefficient. Learning from the adults would give them a far better idea of how the dark elves in this forest thought. If they didn't know the truth, learning about a subject from children was inherently risky.

It's certainly very childlike to get things wrong, so maybe that's the goal here? As children, we're allowed to make mistakes?

Maybe she was overthinking it. But she remembered what Albedo had said before she left—to never stop thinking.

Aura and Mare were the only ones accompanying their liege. That meant they had to think everything through and avoid doing anything that would embarrass the guardians.

She wrapped her hand around the acorn necklace, using its power to talk to Mare. He responded right away.

Aura filled him in on her current thoughts and doubts.

"——*Mm, I agree.*"

Mare did not grip his necklace. That gesture was required only by the person initiating contact—the one who activated the item. The recipient could answer without doing anything special.

"*...There's more to this* playing games *than learning about their culture. But what? He said we had to stay friendly here—is this part of that? Does playing with the children make us look friendly?*"

"*That might be part of it, but...hmm... Oh, are we recruiting the children?*"

"*No way. The grown-ups would be way more useful. They've been bugging me, but several of them seem easy enough to bring over.*"

The point of this was growing still more obscure.

"*Then does Lord Ainz have some plan to use these children?*" Mare asked.

Aura looked up at the kids ahead.

Weak and frail, no real status. She couldn't see what benefit there could be.

"*Use them how? As hostages?*"

"*I can't rule that out, but I doubt it somehow.*"

"*Children...children...using them to gather info?*"

"Hmm. But how much do kids really know?"

"Good point…"

It was hard to imagine they'd have any secrets that really mattered. Or had their master analyzed things from every angle and discovered these children possessed some kind of vital information?

"Also, all you're doing is shooting down my ideas. Don't you have anything of your own?"

"Um…" Mare paused for a beat. *"Oh! Is he thinking about taking these children to E-Rantel?"*

"Oh. That could be it, but even then, adults would be better."

"Children's ideas aren't set in stone, so it could be easier for them to adjust… or maybe it's not just the kids but the whole village?"

"Aha. But if it was all the villagers, I don't see the point in playing with the kids or getting closer to them."

Even if Mare's idea was on the money, it would be better to take the adults under their wings. If the kids were especially opinionated, that might make sense, but she'd been here three days and seen no signs of that.

She just couldn't find any particular value to them.

"Then I guess it must be acting friendly to extract intel," Mare said.

"I guess so… Nothing else makes sense. At least, not that I can think of. Maybe children would let something slip the adults are all keeping under wraps? Mm! Ainz really values information, so that does sound like something he'd think. We'll just have to keep the conversation going."

"Good luck!"

"You'd better help! You can talk easily enough when it's just us. This'll be good practice!"

"We're using the necklace…"

The children ahead stopped.

They were inside the village, but there were no signs of any toys around. Aura had seen enough of the village to know no such thing existed.

She quickly corrected that impression.

The children here might make their toys from trees as needed.

Her ranger senses told her there was only one adult watching.

"*Oh, him. He's watching me again.*"

"*Who?*"

"*Don't look. On our seven. Best hunter here. He's been staring at me from time to time since I showed up. Never comes close.*"

"*He suspects something but doesn't have proof, so he's monitoring what you do?*"

"*Seems likely. Best make sure you don't do anything to rouse his suspicions. We'll have to report that to Lord Ainz later.*"

Aura carefully ignored the man.

Did he actually think she hadn't noticed him? Or did he *want* her to notice? Was the message that he was watching her every move?

As obnoxious as that was, she couldn't just kill him. She needed her master's permission to do that and would have to arrange the death so it looked like the ankyloursus or some other beast got him—ensuring she had an alibi.

She was a beast tamer, though, meaning this wasn't a real challenge.

"…So what are we doing here?"

"Okay!" the biggest boy yelled. "We're playing house."

It almost seemed like he thought if he said it loud enough, they'd agree.

House?

Aura was at least aware of the concept.

A type of role-playing. I remember Lady BubblingTeapot grumbling about Lord Peroroncino saying, I wanna be a baby! Someone be a mommy and pat my head! *Is that what this is?*

Aura pictured herself patting Shalltear's head.

Hmm, could be right. Am I doing that or are they?

Being a mom was one thing, but being the baby would be unbearable. She was a floor guardian, made by one of the Supreme Beings—it would be rude to Lady BubblingTeapot to role-play a baby.

When she told them about Lord Peroroncino, Lady Yamaiko and Lady Ankoro Mocchi Mochi both laughed. But I still bet it would make Lady BubblingTeapot mad.

It was easy enough to say she didn't want to. But—if they needed good info and to loosen up their lips, playing along seemed like a good idea. That was how these things worked. Everyone liked having their suggestions accepted. And playing the same game brought people together.

But what would happen if she refused?

They'd ask what she wanted to play, and Aura didn't have many ideas there.

There were things she could suggest. Racing, climbing, play fighting. But the ability gap was so high, the outcome of all those games was clear as day. There weren't any kids around who could match the two of them—especially Mare—in any physical activity.

It wouldn't be fun when it was obvious how everything would end. If they wanted to keep these kids happy, they could intentionally lose. But Aura had already driven off the ursus lord—officially, anyway—and everyone knew it. If someone that strong lost a race, the children would all know she was just humoring them. If that was all it took to please them, these children were something else.

The only other option was to not play at all, and that wasn't on the table.

Their absolute ruler had told them to go play.

In which case…

"A-Aura, i-is this…?"

He looked very concerned. Likely remembering the same thing she had and reaching the same conclusions.

She flashed her best and brightest smile.

"Our toughest assignment yet, Mare!"

3

With Aura and Mare gone, Ainz finished unpacking. He spent some time gazing absently at the ceiling, occasionally checking the note in his hand.

Killing time.

There hadn't been *that* much to unpack, and he was soon done. Finalizing the interior coordination would require their input.

He'd expected someone would come by soon, but no one had.

Ainz glanced back at his notes.

This contained a list of things he expected to happen here and how to deal with them. Nowhere on the list was the scenario "nobody comes at all."

He had to admit he'd already uncovered a major gap in his projections.

This realization itself was not particularly shocking. Ainz considered himself a thoroughly average mind, and his planning abilities were simply not up to the task. What mattered was how he would recover from this.

He could think of two approaches offhand. First, just sit and wait. The second was get up and go out.

He opted for the former. Didn't want to accidentally miss them.

For a while, Ainz waited, doing nothing in particular. Just as he was starting to fear he'd made the wrong choice, a young dark elf finally poked her head in the door. This was a very tight-knit village, and no one considered this rude. Her eyes met Ainz's, and she looked a bit surprised.

That seemed odd to him.

Why would his presence be surprising?

Or maybe this is a natural reaction to poking your head in someone's house—loaner or not—and finding them staring right at you. But given how they act around one another, I somehow doubt that.

The young woman bobbed her head at him, then turned her eyes to the floor. She stepped inside and set down the plate she'd brought.

Dark elves wore shoes even inside the elf trees. Ainz privately thought it a bit weird to put dishes of food down on the floor, but they also sat there to eat—from what he'd seen, less than half of them used tables—so maybe this was considered normal.

There was something else on his mind now.

Ainz and the woman were already quite close to each other. Another step or two and she could have handed the dish right to him. But she'd set it on the floor without a word. Their eyes never met again after she'd first stepped in.

Ainz knew what that meant.

She had no intention of speaking to him.

This didn't appear to be a gesture of hostility, scorn, loathing, or anything negative like that. The way she'd set the dish down had been perfectly polite. Perhaps she was just…a poor communicator.

Or maybe it's an overabundance of caution. An adult comparable to Aura in power—one they know little about. A measure of caution is commendable. Especially when you consider the gender difference. But I brought gifts to avoid giving any standoffish impressions and put on a whole performance… Dang. Not sure what to do.

He didn't know if this woman had children and didn't want the village women—especially the mothers—telling their kids not to play with the twins.

Children ignored what their parents said all the time, but they also listened.

Ainz thought a moment and decided he wasn't getting anywhere fast.

If I don't know why she's acting this way or how she feels, there's nothing I can do. I don't know how she normally behaves, so speculation is useless. No need to rush to a conclusion.

Once she'd finished setting the dish down, she bowed her head and left the elf tree. Ainz bowed his head in return.

Left alone again, he let a long sigh slip out.

He'd failed to ask.

He couldn't bring himself to confront her about her behavior. Even if he'd let that pass without comment, there'd been other questions or conversations he'd wanted to have. But the wall between them was so obvious, it had made him instinctively recoil.

He would just have to hope the next person would be more receptive.

Waiting for them to come to him seemed more productive than trying to break through that woman's barriers.

Putting the thought out of his mind, he turned his attention to the food she'd left—which brought back memories of being Satoru Suzuki.

I was wrong! It's still not too late! I need to take action before it becomes a problem!

That was how it went at work.

It hurt less to report a mistake to the boss right away than wait for it to be discovered. What seemed like a huge blunder often turned out to be not that big a deal after all. But left unchecked, the wound often festered.

And right now, he had several things he needed to communicate to the dark elves.

Ainz got up and hustled out of the elf tree.

He soon found the retreating woman. Dark elves—or elves in general—had better hearing than humans, so she'd likely heard him coming after her and had already started to turn.

"—Excuse me."

"Y-yes?"

He must have spoken a moment too quickly and startled her; her voice was a squeak.

"About the welcome banquet——"

"——Please bring that up with the elders."

She spoke quite quickly, almost on top of him.

Ainz suspected there was something she didn't want to admit or was actively hiding. Could it be a surprise party? That was the only thing Ainz could think of.

It was pretty weird to try and make a welcome banquet a surprise, but maybe that was how dark elves did things, and he was better off just ignoring that little detail.

"Okay, so…I'm not sure what you call it in this village, but I'm currently on a Kayoukazen's Lament."

"A…Kayoukazen's Lament?"

"Yes, you've heard of it?"

The name and the practice itself were both things Ainz had made up, so she couldn't possibly know it—a fact rather undermined by her response.

"Er, um…no, well… I might have… Yes! It may or may not ring a bell."

This rattled Ainz. Did they have a similar phrase? Then this whole thing could backfire. Especially if their term referred to something bad. He had no clue how he'd wriggle out of that one.

But since the word *lament* itself was often used when mourning some-one, perhaps that alone suggested what he meant. Since *Kayoukazen* was a word he had pulled out of thin air, he should be able to imbue it with what-ever meaning he needed to cover all contingencies.

Incidentally, Ainz hadn't learned the word *lament* at work but from a skill name in *Yggdrasil*. He'd gotten curious about what it meant and looked it up.

"Uh, really? No, that makes sense. We're all dark elves. Perhaps we do share the term. But we can't be sure it means the same thing without further explanation."

"Y-yes, that's a good point. I feel like I've heard the term before, but I can't be sure it's the same *Kayoukazen*."

They were both talking a bit too fast, and their smiles were noticeably strained. Ainz's face was an illusion, so it didn't actually move that much.

"At any rate, this month I'm mourning those I've lost, so I'd rather avoid anything as festive as a banquet. Naturally, I respect your village's customs, so if you insist I make an appearance, I'm willing to do so—just be aware that I won't be consuming anything."

"Ah, you're in mourning? Fasting is completely understandable, then."

Is it? Ainz thought, nodding anyway.

"In any case, I'd like to inform the elders. Do you know where I can find them?"

"I—I can pass along word for you."

"Oh? Then…thank you! Please do!!"

The way the woman had been talking, Ainz had assumed he'd have to go himself, but he wasn't about to point that out. Not even to double-check. Her proposal was very convenient, so he took her up on it.

Now all he had to do was beat a quick retreat before she changed her mind.

He bid her farewell with a speed that left her blinking. Ignoring her reaction, Ainz rushed back to their lodgings. Fortunately, she didn't call out or try to stop him.

Once safely back inside, he picked up the dish she'd left on the floor.

It was heavily laden—though still easy to lift by Ainz's standards—with a massive amount of food. Clearly more than three people could consume.

The likely intention was to provide six servings. Morning and evening meals for three. That went a long way to explaining the sheer volume, but it still seemed like a lot. Maybe that was simply because Satoru Suzuki had never been a big eater, and since becoming Ainz, he'd become unable to eat anything at all. Perhaps this wouldn't seem too much to anyone else.

Living in a place like this, you likely need a substantial calorie intake. There are no nutritionally complete food products.

The meal consisted of cooked meats—*just* roasted with no accoutrements, by the looks of it—and dried fruits. These were paired with some sort of leafy salad. There was also something that resembled mashed potatoes accompanied by a variety of nuts. And what appeared to be fried caterpillars. Rather large ones.

In Aura's opinion, none of it tasted good. And since the ingredients and recipes never changed, she quickly got sick of it.

On the other hand, all this new food whetted Ainz's curiosity.

What *would* these things taste like?

Insects were high in protein, and Satoru Suzuki had often eaten them in his previous life—albeit coated in barbecue flavoring. However, he'd never eaten a whole plump roasted caterpillar before.

Once again regretting his body's inability to eat, he went down a floor and set the tray on a shelf. Then he considered his next move.

They don't seem to have a concept of lunch, so the kids' games shouldn't be stopping anytime soon.

If the children had chores to do, their playtime might be limited, but plenty of people knew Ainz had asked them to play with the twins. In all likelihood, the adults would let the kids play all day today, at least.

That meant Aura and Mare would not be back for a while. Ainz should use this time to pursue whatever interested him.

He'd walked—well, flown—around the village under cover of Perfect Unknowable but hadn't done so while visible. Maybe he'd discover something new. And he had a destination in mind.

I already laid the groundwork for it, too.

He plucked his notes—unlike the previous note, these were in a proper notebook—out of thin air (his item box) and attempted to memorize what was written there.

Namely, how to create potions and what herbs and minerals went into them.

Unfortunately, Ainz's brain was incapable of retaining more than two or three brewing recipes. Feeble as his mind might be, that was hardly the sole problem. As expected, the techniques described were rather detailed and quite difficult to memorize for someone without knowledge or interest in the fundamentals of potion making.

He put the notebook away and spent a minute muttering the recipe under his breath. Then he left the elf tree again, making his way across the village.

A number of dark elves spotted Ainz coming and looked his way. They weren't watching out for him; they were just going about their business and regarding him with interest and curiosity.

If any one of them saw through the illusion, it would be a real headache, but fortunately, it didn't seem like anyone here was skilled enough. If they were, they would've kicked up a fuss the moment he arrived.

Yet, none of the villagers were attempting to speak to him.

Were isolated villages like this just inherently standoffish when dealing with outsiders? No, on second thought, if Ainz—or rather, Satoru Suzuki—had spotted a stranger in the office, he wouldn't have been inclined to go up and start a conversation. If he had, many people would take it as a sign he thought they didn't belong there.

Of course, he didn't personally feel ostracized or anything.

The twins were the stars of the show—Ainz was merely along for the ride. It would never do for him to hog the limelight. More importantly, there would be ample opportunity to make his mark later. Like he'd planned on his arrival, he needed to turn Aura from a hero into a child.

As he had that thought, Ainz noticed a dark elf coming his way.

He'd glanced at Ainz once or twice, but no more than anyone who just happened to cross paths with him.

Good enough. He can help with my cover.

Ainz had spent enough time here with Perfect Unknowable to have a good grasp of how the village was laid out, but "Aura's uncle" had only just arrived. If he looked like he knew where he was going, someone might start to wonder. Naturally, he had any number of excuses. For example, he could simply say Aura had told him. But it was a good idea to head off any suspicion before those proved necessary.

After all, there wasn't anything to be gained by making people cautious.

"Uh, pardon me."

Asking a random dark elf for directions would create the perfect alibi.

"Mm, yes? Can I help with something?"

"Yes, my niece told me your village has a skilled apothecary. Would you mind directing me to the apothecary master's elf tree?"

The man saw nothing amiss with that question and happily pointed the way.

Ainz gave his thanks and followed the directions he didn't need.

On the way, he passed a dark elf extending a hand toward the ground below.

Wondering what he was doing, Ainz paused to watch, and the ground began to heave, the mass of soil climbing the trunk like a slime.

It resembled Mare's Earth Surge, but there were many differences.

Whether it was daily-life magic or a druid's faith spell, neither existed in *Yggdrasil*. These were things that the people of this world had developed during the course of their lives here.

The earth obeyed the man's manipulations, vanishing into the treetops far above.

All that soil would probably go in the dark elves' vegetable gardens.

Their produce was grown in planters nestled inside or above the trees. The planters themselves were made of packed soil, and Ainz had wondered how they got the dirt up there. Clearly, this was the answer.

Pleased by the fascinating discovery, Ainz resumed his walk.

The elf tree at the end of the path was particularly grand—or at least, thick. Possibly the plumpest in the village. This was the home of the apothecary master, one of the village's leaders.

It was separated from the other elf trees by a fair distance. Presumably to mitigate casualties if anything poisonous was accidentally produced.

A high-level apothecary had built up resistances to these toxins, but what they could handle might be unbearable for someone weaker, like children or the sick.

If there was another reason, then...

...*it might be to safeguard his knowledge.*

Ainz had a great deal of respect for any attempts to monopolize knowledge. Both to protect one's vested interests and to avoid problems that might arise if secrets became common knowledge.

Everyone knew medicine could be poisonous at the wrong dosage.

But if someone simply stole the knowledge, would they manage to make effective medicine? Probably not. Inferior facsimiles would not only cause fatalities, they'd teach people to distrust the apothecary's authentic potions.

These concerns more than justified taking protective measures.

"Hello?" Ainz called from outside the elf tree.

No answer.

He knocked on the trunk and called again. Perking up his ears, he could hear a grinding noise.

"Coming in!"

He stepped inside. A pudgier dark elf was seated with his back to the door. Given his status and workload, he was likely well-fed but had little in the way of exercise. Safe to assume he was the man in charge—the apothecary master rather than a disciple.

He was seated at a low table, his arms moving vigorously.

On the table were basic instruments: a mortar and pestle along with some bulkier grinding tools. On the shelves were a number of jars, likely containing medicinal ingredients. Bundles of herbs hung from the ceiling, which lent the space the expected atmosphere of an apothecary.

The acrid scent of dried ingredients mingled with the rich aromas of freshly gathered medicinal plants. When the heady blend reached Ainz's nostrils, it reminded him of Nfirea's workroom.

Dark elves had better hearing than humans, but not by much. It was impossible to tell if the master knew Ainz had come in and was simply ignoring him or if he was too focused on his work to have noticed him at all.

Ainz spoke again.

"Pardon me. Do you have a moment?"

For the first time, the apothecary master stopped his grinding. He glared over his shoulder once, then frowned.

"You're… Oh, I get it. The cloth on your face. The man from the same place as that girl. I heard you were an arcane caster?"

"Indeed I am. I see word has already spread."

He reached for the cloth to remove it.

"Don't," the man said. "Your people's rules, right? I don't need to see. Ain't nothing for me even if I do. Leave it alone. I've acknowledged your greeting. If we're done here, be on your way. I've got work to do."

After that begrudging mutter, the apothecary lost interest and turned back to his desk. It was a curt response that seemed extremely dismissive. But Ainz was actually relieved.

People like this spoke their minds and hid nothing. If he'd merely said, Go away—you're bothering me, all Ainz's salesman tricks would most likely have failed to make the man turn back around.

But that wasn't what he'd said. In other words, Ainz still had a chance.

As the master picked up his pestle, Ainz asked, "What are you making now?"

"Does it matter?"

A bit hostile. He decided to not mince words.

"Perhaps not," Ainz said. After a brief pause, he said, "If I can ask, what herbs are you using to treat an upset stomach here? Quine rind? Candiane root?"

The master's hands paused. His head turned once again, looking over his shoulder.

"Gimme a minute?"

"Of course."

He turned his back to Ainz again and went back to his grinding. But even facing away, it was clear his attitude had changed.

The key was finding common ground in a person's background or their interests—that was the most basic of conversation techniques Satoru Suzuki had learned on the sales grind.

A total stranger or a fellow fan? Even if the product itself, the appearance, the price, and the terms stayed exactly the same, most clients would respond better with the latter.

If this apothecary was passionate about his work, then Ainz had assumed talking shop would be the best way in.

"That's what I'm making now. Can't find quine in these parts, so I'm using azen leaves. You might have heard, but once you crush those, they lose their medicinal properties quickly. But if you grind 'em too fast and they get warm, they're also ruined." Once he'd crushed enough, the man poured some goopy fluid into the bowl. "Sap excreted from a tap on a nelay tree. Mix the two and you get a stable product. But used like this, it doesn't do much; you gotta take it one step further."

The master turned back to Ainz and gave him a long, searching look. He sniffed once and scowled.

"...Don't smell it on you. Show me your hands."

Ainz did as he was told. Pretty sure what this meant, he turned his hands palm up, showing off his fingertips. At this distance, there wasn't much danger he'd try and touch them, but just in case, he prepped excuses to make if the man got up.

"No green scent on you. There ain't an apothecary in the world who can escape it. That and the stains on your fingertips. I heard you were an arcane caster, but you makin' your medicines by other means?"

He'd anticipated this question, so he could have crushed some herbs ahead of time to come wreathed in the right odor and win the master's trust. Ainz's hands were illusions, so he could easily have made them look right as well.

There were two reasons why he hadn't done that.

First, the Baleare home didn't smell like that. Certainly, the odors were quite powerful while they were working, and the workshop as well as their work clothes were similarly intense.

But that smell didn't linger around him all the time. Nfirea in particular took great care in deodorizing. Perhaps that was unique to the Baleares, but in Ainz's experience, when pretending to be something you're not, modeling your false identity on a real individual usually turned out more natural and led to less lying to fill in the gaps.

Secondly, Ainz knew nothing about herbology.

He could fake the smell and the stains and claim to be an apothecary's disciple, but he would only be able to answer precious few questions about the mixing process. It would not take long to catch him out, and that glaring hole in his cover story could bring the whole charade crashing down, forcing them to leave the village.

"No, I don't do anything of the sort. I learned what I do know from an alchemist, and even then, it was just a smattering of knowledge."

Ainz had concocted a cover story to avoid being caught in a lie and skirted the edge of contradiction.

"…Hmm, well, all right."

He could tell the master had lost interest in him.

A reasonable response. Expected, even.

That was why Ainz had prepped a few morsels to keep him curious. As the man turned back to his worktable, Ainz stepped over and laid one of those tidbits down next to him.

"This is a healing potion obtained from a source of mine."

The glass bottle itself had been made in E-Rantel and was the opposite of elegant; the contents, on the other hand, were something the Baleares had made in the process of developing red healing potions. They'd now successfully completed their research on said red potions and were currently working on ways to make them with more cost-effective herbs and alchemical substances. As a result, this potion was not widely circulated.

"It's…purple?" the apothecary asked as he picked up the bottle. "The glass itself isn't colored, so why isn't it blue? Something mixed into it?"

He peered into the bottom and gave it shake.

"Looks like there's some sediment…," he muttered. "Mind if I try it?"

"Go ahead."

Before the words had even left Ainz's mouth, the apothecary opened the bottle, cut his hand with a knife, and doused the wound with the potion. He used quite a bit, almost half the bottle.

The wound was already visibly closing up. Not exactly instant, but…

"That's fast. Don't even need to time it. Assuming herbs and magical solutions…but what's the sediment?"

This guy talks to himself a lot. And wasn't he just using that knife to chop stuff up? Is that safe to use on your own hand? Is magical solution *what dark elves call alchemical tinctures? And the way he used it… Aren't you supposed to use the whole bottle no matter how bad the wound? Or is it just that in the heat of battle, no one can risk eyeballing the severity of an injury to figure out the right dosage?*

The master licked the potion off his hand and sniffed it.

"I smell azen…?"

Before Ainz could even say anything, he realized his error.

"No, that was on my hand already. So why is it odorless? To disguise it?"

Disguise what?

"No…," the apothecary said as he turned toward Ainz. "Are all city potions this color?"

"They are not. I've heard this came from E-Rantel, the city ruled by an undead king. No idea how it reached me, but it's quite valuable. Common potions I've seen are all blue."

The master let out a long breath.

"An undead king? No, that's not the issue here. It sounds like a big issue for somebody else, but so be it. Mm. Mind if I have this?"

He pointed at the half left in the bottle.

"For the right terms." Certain the man was listening now, Ainz added, "I want some information. You're doing this job in this forest, so I'm sure you know a lot about the place. I think that knowledge would be worth trading for. If you're interested, of course."

There was a long silence.

"What would you be doing with this knowledge?" the master asked.

Given the man's attitude thus far, Ainz could imagine what answers he'd find amenable. Anything involving self-improvement or becoming a better apothecary. But those were answers Ainz couldn't provide.

"I don't have a concrete goal here. That knowledge might come in handy for a trade sometime in the future. Plus, it'll slake my curiosity."

Ainz had expected it, but the man's brow furrowed.

"…That's it?"

"Like we discussed earlier, I'm an arcane caster. I'm more than a little good at that, but I was a lousy alchemist. My teacher told me I have no potential. I've got no intention of entering the apothecary game. But the knowledge itself is a whole other story. Knowledge is power and a weapon. Having it makes all the difference. And it's worth having you owe me one."

"…………How so?"

"You know I'm no apothecary. You're not about to teach me any of your biggest secrets. Right?" Ainz didn't even wait for the man's answer. "But I'm offering a mystery healing potion, something extremely rare. Is there anything you're willing to teach me that can match its value? I have my doubts, and if I'm right, you'll end up owing me."

"I might just dole out some basic brewing and medical knowledge and claim my debt is paid. Then maybe I would tell everyone I owe you nothing. I could even say what I provided was worth more and that *you're* the one who owes me."

"Suit yourself."

The apothecary blinked at him.

"There are two downsides to that. First, you can't lie to yourself. If you exchange trivial knowledge for something genuinely valuable, you'll just saddle yourself with guilt."

"Oh, really now?"

"And second, you'll gain a reputation for shamelessness. If we have any future dealings, how you behave now will inform what comes later. If I head back to the city and tell this story, what will other apothecaries—those who know more than I do—think?"

"Aha. They'll think that's all we provincial barbarians know, and then the dark elves and their apothecary will be a laughingstock. I'd be the fool who can't even tell how valuable this potion is, or else I'd be someone who didn't have knowledge worth trading for. Or worse, a man so unscrupulous that I didn't even bother to strike a fair deal."

"Then again, perhaps they'll think you're clever enough to get top-shelf goods at bottom-bin prices."

"…Is that how city apothecaries think? Don't they try to provide good services for fair prices?"

"All sorts of people live in cities, I'm afraid. There may be some blinded by short-term profit, who never spare a thought to where it'll leave them. But I doubt those people last long; no one would ever deal with them again. Merchants who take good care of new customers pave their own way to future success. Like how people say you have to spend to gain."

"Heh-heh-heh," the apothecary chuckled. This was the first time he'd cracked a smile. "You sure know how to talk circles around people. Born with the gift of gab."

Ainz was relieved. He'd thought this dark elf was a bit more emotional.

The fact of the matter was that your average salesman had trouble more often with clients who acted on emotions rather than logic. You could lay out the pros and cons, but if they ultimately went with their gut instead, game over. People like that were far more likely to agree to something one day and change their minds the next.

The best salesmen claimed these people were actually easier to deal with once you won them over, but Ainz—or Satoru Suzuki—had been thoroughly average and preferred to avoid them.

"No one's ever told me that before."

It was a genuine first for Ainz.

"I bet everyone thinks it and just keeps it to themselves."

His mood had certainly improved.

"Really? I find that hard to believe."

"Heh-heh-heh. Well, if I'm trading knowledge worth this potion, it's gonna have to be one serious secret. How long will you be staying?"

"We don't have set plans, but not that long. Seven days at the most."

The master made a face.

"Oh…then…"

He fell silent, thinking for a long time. Ainz said nothing.

"In that length of time, I can't teach you any of the true mysteries. Medicines are usually kept secret because they involve minute changes— you gotta harvest the ingredients at the right time and learn to identify that from small shifts in the odor or texture, make slight adjustments to the amount you use. I'd rather spend a good six months pounding that into your skull."

Ainz would rather the man just wrote the recipe down, but even he could tell that would probably infuriate this master.

"So I can't teach those and I'm not sure it'll be worth the price, but I can share knowledge on how to brew some rare medicines. How's that sound?"

"That'll be just fine. As you see fit."

"Then…you're sleeping here from now on. We've got little time. Gotta make it a part of you."

"——Um, what?"

That would be bad. Really bad.

He wanted to minimize the chances of anyone seeing through his illusion. And he didn't have to eat, sleep, or relieve himself. No matter how good his performance, he'd get caught eventually.

"Sorry, but I have my niece and nephew with me. I don't mind if that means you teach me less. I'll take proper notes."

"…You'll have to memorize them. No writing allowed."

"Oh…?"

Ainz trailed off.

He wasn't sure he could remember things that way.

Certainly, he'd poured his entire self into *Yggdrasil* and had no difficulty recalling vast amounts of information. But this time, he had no real interest in what he was learning. The thought of trying to memorize everything made him shake his head.

And if employees just listened without taking notes, wouldn't that make the boss nervous?

Satoru Suzuki certainly thought so, but his silence was interpreted otherwise.

"That doesn't work for you?" the apothecary master said. "I haven't asked about how that potion was made. Remember that while you consider these terms."

"No notes at all? I dunno. My memory just isn't that reliable. The notes are to help me learn things."

"Absolutely not!" The master's spittle flew. "Your *body* is supposed to remember it! Any apothecary apprentice learns how to measure things by the weight on their palm!"

It felt like insisting that wasn't possible wouldn't go down well. Ainz wondered if he should lie.

He wasn't about to insist lying was inherently wrong. The concept of the white lie existed for a reason. But he did want to avoid any malicious deceptions here.

Well, this is a pain.

The way this was going, Ainz was about to become this man's student and get some intensive training. But he hadn't been planning on committing to anything so grand. All he'd hoped for was a chance to maybe learn something useful if the man was willing to share. Maybe catch a glimpse of dark elf herbology and, if that proved in any way superior to what the Nation of Darkness had, find a way to acquire it later—sending some interns, maybe.

His only real goal here was to acquire a scrap of knowledge to bring home and investigate. Ainz himself had never intended to study anything in depth.

Honestly, when he'd said the payment would be knowledge, he'd have been perfectly happy to simply take home a potion made here and foist it off on Nfirea. That would have been no—well, not much of a—problem. Nfirea would likely have been able to analyze the composition.

Hmm. Maybe I blew my lead-in here. But that was the only way I could think to get his attention. That was why we're talking at all. And there is the possibility we wouldn't manage to reverse engineer a potion, so this approach isn't entirely without merit. What do I do? No, first I've gotta decide if I should lie here and if I do, how.

"Well?"

Didn't look like he had time to mull this over. He'd just have to wing it.

"…The man who taught me did say similar things."

The apothecary master nodded emphatically, pleased that city masters understood the proper way to do things.

"But he also said this: *You're dumb as a post, so write things down. How many times you plan to make me say the same things?*"

"…………Huh?" The master's eyes went wide; then his brows went up. "…*Are* you that dumb?"

"Well, he said as much."

"O-oh. No, no, masters are always harsh on their disciples. I'm sure he didn't mean it. Not entirely. I mean, your arguments were logically sound and smartly blocked all my routes of evasion. That shouldn't be possible if you're truly dumb."

Now he's trying to comfort me.

Dark elves or not, claiming to be an idiot effectively shut any argument down. This world was hardly a kind one, so Ainz thought there was a chance the master might wash his hands of him, but apparently not.

"I'm sure the fault lies with me. My memory is just that poor."

"A-ah…"

Ainz must have really sold that line, because the apothecary looked away in discomfort.

There was a long silence.

It was becoming increasingly likely the master would refuse to teach him at all—if he couldn't even measure things properly, he was liable to end up concocting poison.

But at length, the man said, "Very well, then," like light had dawned.

Ainz wondered why, and the master looked momentarily impressed—but this quickly faded back to his standard grump. A flicker so brief, it might have been entirely in Ainz's mind—but wasn't.

Ainz braced himself. He didn't know what this meant, but it was clear the man had made his decision.

He felt like he saw a familiar demon hovering over the master's shoulder, grinning at him.

What's going on here? This better not be anything weird.

"In that case, we have no choice. Seven days at most—meaning you might leave earlier, right? With that brief a window, I don't want to waste time repeating myself. Just promise to burn the notes once you've got 'em memorized."

Ainz didn't know what had changed the apothecary's mind. That made him cautious, but he didn't let it show.

"You have my word," he said.

"Good. You asked for the hard stuff, so I'll teach it to you. I'm a harsh teacher, but you better not come crying to me later, hear?"

He hadn't remembered asking for anything like that, but he put that argument aside in favor of saying, "I'd rather you be nice?"

The apothecary's jaw dropped, and then he made a face like he'd just swallowed a bug.

Ainz wasn't against harsh instruction but definitely preferred the latter if the option existed.

"Unbelievable…"

"I mean, I don't want to get beaten with a hot poker here."

"D-did your teacher do *that*?!"

"No, he didn't."

"Well, neither will I!"

"That's great to hear."

Ainz held up his hands, grinning, and the master scowled at him.

"Right, I think I've started to figure you out. And I'm beginning to feel sorry for your last teacher. In any case, let's get started. I'm gonna name a few medicines and what they do—teaching you about anything you already know would be a waste... Well, maybe not entirely. If the components are different, there can be value in learning that. Anyway, you can tell me what you wanna learn."

"Thank you. But first—one last question. You're fine with just taking me at my word?"

If he wanted Ainz signing anything, or worse, casting a binding spell of some kind, he might be better off backing out of this whole thing.

"I am. Trust is important. If you turn it into a book, word might get back around to me eventually. I'll lower my opinion of you then. You and all city apothecaries."

"Makes sense. I certainly don't want to cause harm to their reputation, too. I promise I will not be publishing anything learned here."

·

The apothecary master watched the man from the city until he was out of sight, then chuckled to himself.

How long had it been since he saw anyone out? It might have been the very first time since he was appointed head apothecary.

An astonishingly clever man. Is the city full of people like him?

He found that hard to believe. Or rather, hard to imagine.

I knew the city had more people in it than all the dark elves in these woods, but that man has to be among the best of them. Assuming a man of his intelligence is bog standard there, then if our ties to the city deepen and our dealings grow frequent, we'll have to exercise incredible caution or we'll be taken advantage of before we know it.

A modest man, he'd put himself down, but if those words were true, he could never talk like that. Given how the conversation had gone and the information that had been exchanged—that was simply not how a stupid man communicated.

So why had he insisted on writing his teachings down? Had he not been concerned that it would provoke the apothecary master and prevent him from learning anything?

The more he'd insisted he was a fool with a lousy memory, the more the apothecary had started to suspect there was something afoot.

After all, he could have just written things down later on. In other words, he had good reason to risk the master's ire and insist on writing things down before his very eyes. Namely...

It took me a minute, but there were two points he wanted to make clear. First, he's not hiding anything.

Of course, that didn't mean the apothecary master took him at his word. He might be revealing one truth to hide something else. For better or worse, they'd just met today, and the master wasn't quite ready to completely trust a stranger. Yet, the man's attempts to show his hand and prove he wasn't hiding anything went a long way toward building confidence.

The second thing he couldn't say outright—but I took it as a request to teach the hardest brews I can despite the lack of time. Stuff you wouldn't remember just seeing it done a few times.

The man was no dedicated apothecary, so he had a lot of nerve trying to learn challenging brews. And most of those concoctions used valuable ingredients. Perhaps that was why he couldn't ask for them directly.

He was clearly a man of propriety.

But the apothecary master didn't have a problem with that.

From the get-go, this was an exchange for an unknown potion, likely of legendary quality. He'd been ready to share his trade secrets. There were three main categories the dark elves kept under wraps.

First: The brew itself was tricky.

Second: The recipe required extremely rare ingredients.

Third: The potency was too high to be worth the risks.

Those were the three.

He'd mentioned the first as an argument against teaching his secrets. He was now planning on teaching something from the second category.

It was always possible ingredients that were hard to find in the forest were readily available in the city. That sort of thing happened all the time with herbs. But they'd get nowhere if they were too hung up on that little detail. And since the first category was impossible and the third too risky, the second category was the apothecary master's only real option here.

This was a fair trade for what he'd gained, and if the rare ingredients became valued in the city, that could work to his advantage.

If the visitor went home, ended up talking about the brew he'd learned, and it became widely known that the ingredients had value, then traders from the city might come to the dark elf village seeking those out. The purple potion the apothecary master examined seemed to suggest city brewers were very accomplished. Any chance to pick their brains or obtain ingredients they commonly used would benefit the apothecary master in the long run.

He wasn't sure the man's arrival would actually lead to trade with the city. If someone had suggested he agree to this exchange with an eye on profit, he likely would never have gotten on board. If he'd been the kind of man smart enough to break things down in utilitarian pros and cons, the villagers would never have called him ornery and he wouldn't have reached this age without so much as a wife to his name. Even other apothecaries kept their distance, a fact that bothered him, but not enough to make him change his ways.

The visitor had spoken of ventures and gains. The apothecary master usually loathed such topics. But—and this was the fascinating part—the visitor had framed those terms with an apothecary's pride. In spite of himself, the thought that his skills would be discredited in some far-off land without him ever finding out was something the apothecary master could not abide.

For that reason, he felt compelled to value the purple potion accurately and return something of greater worth.

The visitor had certainly been persuasive. He'd come at him from both sides, logical and emotional.

Generally, the teacher had all the advantage and a would-be learner had to bow and scrape.

That sure hadn't happened here.

He had to provide a lesson of comparable value to that potion, but the decision on what counted was entirely up to him. Up to that point, they stood on even ground.

But the man swiftly brought up the subject of notes, exposing himself.

If he did that to prove he had nothing to hide just so he could win my trust… then I've got to do my part to win his. But…

That was tricky.

The master settled down at his worktable, scowling.

…I don't know if I even can.

He was well aware he wasn't the most social dark elf around.

On the rare occasions he'd taught villagers his knowledge, he hadn't been the best teacher.

If I wasn't teaching, I could use those herbs to help myself unclench a bit…

He glanced at a bundle of dried leaves on the shelf and shook his head. They were used to alleviate pain and excelled at banishing stress. But it would hardly be appropriate for a teacher to dose himself before class.

"I'll just have to do what I can," he muttered.

Still, the visitor wasn't much of an actor. He was watching my every move, forgetting to blink… He's just that interested, I guess? Heh-heh. His features make him look younger than me, and the way he acted makes me confident he is. Kinda cute, really.

4

Ainz and the twins were eating together.

Well, Ainz wasn't capable of eating, so it was just Aura and Mare. They had more on the table than the natural flavorings the dark elves had provided.

Ainz had pulled out some Nazarick food from his inventory.

Aura and Mare had taken one bite of each dish the dark elves supplied and written their opinions of it on some paper next to them. Later, they would show these to knowledgeable members of different races in E-Rantel for further investigation.

That said, at the moment, they'd made no discoveries of note—financial or otherwise. It wasn't clear what relations they might have with this village in the future, but they did not seem like they'd be a profitable trade partner.

The reason he was having the twins sample each and record their impressions was so Ainz would have something to say if anyone happened to ask.

This plan had one big problem. Aura and Mare were used to Nazarick food—they had discerning palates. The two of them didn't have a single positive thing to say about the dark elf cuisine so far. But telling the chef, *It tastes terrible*, required you to be either entirely inconsiderate of people's feelings, willing to ruin relations with this village, or possibly a very young child.

So their meal was taking quite a while.

A bite, some chewing, a frown, and then their honest opinion. Then some flipping through their notes, frowning harder, and finally writing something nice. They couldn't exactly say, *Fresh ingredients!* every time. They needed to change it up.

If they'd had a thesaurus available, it would have been soon worn out. By the time they'd pried their impressions out and put it to paper, both kids looked exhausted. Like they'd just completed an eating competition.

"Good work," Ainz said, well aware of the effort involved.

They brightened up immediately.

"No, this is nothi…no big deal, Uncle Ain!"

"R-right. W-we're just eating and writing what we think!"

Mare wasn't wrong, but as someone who couldn't eat, it was hard to just nod agreeably. Especially since their efforts were for his benefit.

They were children, so if they expressed their unvarnished opinions, it would likely not cause (major) issues. Ainz's words were another matter. If he could partake himself, he would likely have been desperately racking his brain for polite phrases, too.

He couldn't thank them enough, but repeating himself would just start becoming oppressive.

So he said nothing more, simply listening to their reviews.

Their honest takes matched up perfectly and never changed. Just to be sure, they went through them anyway.

"Perhaps we should have offered some properly seasoned food and told them this is how we eat? They might have tried to make something similar."

"It's poss— Maybe, yeah?" Aura was still tripping over her word choices every now and then. "When you got to fry meat, all you really need to do is salt it—and it'll be just fine. But the way they keep it fresh isn't all that great, so the meat is still pretty gamey. Perhaps there are people who prefer it that way, but I'm n—I ain't one of 'em."

They'd been in this village a while, but Aura still wasn't used to talking to Ainz this way.

"I—I agree. It smells funny."

"Hmm."

"The veggies are better, but they're lacking in sweetness. Bitter or tart hit you first. Again, people who like that might enjoy that? I wonder if they could make some sauces out of the fruit."

"I could use some dressing, at least."

"Mm-hmm."

Pretty much the same as always.

"Then let me see what you've written down, please."

Glancing them over, he could tell they were trying very hard to say something nice.

Ainz bowed his head again internally.

Once he'd read them through—they weren't particularly long—he did his best to remember the contents and handed the notebooks back. Morning prep complete.

Time to head out to work.

"Okay! It's about time for me to get going. I might be late again, so feel free to eat without me."

They answered as one, but Ainz noticed Aura had almost said something else.

"What is it, Aura? Something on your mind?"

"Uh, well, er...yeah, maybe, Uncle Ain. You're going to study medicine again today?"

"That's correct. Apparently, I'm learning a slightly harder brew today. I used a Gate to ask Nfirea about the medicine's name, but he hadn't heard of it. It would be much faster if we could get them to trust Messages..." Ainz sighed. "But I suppose there is a chance an enemy of Nazarick would use them, so let's just let them have it their way."

"——Will that be an issue?"

Aura's tone shifted, so Ainz matched her.

If she was asking as a floor guardian, then Ainz must answer as the ruler of Nazarick.

"I'm not sure. But I don't plan to make the medicine myself. If any of the components involved existed in *Yggdrasil*, I *know* my brew would fail."

Much like cooking.

Ainz lacked the relevant skill, so he could craft nothing that involved *Yggdrasil* herbs or alchemical solutions. But he *could* make medicine using this world's techniques and herbs found only here. While studying with the apothecary, the first step was to make sure he knew exactly what went into a particular recipe.

Still—

"So many mysteries. We can't use *Yggdrasil* herbs, but what happens if they're cultivated in this world's soil? Do those count as herbs from this world or not?"

"I—I think it's the latter."

"Likely, yes. But what happens if the potency diminishes? Herbs raised by human hands are nowhere near as effective. Nfirea says our efforts to cultivate them around E-Rantel aren't working out because there's something lacking in the soil. A vital nutrient perhaps. That's why they're experimenting with cultivation inside the forest."

"Yes, they are. A little patch of them in the woods. There were lots of logs with mushrooms or moss growing on them, too. I remember seeing those when I went to take a peek. It's actually kinda hard to get close to that village these days...," Aura said.

Enri's goblins were on watch for quite some distance around Carne. There were goblin trap makers, and the traps they made sounded alarms—which were much harder to detect than traps that did damage.

"But if nutrients are the issue, we could just have Mare help or use items."

Both looked at Mare, who shrank visibly.

"Er, um, so, I *can* do that, but I'm not actually sure that's what's needed. I a-actually am sneaking into the E-Rantel Adventurers Guild field at night to see, but I feel like that's not the right approach."

The harvested ingredients might look the same, but once you made a potion from them, the effects were slightly diminished. A particularly unwelcome outcome.

Was Mare *over*supplying them? Was it pure coincidence? Was there something else missing? A better spell for these herbs? There were so many factors involved that no clear answer had emerged.

"We've been here a few years now, but there's still so much we don't know."

"Right."

"R-right."

Each time they learned something, they found more they didn't know. The mysteries only deepened over time. But fortunately—if that was the word for it—they were all things that didn't exactly seem high priority. Quite a lot of them had been left on the back burner.

If these issues could be left to minions or summons, they might have solved them already, but those beings weren't capable of handling all the experiments needed.

It seemed that the bare minimum was an NPC—a being created the same way a player was. But it was possible players and NPCs would have different results. If they really wanted to be thorough, they'd have to do each experiment three times, once with Ainz, once with an NPC, and once with a minion.

"Cultivation experiments might be best left in the hands of those under our control, but we can't have truly vital experiments leaking to anyone who might potentially become a threat to us. That's why we're having those done with Nazarick insiders alone—but our numbers are limited. What a headache."

Keep an eye on other countries for technological breakthroughs, while taking steps within Nazarick to ensure our technological superiority.

Hard work, but...

With Albedo and Demiurge in charge of it, I'm sure it'll be fine. They're both very smart.

In fact, they might already have handled the matter and he was just butting his oar in. Couldn't hurt to bring it up, at least.

I can have a summon write a note and drop it in the suggestion box again.

That way he could avoid the risk of anyone asking, *You just now noticed? —Whoops.*

"Oh dear! It's time! Gotta run!"

Before they could even nod, Ainz burst from the elf tree.

Showing up late was out of the question. Back when he'd been a lowly employee, he'd never once been tardy. No matter how obsessed with *Yggdrasil* he got.

Gotta hustle!

Light struck his face.

A ray of sunshine filtered through the branches above, telling him it was another beautiful day.

•

Aura listened until her master's footsteps were out of earshot before she spoke.

"I feel like Lord... *Haaagh.*"

She trailed off in a sigh. It was hard to keep the act up when it was just the two of them. Not good. Meanwhile, Mare wasn't really doing any kind of act at all.

It was hardly fair. She shot him a look.

"Mm? Aura, wh-what is it?"

"Mm? Nothing. Nothing at all!" Taking out her frustrations on her brother wouldn't help. Aura put her head on right and finished her earlier thought. "Uncle Ain seems to be having fun."

Mare nodded at that.

Aura didn't really get why, though. Her head tilted to one side.

"He's been running to the apothecary every day since we got here, but is it really worth all that effort?"

"Good question. B-but I can't use the druid spells with these trees, so maybe their medicine has some unique qualities, too."

"If someone as smart as Uncle Ain is this interested, maybe. But I find it hard to believe that this poky little town has something so special to offer. I mean, even the tree magic is just something you happen to not have, right? Or is it something other druids can't use, either?"

"Hmm. I don't know. Other people, um, might be able to, but I feel like it's elf-specific magic that originated in this world. Like daily-life magic did. Also, if Uncle Ain is spending this much time on something, it must be worth it, right?"

That went without saying.

"Yeah, that's probably true." Aura looked up at the ceiling, then back at Mare. "So why is it he's having so much fun?"

"W-well, you know. N-new knowledge—gaining information? That's fun? He really likes information."

"Okay, okay. That, I get. That's how he can make such good plans."

Their master wasn't *just* smart. His obsessive hunger for knowledge directly fed the brilliance and foresight that saw so far ahead.

She remembered Demiurge saying their master had plans that spanned a thousand years, and the way he acted made that claim very convincing.

Aura let out a sigh of admiration.

He hadn't led the Supreme Beings for nothing.

BubblingTeapot was still her ultimate master, but Ainz was close behind. Peroroncino lagged a distant third. Ankoro Mocchi Mochi and Yamaiko were tied at fourth and the rest of the Supreme Beings beneath them. Mare ranked everyone below third basically the same.

"That's our uncle! Meanwhile..." Aura's face fell. "We're getting nowhere."

Mare looked just as gloomy.

"Y-yeah. We've learned nothing special, not one piece of information that sounds relevant. And we've gotta try again?"

"What else can we do? I'm getting real sick of playing house. But if we play something else, then what? We'd probably win most games without even trying, and if we pretend to lose, what'll happen if they find out and think we're making fun of them? Technically, we're supposed to be getting along."

A long silence.

Another day of playing house lay before them. But they had no solid reason to back out of playing with the village children and had no alternate proposals. If this wasn't a directive from a Supreme Being, they might have tried faking sick, but that was off the table.

"...............Well, at least we know my tamer skills don't work on dark elves. That's something we didn't know before." Aura saw Mare wince, so she snapped, "I'm including one-hundred-level dark elves, you know."

The reminder made him shudder.

•

Ainz crossed the bridge between trees, bathed in the dappled sunlight filtering down from above.

Every now and then, a dark elf waved at him. Not just that—a dark elf walking his way smiled and said, "Fior, off to the apothecary master again?"

"That I am," Ainz replied.

The fake name had startled him at first, but after a few days, he'd gotten used to it.

"I'm afraid I've got no knack for it, so I'm giving my provisional master no end of headaches."

"Your casting skills are plenty magnificent. If you were an equally skilled apothecary, that would be far more astonishing. Same as how no one's both a skilled druid and a skilled ranger at the same time."

Ainz had slain a beast that approached the village—a giant hypnotism python. This had earned him tremendous respect from the dark elves who lived here.

Ever since then, people waved and came over to chat. Their admiration was evident.

"That certainly makes me feel better. Much as I'd love to stop and talk, I am keeping my provisional master waiting. If you'll excuse me."

"I do apologize. Don't let me delay you further!"

Completing a polite extraction, Ainz pressed on, arriving at the place he'd spent the last few days training.

"Sorry I'm late," he said, stepping into the elf tree.

He was not actually late. Time was entirely subjective in this village; only the hunters were at all strict about it. Most people never promised to be anywhere on time, preferring to play it very loose indeed. No one had specifically told Ainz to be here at this hour.

But he was a little later than usual, so he figured it was worth acknowledging.

In fact—

"You aren't late at all, though?"

Was the only response.

The apothecary master never looked his way. Looking distinctly uncomfortable with the process, he was slowly, gingerly adding crushed herbs to a plate.

Ainz took a seat next to him and, once he was done, picked up the plate and set it on the scale. Then he began adding weights to the opposing plate.

He didn't get it right the first time and had to swap weights in and out several times before the plates balanced properly. Ainz then wrote down the final measurements on the page he kept close at hand.

"Okay, what's next?"

The apothecary had been growing increasingly agitated the whole time, and he snatched the dish of herbs away, moving them to a different dish. He *was* being careful, but it was impossible to get all the herbs off the dish— some residue and fluids remained behind.

The master scowled at that, then tried to use a scraper on it.

If this tool had been made of rubber, perhaps it would have come off clean, but unfortunately, it was made of wood. He got some off, but there was still some left.

"Argh, what a mess!" he yelled, mussing his own hair.

He never would have let Ainz see him this distraught the first day. This was less because the days they'd spent together had brought his guard down than a demonstrative act provoked by his irritation with the workflow Ainz had proposed. It was mostly a hint he'd really like to stop.

"Hang in there, Provisional Master."

The apothecary shot him a sulky look.

That might get one reaction from women or children, but from a grown-ass man, it did not exactly make Ainz's mind waver. No matter how handsome dark elves were.

"...Provisional Disciple, you've turned this into a complete nightmare."

"We've gone over the reasons. And you agreed. I didn't force you into anything."

"......At the time, I thought you had a point. Certainly, our village had no giants. But once I slept on it...I realized that learning to feel it by hand is important. Once you learn that, you can always take measurements later when you're back home."

The apothecary sounded less and less confident as he went on.

Ainz was swearing internally—he'd hoped the master wouldn't pick up on that.

He wasn't sure if this observation came too late or too soon, but he'd certainly hoped to keep him confuddled.

The dish-based approach was the result of the apothecary's attempts to get Ainz to learn by the weight on his palm and then with his tongue.

The hand he could obfuscate—he just had to work harder on the illusion. But flavor was a nonstarter. Put it on your tongue and feel how numb it gets... Easily said, but Ainz didn't *have* a tongue. A fact he could hardly admit here.

So he'd made excuses. "In the city I'm from, we have creatures large and small, from giants to dwarves. Treating them requires different dosages. For that reason, I'd like to take accurate measures of the volume of herbs needed in a single dose, so I can later adjust that to match the body mass of the patient."

The apothecary master had treated only dark elves, so these words rang true.

Ainz thought the story had a grain of truth to it. But he was also well aware it was a deception.

The logic behind it was based more on the world he'd come from and might not apply here.

This world ran on magic, and that warped the laws of physics. Potions clearly had one foot in the realm of magic, so it seemed altogether plausible they would hardly function the way things had where he came from.

He knew for a fact that a small potion could heal a giant's injuries just as well.

Naturally, your average human and your average frost giant's maximum HP were substantially different, so you'd imagine the amount recovered would differ. And yet, in practice, it seemed to be identical. They hadn't experimented to be strictly sure—this was an estimate based on what Ainz knew about *Yggdrasil*, the principles of which were rather similar to this world's. So there *was* a possibility his rationale here was actually true.

In retrospect, I should probably just have said I have no sense of taste.

That would have saved them a lot of trouble. But if he'd gone that route, it probably would have led to other problems somewhere.

No use crying over spilled milk. What I need now is something that'll silence his complaints and convince him…but nothing springs to mind. I thought I had him where I wanted him so didn't prep any other excuses. Big mistake.

Ainz adjusted his facial illusion, closing the eyes. Since it *was* just an illusion, he could still see just fine.

The twins had said his face didn't move nearly enough—*It's like you're wearing a mask.* So he was making a point of closing his eyes sometimes. The parts left uncovered by the cloth—his brows and eyelids—were particularly vital in conveying emotion, so if they never moved, it was just like he was staring fixedly at a single point and rather unsettling. He'd had no idea.

With them supervising, he'd practiced until he was capable of producing things that looked enough like emotion to pass rudimentary inspection. Even then, that was true only when he was consciously controlling it. The movements were still rather clunky, and he definitely couldn't do anything at all if he wasn't focused on it.

It wasn't clear how the apothecary had interpreted this bout of silence, but he said, "And doing it this way—you know it's unproductive. Far less medicine produced a day is bad for the village!"

A fair assessment.

The village had a number of druids, albeit low-level ones, and they could heal most urgent injuries. The demand for medicine came from hunters and anyone else leaving the village proper—people who necessarily would be far from the druids.

If the druids accompanied the hunters, they might help when injuries occurred, but since they weren't good at concealing themselves, they'd get in the way of the actual hunts.

Ainz didn't know much about hunting, so he was of the opinion they should just make a base camp and leave the druids on standby there, but this village had its own way of doing things. Likely the result of trying things out and seeing what worked. An outsider with little knowledge of the forest itself really shouldn't be sticking his nose in.

"And can anyone truly say that the properties don't change while the mixture is sitting on this dish? They cannot."

The scale and its dishes were a retired model taken from the Baleares— to Ainz's knowledge, the most accomplished alchemists this world had to offer. If they'd used them without issues, there likely wouldn't be any issues. He'd said as much already—specifically, that he'd been given it by his master, so it should be fine.

But when asked, "Did your master use the same herbs? Can you say these herbs won't be affected?" he'd been at a loss. Without asking, he couldn't really know.

"Like I said before, it should be fine."

"*Should* isn't *will be*. You aren't completely sure! You have doubts yourself! Are doubts allowed? Medicine can be harmful. What if this dish causes a reaction and the result winds up hurting someone?"

"............That seems highly unlikely."

"Yeah, maybe so. But to be absolutely sure, we'd have to make every kind of medicine and double-check. And even if we did, the change might be minor enough that we wouldn't even notice! But after days or weeks pass, the change could become much more significant. Then we go use it on someone in critical condition and the changes wind up killing someone it should have saved."

His reasoning was perfectly sound.

Ainz had no basis to make clear declarations against any of these hypotheticals. He could not defeat this argument.

And what Ainz did know was stopgap knowledge. How was that supposed to compete with the wealth of knowledge a true master had? If either Baleare had been here, they'd likely have made swift work of things.

But he couldn't afford to back down.

Especially given the potential involvement of the tongue he didn't have.

"Then you just keep doing it your way. I'll take the raw data back to the city and follow up on your suggestions to investigate things."

Ainz rattled all this off before the apothecary could say anything else. Only a fool would let his opponent fire back. Ainz *was* a fool and frequently got hit with return fire—or shot in the back. Mostly by Demiurge.

"There are more apothecaries in the city. With their help, we can make a lot of medicine rapidly. And there are all sorts of races, so I can borrow the help of apothecaries from those races to ensure it's safe for all."

The master looked a bit disgruntled. These medicines were passed down from generation to generation in his tribe and considered trade secrets. He likely wasn't thrilled about them being shared with that many people. Ainz sympathized. Albeit less concerned about vested interests than sharing knowledge with those who might prove a threat to him.

Ainz did not actually intend to do anything he'd claimed. It was simply a rationale he'd concocted to get through this impasse.

Ainz's friends had taught him well.

The true value in knowledge came from monopolizing it.

If he shared the knowledge he'd gained here with anyone, it would be with the inhabitants of Nazarick.

"If you've got no arguments, Master, let's proceed."

The apothecary looked less than pleased by this assault. But he didn't have a decisive argument, so he shrugged and went back to putting herbs on the dish.

He moved fast. It was not easy for Ainz to play his part and take notes.

Perhaps that was the goal.

If he finished his side of things and Ainz still wasn't done, then he'd have an excuse to jeer. Less because he was trying to get through a job he didn't like than payback for having argued him down.

Not so fast, buddy.

Sure, Ainz wasn't as fast as a professional apothecary. But he *had* spent the last few days performing the same basic tasks repeatedly. He wasn't about to call it quits now.

Getting fired up, he threw himself into his work.

When the herbs came his way, he put the appropriate weights on the scale, relying on applied experience to get it right on the first try. If he didn't have time to write things down, then he'd just have to pound those numbers into his mind. Ainz was not exactly a brainiac, but it wasn't like his short-term memory was completely lacking.

When Ainz got faster, so did the master.

Neither spoke a word. They focused purely on their tasks. If anyone else had stopped by, they would likely have been shocked by how fast the two of them were going.

But…that's the fun.

As he learned how to make the medicine, he considered the effects of it.

This medicine doesn't do that much. But if we combined it with other things...there could be some synergy.

Yggdrasil had been a game with an immense wealth of data, and players had loved nothing more than finding new ways to gain an advantage. Ainz—or Satoru Suzuki—had been but one of them.

And medicines *Yggdrasil* lacked, made with this world's original techniques—they had potential.

Compensate for the weaknesses with magic items rather than spells...but that would take time. It needs more zip...

They'd first have to investigate whether synergy was actually possible. But the potential for new methods and techniques got him excited.

I should have looked into this sooner. Ainz pictured Nfirea's face. *I have the connections. He'd tell me more if I asked...*

But Ainz had been focusing his study time on other matters. He'd left acquiring knowledge of this world's techniques to Titus, et al.

Honestly, I'm not capable of running anything, let alone a nation. I'd be better off putting myself in the research department. That's what I like doing anyway...

He'd had vague thoughts along these lines when he'd first started learning here.

If Satoru Suzuki had actually had a good brain—Ainz's skull was thoroughly empty—perhaps he could have learned both. But that had not been the case. And so he was devoting his efforts to a field he was ill-suited for—and that was arguably a complete waste of time.

I've thought about fleeing my duties before. But this isn't that. All of us have a place we're meant to be. When I get back to Nazarick, I should tell Albedo I'm transferring...but what then? Would that not be a betrayal of the NPCs' trust? I'm the guild master; I'm calling myself Ainz Ooal Gown—is that any way for me to behave? What would...the others say...? Ah!

The apothecary master's hands stopped—and with it, their competition and Ainz's line of thought.

The master had turned to face the door.

Ainz had been about to grin triumphantly but quickly hid that, following his seven-day-master's gaze. There was no one there—so he listened instead.

There was a commotion in the distance. It didn't sound urgent—at least, not like a monster attack or serious injury.

"You're the last arrivals from the city?"

"Mm? Uh, yes, we should be. I don't know of anyone else headed here. You mean…?"

"Yeah, I do. This is what it's like when someone arrives—and it's a newcomer. If it was a neighboring dark elf, it wouldn't sound like this. Might be an elf."

Could it be someone from Nazarick?

No, Ainz dismissed the thought. If they wanted to get in touch, they'd send a Message. It was hard to imagine them just popping by. But if this was an elf, he had an idea.

"An elf merchant?"

"Could…be. But…this feels different. Well, not our problem. If it was, someone would come to fetch me."

He seemed to be trying to convince himself. He turned back to the table.

"Let's keep going. I'm sure your teacher told you the potency of many brews diminishes the longer they take."

He was going much slower than a minute ago, but this didn't last long. A dark elf villager burst in, out of breath.

"Mango!" the interloper yelled. Then he saw Ainz and slowed down. "Oh, and Fior. Sorry to interrupt."

Everyone in the village knew Ainz was making regular visits here. But whatever was going on had made that fact slip his mind.

"You apologize to my provisional disciple but not to me? What's the meaning of this?" the apothecary grumbled. He didn't take any real offense. He was scowling but clearly toying with the man.

"Ah, sorry, Mango. I'm interrupting your work."

Mango Gilena—that was the apothecary master's name.

The apologetic dark elf glanced at Ainz once more but remained silent.

"Uh, if I shouldn't hear this, I can leave?"

"No, that's not it; it's just... Mango, an elf came to visit. Apparently, the human country near the forest is attacking us."

He glanced at Ainz again.

"Ah, in that case, I can promise it isn't *my* country. This is likely the Theocracy—they lie between the woods and my home. I'd heard they were at war with the elves."

The dark elf looked relieved.

"Well, the elves want us to send troops. They've got other villages to visit, so they've left already, but the elders called a meeting to decide what we should do."

5

There were quite a few dark elves in the clearing. Possibly everyone but the children.

They always gathered here for meetings.

But this clearing was not on the ground. It was like a tray suspended in the air, attached to the bridges between trees. That hardly seemed ideal if it was raining, but there was nowhere else to meet. No elf tree could handle this crowd. Possibly there were smaller meetings that took place in some elf tree or another, but now was not the time to ask.

Ainz had joined the meeting as an adviser.

This was the last role he wanted to play.

He preferred to avoid anything resembling responsibility. He wasn't getting paid a consulting fee, so why would he be happy?

He'd have preferred to join in as an observer, but they'd wanted an adviser instead. Ainz was interested enough in the content of this meeting to fret about it for a long, long, long moment and finally nod.

He was primarily interested in the outcome. Knowing that would make all the difference.

It might also be helpful to know who'd been for and against certain proposals. And what the mood of the discussion had been. The things you couldn't learn from the meeting minutes...or by hearing about it secondhand.

Even if the village reached a consensus, there might be those nursing resentment or who were just plain unconvinced. Ainz hadn't decided what they'd do with this village in the future, but it couldn't hurt to dispose of those who wouldn't benefit Nazarick and take in those who would.

Perhaps Albedo or Demiurge could have joined the meeting surreptitiously, but Ainz was better off just inviting himself along.

Glancing around the crowd, he found himself remembering his days in Ainz Ooal Gown. Faces hadn't moved in that virtual world, but during meetings, you'd sensed things anyway.

But that didn't change anything. The guild had decided things through majority vote, so it didn't really matter if you could pick up on a vibe. Here, it did.

This might be a better position than I thought. If I depart midway, leaving the decision to them, I can avoid taking the blame. And I don't have many chances to attend meetings where I'm only moderately influential.

Honestly, he didn't really get meetings. He'd been in his share of them. Satoru Suzuki had been an office drone. Few companies could avoid having meetings entirely. But those he'd joined had been all things he'd had no vote in. Meetings designed to pass down what the higher-ups had already set in stone. He'd just warmed a seat.

But once in this world?

Meetings in the Great Tomb of Nazarick were pure hell.

He was their ruler, and no matter how wrong he was, they took his word as gospel. He couldn't afford to make mistakes. But his guardians believed he was their absolute ruler, a genius capable of plotting everything out to perfection—and constantly asked for his views on things. The resulting pressure steadily ate away at him.

But here, nobody's deferring to an absolute ruler. Maybe I'll actually learn something about meetings. Nazarick ones just end with a plan of action based on whatever I suggest.

He wasn't sure what he could get out of it or even what he wanted. Perhaps just a broader perspective.

At last, the elders arrived.

They stood at the center, with the dark elves assembled in a semicircle around them. Ainz was off to the side of the elder zone.

Hmm, I might have messed this up. I ended up spending so much time at my temp master's place that I don't really know who's who.

He'd said hi to plenty of villagers whose names eluded him.

Ainz had made a point of trying to learn about the village leaders. But that had not extended to a solid grasp of who they surrounded themselves with.

He considered that a lost cause. No matter how hard he tried to make friends, he hadn't been here long enough for anyone to really open up.

Grown-ups…all have baggage. I hope the kids aren't the same.

From what little he did know, the standing arrangements were not particularly significant. Friends, family—people just stood with those they were close to.

Wishing they wore name tags, Ainz settled for making his facial illusion look grave and waited for the meeting to begin.

"Let's get started," one of the elders said—the younger man. "I'm sure everyone's heard already. But in the interest of accuracy, let me explain again. A messenger from the elf king arrived today. He said a human country to the north is advancing on the elf capital. Yes—"

Lots of people looked at Ainz here.

Likely thinking the same thing as the man who'd come by the apothecary. Should he deny it immediately? Letting confusion fester was not good.

"Sorry," Ainz said, raising a hand. There was no such rule, but he was interrupting an elder here. Best to look mindful of that. "Just to be clear, this is not the country I'm from. The invading country is exclusively human—a single-race country that regularly enslaves elves."

That word sure got a hostile reaction. But he also heard a number of meaningless whispers. "Elves," or "I knew that." Didn't seem like they discouraged chatter much.

"Like I said before, the place where I live has all sort of races in it. There are laws forbidding the residents from fighting or attacking one another. Uh, no one race gets targeted by others. There's not much crime, but…well, there's always some. Walking somewhere dangerous alone…I can't say it's entirely risk-free. Sorry, I'm getting off topic."

Ainz bobbed his head to the elders, and they returned the favor.

"So to fight these invaders, they've requested that the dark elves muster soldiers."

"It wasn't a request," a younger man said, scowling. "It was an order."

Several grunts of agreement rang out.

The elders made no attempt to stop this. They likely felt much the same.

"We called this meeting to discuss what we should do. Once we reach a conclusion here, we'll consult the other villages, too. In other words, our decision may not become the decision of all dark elves. We can take our thoughts to the other villages, but they may not accept our proposal and may not reach any conclusion at all."

Another elder took over here.

"I'd wager that's actually very likely. We all know one another here, but even we struggle to reach a consensus." At this point, he glanced at Ainz. "It's not necessarily bad that opinions are divided. Just try not to get caught up in your own point of view. Listen to what others have to say and examine their perspectives. Be aware that you must make your choice while taking into account everyone else's circumstances."

Ainz had been a guild master, and he had some doubts about this approach.

Should a leader really be letting conflicts fester and encouraging everyone to go their own ways?

If people went against the guild's decision for selfish reasons, then there was no point in forming a guild in the first place. Their strength lay in unity. Divided, they could be taken out one at a time.

But Ainz left this unsaid.

It was not the time for an outsider to impose their ideology. How would he feel if their positions were reversed?

And the woods were a dangerous place. Perhaps that had led to them prioritizing self-determination.

Even the week he'd spent here had been enough to leave Ainz with the impression that dark elves took a lot more responsibility for their own actions than humans.

A philosophy arrived at over decades and centuries would not be disrupted by the voice of one lone visitor—if it did, that was a problem in and of itself.

Besides…

Infighting among the dark elves is good for Nazarick.

"For that reason, we asked someone who knows more about the world outside to join us."

He hadn't expected to be roped in yet but managed to avoid acting flustered.

"I'm not sure how useful I'll be, but I'm certainly happy to share what I know."

An appreciative murmur went up, and one dark elf threw out a question.

"What are your thoughts, elders? We have no 'troops,' but are we sending someone?"

"We think we should," the female elder replied. "We've heard of no dark elf villages being attacked, but that could simply be because they haven't been targeted yet. I'm sure you're all aware, but we're on the outskirts of the elf country. The southeast edge of it. If these invaders march steadily forward, we'd be the last they reach."

"And if they wipe out the elves, then we'd likely not escape unscathed. In which case, it'd be a good idea to help drive them back now."

"…That's my concern, elders. Just because the elves are getting attacked, does that really mean we would be?"

Fair. From what Ainz—and Nazarick—had discovered, there had been no dark elves sold as slaves.

"In fact, if we join the elves in the war, that might convince these humans the dark elves are their enemy. Worse—can we even *beat* these humans?"

A ripple ran through the crowd.

A natural question.

This invasion was knocking at the door of the elf capital. It would be hard to turn things around. Anyone could guess this was a losing battle.

"I agree with the elders," a dark elf said, looking displeased. "Melon, when we fled to these woods, the elves took us in. You intend to forget that debt?"

Melon appeared to be the previous speaker. He hastily corrected himself. "Nah, I didn't mean that. To fight or not to fight ain't our only options. Off the top of my head, we could invite the elves to run with us. The forest ain't exactly small. I dunno the first thing about humans, but I bet they're not built for living here the way we are. If we head farther in, they might not chase after…and there's always the option of moving to a forest that's even farther away. Why are these humans attacking the elves anyway? For all we know, the elves started it."

"…In that case, it serves them right," the apothecary master muttered. Not that loud, but loud enough to make an impact.

"Yes, the cause of this conflict is a concern. Do humans dwell in these woods, too?" The elder looked at Ainz.

"——I'm afraid I don't know the cause of the war. I wasn't even aware their invasion had made such significant inroads. But I can say the human country lies *outside* the forest. I don't believe this is a war over the necessities for survival."

"Understood. This forest is so vast, even we do not know the extent of it. And the world outside is larger still. So what do you think we should do?"

Huh? I'm an outsider; you're gonna ask me that? Uh-oh. Well, it's not like the dark elves are a particularly vital race…

The elf trees themselves and what the apothecary master knew were things he'd like to have, but he didn't *need* them.

But it's not like I want them to die off, either. Let's avoid lying and direct them to a less permanent solution.

Aura's and Mare's faces floated across his mind's eye.

He wasn't sure his plan was going well, but perhaps they'd be sad if the children they were playing with died.

Ainz thought a moment, considering his answer.

Mm. Can't really provide guidance here. I don't have the data available.

He wanted to avoid hastily throwing together a messy plan and having it lead to disaster. Best to just go with his gut.

"I'd say if you owe them, you can't afford to abandon them here. If you do, they'll deem the dark elves untrustworthy and refuse to help you when you need it."

The elders nodded.

"But there's no guarantee you can win. By that I don't mean what the elves believe, but a rational conclusion based on evidence you've gathered yourselves. Without that, sending everyone off to fight would be downright reckless."

The younger villagers nodded.

"So I'd recommend neither option."

Everyone looked puzzled. Feeling their eyes on him, Ainz remembered a guild war back in *Yggdrasil*, where he and his guildmates had played both warring sides against each other so they could profit no matter who won.

They'd employed some vicious strategies, but those had taken advantage of their unique position—that approach wouldn't work for the dark elves.

"First, each village should send a handful of reinforcements. Those people are highly likely to die in battle. But they have to go. The elves may grumble that you aren't sending enough, but if you say that's all you can afford without risking the safety of your village, it should silence them. You have nominally contributed, after all. Then those who remain should evacuate."

As he wrapped things up, he heard approving voices. And a few suggesting it wasn't exactly playing fair. But the majority seemed in favor of the idea.

"City life has served you well," an elder said. "We would never have thought of that."

Ainz made his illusory face wince.

That didn't feel like a compliment…

But the elder wasn't being spiteful or sarcastic, either.

That was the first thing I thought of—if they really couldn't manage that, does that mean they are really that inexperienced? But I feel like the lizardmen adopted similar tactics… Oops, almost forgot to respond!

"I think it's less about city life than natural cunning."

"I wouldn't say that," the apothecary master said. "Cut away a piece to save the whole—common enough in gardening."

Several dark elves looked shocked by this. Perhaps he rarely spoke at these meetings—or even bothered to show.

"Thanks, Provisional Master. And I forgot to add something important—make sure you remember it." Ainz double-checked all eyes and ears were on him before continuing. "This is just a suggestion. My opinion and mine alone. This is your village's problem, and the final choice should lie with you. Your lives are your responsibility."

This had to be said to drive the point home.

Ainz was not about to take the blame for his proposal.

If they ran with it, quite a few dark elves would lose their lives. Their deaths would help sell the other elves on the meager reinforcements. But the bereaved might hold a grudge against Ainz.

Thus, he had to ensure this was their decision. So he could insist as much later.

That won't work against anyone vindictive, but there's no need to maintain cordial relations with people like that. Squishy Moe once said it was impossible to have everyone like you. If they send the parents of the kids Aura and Mare are playing with, that could leave a bad taste…but it wouldn't be a good idea for me to stick my nose in any further. I'll check up on that later…although we may not have time.

There was no huge benefit to Nazarick here. If there was one, he would've spoken up, lay claim to anything worthwhile, and help keep the villagers alive. But the dark elves just weren't worth the effort. If their loss was no big deal, then why lift a finger?

It had occurred to him to suggest they surrender to the Theocracy, but that was not for him to say. He had no clue if that would actually save their lives or lead to any happy outcome.

"Your input is greatly appreciated," the elder said, turning away from Ainz to the assembled crowd. "Does anyone else have something to say?"

No one argued.

Looked like they were going with his proposal.

They moved on to how many they should send and who and where the rest should go.

Since they'd mentioned consulting the other villagers, perhaps it was too soon to settle those questions. But once the other villages were on board, it would be too late.

Ainz stood watching this, unsure how he should feel.

Having his idea adopted was satisfying on some level, but it failed to bring the joy of a successful pitch. Perhaps because he'd had no clear goal in mind.

He wasn't leading them toward anything that would benefit Nazarick; he'd just been stuck in a position where he had to say something. He'd prefer to back out here and leave the rest of the decision-making to them. And—time was running out. He wanted to get going.

"——If you'll excuse me, I think my role here is done. I'll go check in on the kids."

"You've been a great help to us," the eldest elder said. "We'll hash out the details here and then relay the proposal to the other villages."

No need to be obsequious about it, Ainz thought.

"May I ask that you not include my name?" he said.

"Wh-whyever not?"

"If they learn the suggestion came from someone who's not from this village and has little to do with this forest's dark elves, there may be those who reject the idea out of hand."

That was not the real reason. He simply wanted to avoid incurring unneeded grudges.

"They would never! Our forests may be different, but our ancestors are the same. No one would think less of your ideas. But—I'll do as you suggest and leave your name out."

"Glad to hear it. Well, it's a little sooner than expected, but I think it's high time we left the village and headed on home."

"What?!"

"An abrupt departure, I realize, but if anything happened to the kids, I'd be letting their mother down."

"…If they're making you this cautious, Fior, I take it these humans are powerful indeed?"

This momentarily baffled him, but then he realized that given their skill levels, the implication that they were fleeing the war had suggested they feared the Theocracy's might.

"That, I can't say. I'm pretty sure we could handle most threats, but it's not like I know every champion the humans have or can predict the outcome of a major conflict like this. I'm simply avoiding any risks we don't have to take."

The elders nodded.

"It's a shame to leave, but once we're packed, we'll be on our way."

"Then…at least a farewell dinner…? We never even held the welcoming one, so it would shame us to let you leave without any show of hospitality."

"No, no, don't trouble yourselves. The situation being what it is, we couldn't possibly add to your burden."

They went back and forth a few times on this point, and finally he scored a victory by insisting this was hardly the last time they'd meet. Blueberry was doing a weird dance in the corner of his vision—perhaps he'd planned to show that off during the banquet.

Ainz made to walk off, but the eldest elder stopped him.

"Um, Fior, I meant to ask this away from prying ears, and it's unrelated to the matter at hand, but do you mind?"

"What?"

"Are you married?"

Ainz blinked at him.

"If not, are you at all inclined to wed someone from this village?"

A quick glance around found no dark elves opposed to the notion. The women actually looked rather hopeful. It wasn't that they were willing to sacrifice themselves for the sake of the village—they were outright in favor of the idea.

Ainz didn't know a lot about women. Actually, he knew nothing about them. But he felt quite sure these smiles were not just for show.

"N-no, thanks. Honestly, I have a number of girls interested in me already. It's a real hassle, ha-ha."

This ambush had rattled him, and he wasn't exactly picking his words carefully. The elder appeared unperturbed.

"Is that so? Well, it's only natural a man of your considerable skills would capture the interest of many ladies."

Talent certainly affected people's prospects in human society, too. Judging by the reaction here, that was even more pronounced in this dangerous locale. But his excuse seemed to have convinced everyone.

There was only one last thing to say.

"We may be leaving here, but if you chose to abandon your village and flee to my city, I wouldn't mind lending a helping hand. You only need to say the word. Might be a few months from now, but I plan to come back in due time. If you've been forced to leave the place behind, bury a map of your new location outside the tree I borrowed."

"……We're all hoping it won't come to that, but if it does, thank you."

The elders bowed their heads, and the rest of the dark elves followed their lead.

Once their heads were back up, Ainz said, "Then this is me," and bowed his head once, followed by a deeper bow to the apothecary master.

Then he walked away.

No one called after him—he hadn't expected anyone to—and he kept going until he was out of sight.

There, he found Aura and Mare waiting, obviously done pretending he was their uncle. They were clearly back in floor-guardian mode. Aura even gave him a quick look over, her eyes watchful.

"Lord Ainz, I'm glad you're safe. Did they do something to you? I caught a strange vibe from you shortly before you headed our way. Like a hunter nocking a bow."

He could think of only one reason.

"Uh, there was an awkward moment. The ladies may have set their sights on me. But don't worry—I talked myself out of it."

"You…did? I'm still sensing a strange tension… It might even be getting stronger…"

Ainz frowned. He'd thought the women looked convinced, but perhaps he'd misread things. But he didn't know what else to do. They were leaving. No better approach existed.

"I should probably have asked this first, but is anyone monitoring us now?"

"No, we're fine," Aura declared.

That meant they were in the clear. Aura had known that, which was why she'd acted this way.

"——I'm sure you heard the discussion?"

"Yes, Lord Ainz. I've already relayed the matter to Mare."

Better to head back to the house they'd borrowed than talk here. But it was possible the two of them had picked up on something Ainz had missed. If so, it would be egg on his face, but he might have to turn back and rejoin the discussion. In which case, heading to their tree would delay that even further. For that reason, it was worth the risk of talking here.

"Anything catch your attention? Feel free to share."

The twins exchanged glances.

"Nothing seemed noteworthy. Your proposal was ideal, Lord Ainz."

"Y-yes. When Aura told me about it, I thought the same thing."

Mm? Have they not realized the children they were playing with might be about to watch their parents head off to die in battle? Or have they noticed and aren't in a position to argue with my idea? He studied their expressions. *I'm not sure. Perhaps I should double-check?*

If it was the former, this might make them sad and cause fractures in their newfound friendships. It never hurt to ask.

"They might end up sending the parents of the children you played with."

Both looked confused. The twins glanced at each other and then back at him. Aura spoke for them both.

"That's true. What of it?" She looked genuinely baffled. "Is that a problem?"

"…No, not at all."

Ainz didn't ask why they'd reacted that way.

He just assumed they hadn't made friends.

Or like how my friends wound up prioritizing real life, these two always place Nazarick first. In which case, what should I do?

He hesitated, but then Aura put a hand to her ear, listening to something distant. Were they saying something important? Ainz and Mare stayed quiet so as not to interfere.

"Lord Ainz, they're discussing you."

"Can you hear what they're saying?"

"Yes, more or less this—" Aura changed up her voice, doing a (bad) imitation. "You ask why we must keep it secret that this proposal came from him? He hails from a land near this human country. If word reaches the humans that he proposed this, might that not cause problems for him in the future? Do you think that might happen, elders? We can't be sure. But it's our duty to take precautions against the possibility—— Other villagers are agreeing with that. They intend to keep the secret."

"I see. Thank you, Aura."

"Er, um…this way nobody will find out you manipulated them?"

He hadn't *manipulated* anything, so why did Mare think this? He considered asking. He'd merely offered a suggestion. But there were more pressing matters at hand.

"As long as mind-control spells exist, death is the only way to completely contain information."

"Should we?" Aura asked.

"No, we shouldn't. There's no benefit to doing so. Or let me put it this way—there's no downside to the Theocracy learning about what happened here. They're already a potential enemy. We have no plans to ally ourselves with them, and supporting the enemy of your enemy is only natural. In fact, that's the upside—my name and face are lies. They might end up fruitlessly searching for a man who doesn't exist."

Ainz paused to gauge their reactions.

"…Still…it's a shame. If the Theocracy had attacked this village directly, we could have profited further."

The twins looked at each other, lost. Mare asked this time.

"Er, um, Lord Ainz? Why didn't we make them attack this village? Like, um, killing Theocracy soldiers disguised as a dark elf and then leading them here."

Good question.

That would have been far more beneficial to Nazarick. Ainz was well aware. Conceptually, it was similar to baiting monsters into other parties. The reason he hadn't…

I didn't want to.

Ainz had enjoyed his time in this village. And he was reluctant to set the place aflame himself.

This sentiment was only natural. No one wanted to do unpleasant things. But that was a luxury not afforded to the ruler of the Great Tomb of Nazarick. As their leader, he must always prioritize his organization's profits. But this time, he'd gone with his gut.

Perhaps that amounted to betraying Nazarick.

I talked about them making friends, but I had all the fun.

He would have to ensure this did not happen again. He would make Nazarick's gains his top priority and act accordingly.

That was his duty as the sole remaining guild member, the master of the NPCs.

Swearing a solemn vow inside, he waffled on how to answer Mare. Perhaps it was better to just admit he'd made the wrong call.

"…Yes, I considered it. Perhaps for Nazarick, we should have. Yet, my own weakness stayed my hand. Unbefitting of Nazarick's ruler. It shall not happen again."

They both looked shocked.

"Er, um…I don't think that's true!"

"Yeah, everything you do is right, Lord Ainz!"

As they consoled him, they reached the home they'd been borrowing for a week. They merely had to gather up the things left here and they'd be ready to pull out.

They hadn't brought all that much, so this took no time. Baggage in hand, they stepped outside. Aura looked up. Ainz followed her gaze and spotted the apothecary master running their way.

His weeklong master soon reached them.

He was slightly out of breath. Given his apothecary skills, he was probably high level, but his physique was not impressive. It was hard to judge what classes he'd taken, but his stats were likely not much different from an arcane caster's.

This did not seem to be a parting gift. He'd come directly here from the meeting. A last good-bye?

"What's wrong? Forgive me for not directly saying farewell—"

"No, I figured I should do my provisional student one last favor. Several of the women are intent on accompanying you back to the city. I saw them racing off to their homes. If you don't plan on entertaining their companionship, you'd better leave quickly."

"Huh?"

"*Huh,* my ass. They're likely not *just* trying to hang off your coattails, but you'll be the only person they can rely on in a whole new town, and they know that might help seal the deal. And in our culture, many wives or many husbands are perfectly acceptable as long as you can provide for them. And you're from a clan that split off from ours; it wouldn't hurt to bridge that gap. If the other villages knew… Well, I'm on your side, but you get my drift."

This was a disaster.

If they laid so much as a single hand on him, his disguise would be ruined. And he couldn't be sure these ladies wouldn't try.

The elves saw undead as mortal enemies, and dark elves likely shared that attitude.

Ainz could not reveal himself until he had fully placed the dark elves under his wing. And since he had plans to do so eventually, he couldn't exactly harm the women intent on leading the way.

"Uh, did you seriously not see this coming? Not even a bit? Come on, man! You're supposed to be smarter than that! I thought you realized that this could happen, but just didn't think they'd be this quick to act. Get a grip. Be grateful I warned you."

Ainz had only one option.

"......Come on, kids! Move out! Bye, Provisional Master!"

Time to run for the hills.

Without a further word, the three of them raced off.

They were soon in the woods and kept on going. They ran until they were sure they'd not be followed and at last drew to a halt.

"...We're good. No one's coming after us. Are we going back to Nazarick now?" Aura asked.

Relieved by this news, Ainz grinned. Well, his face didn't actually move. He hadn't even bothered manipulating the illusion.

"We will not. Going back to Nazarick and procuring troops would have its advantages, but I don't want to waste the opportunity. The three of us are going to pull off a trick Squishy Moe once taught me."

"A-and what is that?!"

Mare's eyes were sparkling. Ainz was quite pleased with himself. If their reactions had been dismissive or uninterested, his emotions probably would've triggered the automatic calming.

Proudly, he answered.

"A variation on a kill steal."

Chapter 5 **Kill Steal**

Chapter 5 | Kill Steal

1

At the top of the Theocracy military stood the generalissimo and directly beneath him—two marshals, Valerian Ein Aubigne and Gael Lazerus Bulgari. The former was in charge of the campaign against the elves.

Central command was run out of a tent quite close to the elf capital, and Valerian was seated within, accompanied by six strategists. While he was in his fifties, all of them were still in their twenties.

Age was hardly a reliable indicator of strength, but in a position requiring intelligence and experience, it could serve as a sort of benchmark. By that logic, these strategists were arguably far too young.

Each had deep circles below their eyes and furrowed brows. They wore the faces of men who'd long labored under a heavy psychological burden.

Valerian ran his eyes over documents that were the most likely causes of their fatigue.

These were the casualty reports stemming from the elves' night raid. Considering the early-morning hour, the attack had happened mere hours ago.

"——That's a lot."

He'd expected it, but no other words came to mind.

Still, the Theocracy had far more faith casters than other countries, so any casualties who still lived and could be recovered, even the critically injured, could be made whole. As a result, the killed column was a far smaller figure than the wounded. And the majority of those wounded were currently getting treatment.

But the number of elf dead left on their side was even less than the Theocracy.

It seemed unlikely they'd recovered the bodies and retreated while conducting a night raid. Thus, the reported fatality count was likely accurate.

An extremely poor kill ratio.

"Yes. This close to the elf capital, they're clearly sending in their strongest; these casualties are the result." The speaker was the man who'd drawn up the figures. "But the enemy seems to be operating with a smaller, more elite force, so we believe even these losses are significant."

One hero was worth a thousand soldiers. On the other hand, the loss of even one hero was painful. The raw number of dead didn't reflect the true impact on military capability.

That was the strategist's point, but this was hardly a comfort.

"I can already imagine how the troops will look at us now," another one muttered.

"It's only natural for them to hold a grudge." Valerian sighed. "They've all lost friends."

Everyone wanted people to like them, and a commander who lost the faith of their troops was at a major disadvantage. For those with a commanding class like Valerian, their support power functioned only if the troops were following them willingly.

"We've been fending off their night raids thus far, so the issue is less with our defensive formations than the simple fact that if they send in their elites, we need comparable defenders to counter them."

"Exactly. Our side has a number of powerful soldiers, but the bulk of them are faith casters. If the classes are different—you need a more substantial power differential."

In a frontal assault, those faith casters would be a huge asset. But in a night raid, ranger skills had the clear advantage. They didn't need to look any further than these casualty counts for proof of that.

"What we need to do is increase our defenses so that no additional night raids can occur. Anyone have any ideas?"

The raid itself must have put that idea in their heads; the strategists all had proposals ready.

Valerian had thought of several himself, and they had some that hadn't occurred to him. If they could incorporate all of these, the result would be a substantially stronger defensive position. Problem was, doing so would require significant labor, resources, and time. They would have to prioritize the most efficient measures and discard the others.

Worse—

"Sir, defenses are all well and good, but is there actually a point in spending the time to stay and fight here?"

That was the obvious question.

"The top brass have sent their orders." He looked around the table. "You've all read them. They need us to stand our ground a while longer. Understood?"

No one disagreed. But their silence was not acceptance.

He had not expected them to be on board. He knew exactly how each of them felt, and despite his many years, he knew he could not dismiss this as the folly of youth.

Frankly, they were entirely justified.

The lives lost in last night's attacks had simply been wasted. These losses had been entirely avoidable.

The Theocracy armies had placed their camp close to the capital, virtually on the front lines. It could be argued that this meant information reached them quickly and they could respond to enemy actions promptly— but it also carried the risk of their headquarters falling if a particularly strong elf made a suicidal charge directly at them. The elves were on the ropes and increasingly likely to employ such tactics. No question about it— the Theocracy should be launching their full assault as soon as possible.

Simply put, if the enemy's most powerful fighters were forced to take up defensive positions, the risk of the Theocracy headquarters falling was significantly diminished.

But the leadership had ordered them to sit here and merely probe the enemy lines. They must have been aware that would lead to elven night raids.

Certainly, the collapse of their front could lead to evacuations or desertions, and orders to park themselves close by and swiftly move to prevent that made a certain amount of sense. Valerian was even on board with the idea of dangling bait before the elven elite or the elf king—who had barely shown himself. But those strategies were contingent on the participation of the Firestorm Scripture.

Why were they not here, helping?

Certainly not because their subleader had perished at the hands of the elf king.

Supreme command had sent word that the Firestorm Scripture were busy with another mission, but nobody here took that at face value.

Valerian knew the truth, and though young, these strategists were all brilliant and knew exactly what the top brass were thinking.

Withholding the Firestorm Scripture had several effects.

First, experience.

For humans used to city life, survival in this forest was much harder than they'd imagined. A far cry from the safety of home, here they always had to be on the lookout.

This battle was one big lesson.

Elves had merely taken the place of forest beasts.

If there were future opportunities to gain similar experience, they likely wouldn't bother—but it also wasn't something you wanted happening often.

But that goal did not require actual losses.

If experience was the only goal, they need merely train somewhere safe. They could have the Firestorm Scripture fill the same roles as the elves. Obviously, high command knew that, too. So why take this approach? Did they not care about the losses it incurred?

No—

It's all about their state of mind.

If a soldier was to protect anyone, they needed techniques used by hunters and rangers.

By going up against creatures who excelled at forest combat—like the elves—the rank and file learned ways to fight in this environment. Some might learn enough to acquire the ranger class. And fatalities were a real incentive. The more friends they lost, the more threatened the survivors felt.

For that reason, command had refused to send in the six scriptures—especially the Firestorm—on the grounds that they would make short work of the elves.

The very thought of this cold logic made Valerian want to grimace.

He understood why. But that didn't mean he liked it.

"Sir, a proposal."

The strategist's tone was pretty stiff. He was the youngest man here. This war had gathered the youngest strategists together—for the goal of fundamentally changing how they think.

Valerian urged him to continue.

"Naturally, we expected all of this. But the death toll has reached the absolute limit. Under these circumstances, even if we attack the enemy stronghold, actually seizing it will be extremely difficult. Since we haven't killed all the elves from that night raid, we can expect fierce resistance from them. I cannot accept incurring further losses. Can you please ask the higher-ups to change strategies?"

He knew this was impossible. But seeing men die before his very eyes had weakened his spirit.

Valerian suppressed the urge to sigh. He got what this man was going through. Every officer had to work through it at some point.

Life—here defined as that of your countryman—was precious.

That was, perhaps, a flaw in the Theocracy.

By itself, that could hardly be considered a bad thing. It was, in fact, unquestionably *good*. Faced with the choice between a country that valued its citizens' lives and one that did not, anyone would pick the former.

Arguably, the Theocracy armed forces had grown soft under the protection of their heroes, but the desire to minimize losses was not morally wrong. But that was the logic of those without weapons. It was a soldier's job to kill or be killed. Could the members of the military afford to think like that?

Inevitably, there would come a time when victory could not be obtained without sacrifices.

A time when they would have to fight without the six scriptures backing them.

If overvaluing life made them timid and unable to act decisively, that was a fatal flaw.

Valerian did not want them to treat soldiers as disposable commodities. He wanted them to know the pain of command—pain Valerian and his superiors grappled with—and learn to deal with it.

All of them were wrestling with this pain, making it their own. And the results were showing on every gathered face.

Presumably, none of them had enjoyed a good night's sleep. It would be hard to while the suffering of the soldiers filled their ears.

Valerian did feel a modicum of pity.

If they had not been forced into this tactical situation abruptly, it would have been possible to ease them into it. That would have taken far less toll on their spirits.

But circumstances didn't allow for such leisurely approaches. They not only had to whip each soldier into shape, they needed their commanding officers at the top of their game. The troops needed to be strong, and their officers needed to be stern enough to order them to their deaths.

We'll be challenging the Nation of Darkness in due time, and countless soldiers will die in those battles to come. We expect there to be casualties among the civilian population, too. That's why the brass want them to familiarize themselves with death here. As cruel as that may be.

"I feel your pain," he said. Every officer here did. "But we cannot stop now. Look not at the present but at the future."

"........................."

The youngest strategist hung his head, then looked up at Valerian once more, desperation in his eyes.

"…At least, at the very least, when we do attack the elves' capital, let it be a full-scale assault. Our strongest spells, destroying the enemy's outer perimeters. If we're forbidden the use of not only catapults and siege engines but even fire arrows—far more soldiers will die."

"——That, too, I cannot permit. And you can imagine why."

These were the finest minds their country had to offer. They knew where the Theocracy stood and could surmise the reasons for their orders. Valerian felt spelling it out for them would be redundant, but perhaps it was worth stating in so many words.

"We cannot avoid a conflict with the vile Nation of Darkness. If this city is in our hands, intact—then we *might* have the option of evacuating our people here. That is why we stopped felling the trees in our path. That is why we are not allowed to do significant damage to the city itself. Understood?"

"I thought so. Every choice the higher-ups are making is to lay the groundwork for the next war. But the elves made this city with their spells. Even if we raze portions of it to the ground, I believe our prisoners could restore it. Is that not an option?"

This came from a different strategist, and Valerian nodded.

"They could," he said. "Several people have proposed as much. Others suggested those elves could rebuild elsewhere. But given the time frame we're working with, those plans are untenable."

They did have plans for any elves they captured. It was not difficult to force them to cooperate using Charm or similar spells. But using mind-control magic repeatedly in a short time frame made it easy for them to build up resistance to it.

They had already performed some experiments and found that while the elves' magic worked on trees, it took ages to grow one from scratch. No one knew when war with the Nation of Darkness would begin, but the math suggested they'd never complete a city capable of housing a whole country's worth of evacuees in time.

They would have to use what already existed and could not afford to waste a thing.

"Our sole course of action is to force our way through their last lines of defense, despite the casualties that will occur. Obviously, nobody *wants* this loss of life. We'll need every fighting body we can get in the war against the Nation of Darkness. We can't waste them here."

What command wanted was truly a paradox.

Valerian was conscious of the contradiction. But he also knew it plagued his superiors.

"...Sir, more than that, those who survive certain death come back stronger."

"Yes...true words. They will do that."

This came from the strategist ranked second only to Valerian himself in the commander class. Valerian agreed entirely.

The Theocracy had long held that a single hero was worth a thousand soldiers. But that would no longer be enough. They had to make each soldier stronger—thus, the cruelty of this campaign.

Everything was to prepare for the coming war with the Nation.

A conflict that most certainly would come to pass.

"I know it's hard for all of you, but wring out your brains and do whatever you must to ensure your troops live to walk on Theocracy soil once more."

Valerian bowed his head, and all responded favorably.

This was not all.

There was another reason to dawdle here.

An individual no one but Valerian knew about—had been *allowed* to know about. They were waiting for her arrival.

The elf king was a powerful foe. Strong enough to slaughter veritable heroes in a single blow. Yet, the Theocracy had a card capable of beating him.

Using it was strategically sound. Champion against champion, hero against hero, and for those who surpassed that—

But the Theocracy leadership was hell-bent on pitting her against the elf king, for reasons beyond the mere militaristic advantage.

He did not know why.

But Valerian waited.

Waited for the final card to arrive.

As he did, a messenger interrupted the meeting. An urgent look on their face, they came up to Valerian, whispering, "Sir, reinforcements from home."

"Ah, at last," Valerian said and rose to his feet. The strategists looked up, and he said, "Men, we no longer need defensive measures. Throw all troops assigned there to the front lines. Prepare for the main assault."

The long campaign was approaching its end. The battle was entering its final stage.

•

Why are they fighting like this? Does the Theocracy have no concern for losses?

A week after they'd left the dark elf village, Ainz was observing the Theocracy assault on the elf capital and musing to himself.

They'd made wall-like structures from wood and were pushing those ahead of them as they advanced. He knew this was an attempt to shield themselves from the elf archers' uncanny accuracy, but it felt extremely inefficient.

And they didn't even have anything overhead so were unable to block skilled shots that arced over their mobile cover. There weren't all *that* many of these, so perhaps the losses were acceptable, but still—

"——The Theocracy has a lot of faith casters. Why aren't they just flinging out AOE spells? As it is, the elves have the terrain advantage. To counter that, they could just summon angels or the like and have them attack from above. Or smarter still, simply burn them out of their homes. There's no shortage of wood to make siege engines from. They could easily set the place ablaze from a distance."

Trees that size might not burn that easily, but the smaller branches and leaves certainly would. The smoke from that would harm the elves and impair the aim of their archers. The Theocracy's failure to do so struck Ainz as downright unnatural.

Why not send in their champions? If they had high-level units like Fluder or Gazef, they could cast larger spells, attack in force, help the troops break through. I see no reason to hold them in reserve.

"Hmm, it makes no sense to me. Have either of you spotted anything in their movements? Any insights to offer?"

The twins were watching the same thing he was. After a pause, Mare answered.

"Er, um…maybe they just *aren't* thinking?"

"Please, that can't be true. An army this size has any number of commanders and strategists. I find it hard to believe none of them has a plan. There must be a specific reason for this."

But Ainz literally couldn't think of one. It was certainly possible that an idiot had been placed in charge for political reasons and was ignoring the advice of his strategists, but given the sensible measures they'd taken on the advance to this location—felling the trees, etc.—it didn't feel like the right answer.

"Hmm, they're attacking from other directions, too, but the methods they're using don't seem much different."

They had the elf capital half surrounded and a number of units stationed on the far shore of the lake behind the city.

"They don't seem to be placing any POWs on the front lines… Are the soldiers leading the advance disposable? Does the Theocracy have a slave caste?"

"No, they've been known to sell elves as slaves, but I haven't heard anything about human warrior slaves. We've got a solid grasp on their political structures, but…it's not like we know everything. Still…I doubt that's it."

"C-could those soldiers have been s-summoned?"

"Those hit by arrows are still lying there, so probably not."

Other soldiers were dragging the fallen to the rear—to the Theocracy base camp. That suggested they weren't expected to die on the front lines.

So why let them? Why not do everything possible to avoid that?

Ainz racked his brain, found something that seemed plausible, and voiced it.

"Maybe—just maybe—they've realized we're here? And that's why they're fighting like this?"

"Huh?"

"B-but that's..."

"No, we can't say it's *us*. But if they're trying to make enemy countries or groups think they're fools or pulling some subterfuge to hide the presence of their champions—it might look like this."

The Nation of Darkness might not be the only target of a potential misinformation campaign. The Theocracy might have other enemies Ainz was unaware of, leading to what they were seeing.

Nazarick had done similar things in the past, so it stood to reason their enemies might, too.

The Theocracy has some history behind it. That creates enemies. Is that what this is? But I can't think of any other reason to hold the champions back. In which case...could it be that place north of the Nation and kingdom? The Council State? The Theocracy are human supremacists, so there's no way they get along with that melting-pot country. Hmm, then perhaps we should ally ourselves— No, Albedo and Demiurge would have considered that already. Still, if I leave everything to them, I can hardly call myself their boss. I'll have to broach the subject.

Toward the end of the war with the kingdom, a mysterious being calling himself Rik Aganeia had appeared—and their speculation suggested he might be related to the Council State's Platinum Dragonlord.

This was based solely on the color of his armor, but in that case, allying with the Theocracy against the Council State might work. Or they could do the opposite, allying with the Council State against the Theocracy and using that as an excuse to find out how they operated.

Either way, perhaps they should do something before those two countries teamed up against the Nation. Still, if this had occurred to Ainz, odds were those two great minds of Nazarick had long since thought of it.

...Hmm. If they have laid the groundwork for an alliance, we should take care to not let the Theocracy find out we're here. Kill any witnesses.

"Lord Ainz, should we infiltrate the Theocracy camp and steal information?" Aura suggested.

"No, absolutely not," he said, shaking his head. He explained his idea. "See...assume an entity comparable to me was opposed to us. Do you think they could sneak into Nazarick and make off with the information they wanted?"

"Yes, absolutely!"

"I think so, too. If someone as incredible as you actually existed, Lord Ainz, then they can do anything."

"Oh, um…"

They seemed confident. Mare uncharacteristically so. But this was not what Ainz had wanted to hear.

"Um, forget that question. Um, instead, say, Shall—"

No!

He already knew that answer.

If he suggested someone equivalent to Shalltear, Aura would insist it was impossible. Certainly, that was the answer Ainz was looking for, but he didn't want what led to that answer. Not at all.

So who? he wondered.

Pandora's Actor…can transform into any guild member, so they might think it possible. Then Demiurge…? Hmm, he does seem like he could steal anything. Aura…or Mare are bad choices here. Then…

"Same basic question, but let's say instead that a being equivalent to Albedo was hostile to Nazarick. Do you think they could steal all the information Nazarick has?"

"Um, Albedo…?"

"Er, um…do you suspect something?"

"N-no! I don't imagine she'd ever betray us!" He was a bit flustered by that response. "This is a hypothetical, an imaginary someone of similar abilities. Merely for comparison's sake."

The twins glanced at each other, like they weren't buying it. Finally, Aura spoke for both of them.

"I think even Albedo couldn't manage it. She hasn't raised her stealth skills, and I've not heard of her having any equipment with effects like that."

"Yeah…that's true…Albedo's a tank. No relevant skills." Once again, Ainz had chosen a bad example. "Let's put skills aside for the moment. Do you think it's impossible even with her brilliance?"

"S-still impossible."

Fine. He couldn't think of any better names. Offering a silent apology to Albedo, he decided to move on.

"Mm, yes. I agree it's impossible. Nazarick has many defensive measures, and those are beyond what any one person could handle. In which case—are there not other places like that?"

"I doubt it! The Great Tomb of Nazarick was designed by the Supreme Beings themselves. It's very…special. I don't think anywhere else is like it."

Mare was so firm on this, Ainz nearly agreed with him.

He himself had helped create Nazarick, so Mare's faith pleased him, but that was not the point he was trying to make here. And he couldn't exactly say, *Take a hint and guess what your boss wants.*

He decided to just ignore Mare.

"Um, so this is how I view things. If we could pull it off with Nazarick, it makes sense people could pull it off elsewhere."

Ainz wouldn't be able to pilfer Nazarick's secrets if he was working alone. Was it wrong to believe that other players' homes would be just as difficult to infiltrate?

He didn't think so.

If they could keep information from their foes, their foes could keep information from them. Only a fool would act without that assumption in place.

This was why Ainz had not dispatched spies to the Theocracy—a place where multiple clues hinted at a player's presence. This country had existed for a long time. If a player lived there, then those years would give them a serious advantage.

As it was, they'd developed spells he didn't know—like the one that killed you after you answered three questions.

"Naturally, there are times when we must take a risk despite the dangers. But that leaves the question—is that time now? Aura, Mare?"

""Yes,"" they chorused.

"The Great Tomb of Nazarick—we are *strong*. But we may not be *unrivaled*. Never underestimate your foes. Never neglect to gather information."

Both agreed, and he nodded.

"Okay! In that case, let's watch a while longer. As it stands, we can't achieve our goal."

They were here for a kill steal. Well, technically, they were here for something else.

A kill was considered stolen if you spotted someone else fighting a monster and you jumped in and slew that monster yourself, making off with all the experience. To do that here, they'd have to attack either the elves or the Theocracy and do significant damage.

But that was not what Ainz was after.

He was targeting the magic items in the elf castle.

Any half-decent royalty likely had a sizable collection of valuable magic items. And those could be powerful indeed. In this case, he really meant that they'd be swooping to grab the treasure while everyone else was busy fighting.

If the Theocracy had advanced this far, odds were they'd win. The elves' magic items would fall into Theocracy hands if Ainz did nothing. The last thing he wanted to do was give a potential enemy any advantages. So before they got to any hoard of magical items, he planned to rob the elves first.

One other advantage of this strategy was that he would not be directly opposing the Theocracy. Certainly, if he was caught, they would vehemently reproach him for it. But since they weren't the Theocracy's possessions *yet*, he could make excuses.

So this was less a kill steal and more simple looting.

Ainz had done much the same thing several times in *Yggdrasil*. He could recall laughing at the sight of an attacking guild occupying the enemy base only to discover the treasury was already empty. That's why the idea had come readily this time.

Just one problem.

He had no idea what sort of magic items the elf country or castle contained. He should not just assume they had some. They might not! In which case, he was taking a risk for nothing and possibly worsening relations with the Theocracy in the bargain. He would have preferred to gather information before acting.

Even if the elf king did have a collection of magic items, there was a solid chance they weren't stuck in the treasury during what was essentially their last stand. It would make perfect sense to use them against the invading Theocracy forces. Or even sent off to some other place for safekeeping.

But they didn't have much time to investigate.

"...Let's watch a bit longer, then head into the palace. I don't want them removing the magic items."

"If they do, I can track 'em."

"Yes, right. I'm sure you can...but no guarantee they don't have Forestwalk or the like. Best if we get our hands on them before that happens. Hmm, we'll have to locate them, too...so perhaps sooner is better."

"Th-then...?"

"Yes, let's go now."

Ainz glanced at the invasion once more.

It had been a week now, so depending on discussions with the other villagers, the dark elves might already be here, fighting.

Part of him wanted to know if they were and where they were posted, but he had just regretted acting inappropriately for his role as ruler of Nazarick. He should focus purely on what they stood to gain from all this.

He turned from the palace to Mare.

"Mare, if the need arises, we might station you on the front line as our tank. Do you mind?"

Best to make sure.

"N-no, I can handle it. Like the village, it, um...the elf capital counts as nature, so there's no issue. I'll do my best!"

Neither Aura nor Mare was dressed in their usual equipment. The armor in particular was quite different. Aura was in archer gear, and Mare had switched to a defense set.

These outfits were not provided by Ainz but from the stash Bubbling-Teapot had left them. They weren't quite as good as their typical equipment.

But they'd been tailored specifically for the twins, so their overall abilities hadn't taken a major hit.

Still, this was a stealth mission. It would probably be best if Ainz changed up his gear, wearing items called secret shoes like they both were and all three wearing masks. But he had done no such thing.

The main reason was that despite being the most recognizable of them, he'd decided to go with his usual equipment. This was because the two of them *had* changed their gear and were a bit weaker than usual. If Ainz *also* changed his and was similarly weakened, that would be too big a risk.

He thought for a long while and eventually settled on the super-reductive idea of just killing any and all witnesses. That eliminated the need for any disguises.

The twins' armor choices were a lesser motivation.

For backup gear, they had decent stats for one reason—they used data crystals that raised the armor's total parameters but eliminated gear slots at specific locations. In Mare's case, he was unable to equip anything to his face, so he couldn't wear a mask in this armor.

As for the armor itself...

......*This is definitely another gender-swapped arrangement.*

That was hardly the only eyebrow-raising element.

The only reasonable response was, *What the hell kinda armor is* that?

Especially Mare's.

It put the *dress* in *dress armor,* and the very eye-catching, skin-flaunting design left his entire midriff exposed.

Yggdrasil armor derived their defensive ratings from three values: the quality of the metal used, the quantity of the metal used, and the data crystal. So it wasn't like Mare's torso was actually unprotected; the data crystal portion did provide some coverage there. Essentially a magical defense aura.

It was likely none of the regular soldiers fighting here could even scratch him. But back in *Yggdrasil,* these exposed points had been designed to make critical hits easier to land.

This was not exactly gear for a tank.

Tanks should be wearing bulky armor like Albedo's.

BubblingTeapot's racial weakness in *Yggdrasil* was an inability to equip armor, but she'd carried a shield in each hand and had a skill that hardened her ooze.

She was a tank herself, so what had she been thinking when she picked this gear for Mare?

She most likely hadn't been thinking at all.

On second thought, Ainz realized she'd probably put a lot of thought into it. Just…based on her personal predilections rather than combat potential.

Like brother, like sister was what Ainz instinctively thought, but he fought off that impulse, rising to their defense. Mare had originally just been an NPC and was not capable of changing his own gear.

In other words, what he had on now had simply been an alternate skin, just some variety in his wardrobe. Most players likely wouldn't have bothered making actually viable equipment. That BubblingTeapot had was likely to her credit. This was purely a fashion statement, but the stats were still solid.

Ainz could just see her beautiful smile—not that she had a face—and her brother's look of horror.

2

The Theocracy shored up their assault and finally broke though the elf capital's defenses.

Ainz spotted Theocracy troops in the city itself and hastily took action.

Under cover of Perfect Unknowable, the first thing Ainz did was find an elf on their own and capture them while there were no witnesses around.

When he finally got his opportunity, he found himself with a female elf, likely a servant.

He used Charm on her and took her through a Gate back to where Aura and Mare waited. Like the elf they'd captured previously, they asked a few questions, but she didn't have much valuable information.

Deciding they'd get nothing more from her, Ainz didn't hesitate to use Death on her. He figured no one would notice a missing servant in a castle about to fall.

Stripping off the clothes and anything else that would identify the corpse, he sent it through a Gate to a far-off land—specifically, to where they'd found the ursus. He figured the wild things would eventually take care of the body, and if anyone did stumble across it, it would just be some mysterious remains with no visible injuries. Nothing connected it to Ainz himself.

It might have been more natural to move it to the air above the castle and drop it—making it look like a suicide—but he decided that if she was missing, then perhaps he could use that knowledge to his advantage later.

He'd used a little MP disposing of the body, but given his recovery speed, there was nothing to worry about. They had neither the need nor the time to sit and watch further.

The surviving elves were employing guerrilla tactics throughout the city, and the Theocracy forces were struggling to advance, but given the numbers advantage, it was only a matter of time. There were no signs of champions strong enough to turn the tide, suggesting neither side had any to put into play.

The elf king himself was supposed to be formidable, but if he wasn't out there fighting, perhaps he'd already made his escape.

In which case, he might have taken the magic items with him, and they were wasting their time. As he pondered this, Ainz turned to the twins.

"Let's go."

They knew the approximate location. It was a pity they'd been unable to find any concrete information on what items the treasury held or what powers this superstrong king actually had. Perhaps he should have targeted a higher-ranking elf, but they hadn't had time to be choosey.

Only one real problem.

How—? Or rather, who should hide?

This was enemy territory, and he wasn't about to let them split up.

They'd taken pains to keep themselves concealed, so if they just waltzed into the place, that would all be for naught.

It would be best if all three could remain hidden.

There were ways to accomplish that. But all had their downsides.

If Ainz had Perfect Unknowable active, only Aura could tell where he was. And even then, she would only have a vague impression of his general location. Druids were capable of acquiring a skill that could see through Perfect Unknowable, but Mare didn't have that—his build was all offensive magic, with precious few exceptions.

When Aura had the Ghillie Guise Cloak on, neither Ainz nor Mare could find her.

Mare's standard outfit included a Dappled Cape, which provided excellent concealment outside, especially in forests, but the effect was halved indoors. The castle might be carved out of a living tree, but it still counted as inside, and the cape's cloaking ability was reduced to the point where even Ainz could sort of tell where he was. Aura and Ainz knowing Mare's location was fine, but this meant it was easier for enemies to spot him and thus sort of pointless.

If Ainz hid, Aura could see him, but Mare couldn't.

If Aura hid, neither Ainz nor Mare could spot her.

Mare's Dappled Cape didn't offer particularly strong concealment, and that wasn't really improved if he used the Ghillie Guise Cloak—either way, odds were high someone else could spot him.

There was no way for all three to hide, so it was better if one person stayed hidden in case of emergencies. But who? Aura was probably best for that role, but in a pinch, it might be a problem if the other two didn't know where she was. They might accidentally turn her way and run into her.

This is a huge mess.

He'd had a week to prepare. They really should have talked this through at some point.

Ainz had done plenty of stealth missions back in *Yggdrasil*. On their initial conquest of Nazarick, his whole party had snuck through the marshes filled with lurking tsveik. But with other players, they'd prepped their own stealth measures and mostly knew how it worked—there'd been no need to preplan, just a quick confirmation before leaping into action.

Perhaps the kill-steal idea had left Ainz a bit giddy and forgotten that he wasn't playing *Yggdrasil* anymore because he had completely forgotten to run his plan by the twins.

So why had neither of them brought it up? The most plausible explanation was that it was a side effect of their absolute faith in him. *Lord Ainz must have a plan!* (He was too scared to ask if that was actually the case.) He glanced at them and found their eyes gleaming with trust.

He was too ashamed to admit it simply hadn't occurred to him. Ainz's brain—not that he had one—went into overdrive, running fever hot. He could try asking their opinion but didn't want to waste any more time on this. So he went with the best idea he could come up with.

"I'll use Perfect Unknowable. Aura, you take the lead."

That settled it.

The twins would not hide. They would have to rely on Aura's senses and do their best to avoid running into anyone. If that did happen, they'd handle it, and Ainz would stand by, ready to back them up as necessary. Since they couldn't see each other, the risk of them getting split up during an attack was greater than the risk of the twins getting spotted.

Neither argued.

Are you really fine with that? Go ahead—offer feedback!

Ainz was always happy to be argued with.

Putting their heads together would assuredly result in a better idea.

And they agreed because it was his suggestion and they trusted him. That was tantamount to an abandonment of thought. If Ainz had missed something or picked a bad plan—and that happened plenty—then what? They'd likely not say anything even if it did go south, but that was hardly a good thing.

This is the downside to NPCs. Still…I could insist they offer their two cents, but we really don't have time to discuss them. Best we leave this problem for another day and just have them be extra careful.

He ran several strategies by them, then activated his spell, following Aura and Mare into the castle.

There were very few elves here—it had been the same when he entered on his own—so they didn't run into anyone. It helped that Aura was listening closely and moving when there was no one around.

The Re-Estize Kingdom's castle was also largely deserted at the end, but at least they'd barricaded the entrance and tried.

The Theocracy was already in the city, but no one was putting up any resistance. It was like nothing was happening.

No one moving to defend themselves…because their leaders have already abandoned the city? I've heard this is the only elf-led country around, but the woods are vast. Maybe they have territory to the south. Could even be another city.

In that case, this was a futile effort.

But Ainz would find out soon enough. No point speculating, so he abandoned the line of thought.

The treasury was upstairs, on a floor no one was allowed to enter.

It was two stories above the king's own chambers, at the very top of the palace. He'd considered accessing it from outside, but naturally, there were no windows.

The three of them climbed on.

Up stair after stair, no sign of anyone here. When they reached their destination floor, Aura muttered, "What the…?"

The ceilings were a good fifteen yards high and glowed like they had lights fitted all over. There were no windows anywhere, so this light was clearly of a magical source.

But it wasn't exactly bright.

Ainz moved around a bit, making sure no debuffs had hit him.

This wasn't the kind of light priests used against undead. This was the elf country, so odds were it was some sort of druid faith spell.

That wasn't the odd part. The sixth floor of the Great Tomb of Nazarick was much the same. Arcane and psychic magic both had light spells, too. But with no side effects, it was hard to pinpoint the spell, much less what type of magic.

Aura's question had been prompted not by the ceiling but the floor.

——It was covered in dirt.

The whole floor was one vast open space, no walls or partitions—a solid hundred yards in every direction—and dirt was scattered across the breadth of it.

Not every inch, but the area around the doors in back had especially thick layers of soil.

Aura kicked the ground a couple of times, turning the dirt over. The floor was right below it. It wasn't that thick a layer.

"Is this in lieu of carpeting?"

It did give that impression. The dark elves hadn't used any rugs, either. At most, they had cushions of woven grass.

"Ugh, man… I guess it takes all kinds, but this seems pretty uncultured? Or is this a security system? Ensuring we leave footprints?"

"B-but wouldn't it be better to just leave guards?"

Ainz agreed with Mare on that point. He'd glanced around, but the place was deserted.

So lax… If there's no one here— No, maybe there usually is, but they're busy fighting the invaders. The servant said they weren't allowed up here. Then again, there wasn't any mention of guards, either.

"Um, what if they were planning for a siege and thinking about growing vegetables in here?" Mare suggested.

"Oh!" Aura said, nodding. Ainz did the same.

There might not be sunlight, but with druids around, they could easily make fields. The light above might work like sunlight and allow crops to grow.

Aura had dug up the very edge, so perhaps toward the center, it was deep enough for crops to take root.

If we had a race that takes debuffs from sunlight, like Shalltear, we might learn more. Or if it's a magic item, I could use Appraise Any Magic Item.

If they checked the treasury and found nothing worthwhile, perhaps it would be worth seeing if they could bring those home.

His mind made up, he began following them across the floor. The twins both had skills that prevented them from making tracks, and Ainz was using Perfect Unknowable and Fly, so he had no tracks to leave.

As they reached the center—

"——Hmm, I sensed something off and came to see what was wrong, only to find that we have some dark elves. Twin children?"

A voice called out from nowhere.

They spun around and found an elf standing a good ten yards off.

He possessed a cold sort of beauty, with eyes of different colors. Clearly not a servant.

His attitude alone made it clear he gave the orders. He was just that arrogant.

"——How?" Ainz whispered, too quietly for anyone to hear.

No such man had been here. He was sure of it. Ainz or Mare might have missed him, but Aura definitely wouldn't.

He had not been invisible. Ainz would've see through that.

Perhaps he'd used some sort of concealment skill to evade Ainz's detection and also invisibility powerful enough to escape Aura's, or else…

——A teleport? Damn, I should have had Delay Teleportation active.

Aura smoothly moved to stand between Ainz and the elf. Mare's knuckles were tightening on his staff.

They were clearly bracing for a fight, but the elf did no such thing. To Ainz, he looked entirely exposed, but perhaps that was merely a ruse to bait them in. If he'd had a warrior's talents, the difference might have been apparent.

Ainz moved away from the twins, waving at the man.

The man's gaze never budged.

He had not seen through Perfect Unknowable.

Ainz glanced at the twins.

Before they'd started this mission, he'd told them to gather information when encountering anything unknown—unless they detected clear hostile action.

Aura unobtrusively reached for her necklace, gripping it. Likely intent on discussing how to approach this with Mare.

Ainz understood the intent, but it was careless.

If an intruder made any suspicious moves, Ainz would have attacked on sight. Touching your equipment was tantamount to pulling a gun.

Expecting the mystery elf to attack, Ainz got ready to use an appropriate spell…and then craned his head to the side out of confusion.

The elf man hadn't budged.

He'd clearly seen how Aura had moved but didn't seem bothered by it.

Was that extreme confidence in his own abilities? Had he just not understood the implications of her action? Or was he also hesitant to attack without learning something first?

"——Mm? What's this? Your eyes… I have no memory of lying with a dark elf. Or did I…? Mm, mm, mm. Let's just make sure."

The man's…intimidation factor, perhaps, seemed to rise. It felt like his entire body grew larger.

Aura clicked her tongue.

"Body of Effulgent Beryl."

"My, my, my. You can stand up to this? That might be a first!"

"Um, why are you acting all hostile? I *will* kill you."

"Indomitability."

"——Ha! Ha-ha-ha-ha-ha-ha-ha!"

The man threw back his head, laughing like he'd never heard anything so funny. Aura's frown grew dangerously pointy. Her fist clenched very tight, but as Ainz watched, she slowly unclenched.

"Greater Resistance."

"Splendid! No, no, that explains it. It never occurred to me! Grandchildren! Of course. Even if the children are worthless, the blood might awaken in the next generation! How foolish of me to have let that possibility go unnoticed."

"What the hell are you talking about?"

"Greater Full Potential."

"Yes, indeed. I was barking up the wrong tree! Isn't that right, grandchildren?"

Grandchildren? What the hell? Why would he think that?

"Huh? Are you Lady Teapot's?"

Ainz felt a wave of panic. It suddenly occurred to him that Bubbling-Teapot might have been flung here on her own and left this man behind. But—

——*But there's no trace of slime here. Is he a shapeshifter, like Solution?*

"Teapot? What are you on about?"

No...? Then...is Akemi...?!

Akemi was Yamaiko's little sister. She'd made an elf character but hadn't gotten that into *Yggdrasil*, so he'd spent little time with her.

"Mm...you're a purebred elf, right?"

"...Whoops. Caster's Blessing."

"What an odd ques— Do you not know who I am? That can't be possible."

"We do!"

"Y-yes, of course."

"You're both terrible actors!" Ainz wailed. They'd sounded like they were reading off cue cards. In fact, they hadn't fooled this elf a bit, and his jaw dropped.

"Y-you really don't? Impossible! Honestly, I heard the dark elves lived at the very outskirts, but you are remarkably uncivilized."

He glared at them.

"Since you're my grandchildren, I'll forgive it once, but ignorance is a sin. I shall ensure you're properly educated."

"Educated, huh? But who are you actually? Just to be clear, I'm assuming you're the elf king?"

Aura suggested as much because the elf king was the only person who seemed likely to have any real strength.

"Life Essence. Oh!"

Ainz let out a yelp of surprise. The man had quite a substantial health pool. Easily higher than the Pleiades. In *Yggdrasil* terms, he'd be at least level 70. Definitely not a foe to be taken lightly.

"Sigh... How sad. Did your parents teach you nothing? What could possibly be more important than knowing the name of the king, the pinnacle of the elf species? Decem Hougan!"

"Shit."

Ainz swore under his breath.

He'd seen it coming, but the confirmation was worth a little swearing. So much for all that sneaking around. It felt like a huge wasted effort.

A major threat—probably—who should have been out there diminishing their future enemy's forces, but instead? He was going to have to eliminate the man himself.

It was hard to find any excuse to let the king live now. If he'd been weaker, perhaps overpowering him and erasing his memories would have been an option, but Life Essence suggested this man's combat abilities—or at least his HP—were astonishingly high by the standards of this world.

Naturally, if it came to a fight, the Nazarick denizens would certainly win. The three of them were all level 100. But capturing him? That was another story. They couldn't afford to let their guards down.

Like his sudden appearance, this elf—Decem—likely had some previously unknown abilities. Without adequate information, trying to capture instead of kill...was far too risky.

But at least Akemi's name hadn't come out, which meant there was a solid 90-percent chance she wasn't involved. If she was, her name would have been in there somewhere.

If this elf was the son of Yamaiko's sister, killing him would have been a last resort.

"You're the king? Then why are you here? The humans are attacking! Go out and fight—protect your citizens."

"Mana Essence... Interesting."

Decem's magic pool was also huge for someone from here. Almost as large as Shalltear's.

Given elven culture, if Decem had sizable pools of HP and MP, then he was most likely a druid, like Mare. And probably a back-line type.

"Why should I do that? You have some odd ideas about kings. A king is an exalted being who the populace must pay tribute to. Not someone who cleans up after them. Superior beings show those beneath them *mercy*. And mercy is something you beg for, not demand. Even if it is not granted, lesser beings must come to terms with that fact."

The hell was he on about?

Ainz couldn't believe his ears. If he meant anything he was saying, this king had bats in the belfry. He felt sorry for the elves suffering under his rule.

"So you're not gonna help them? But, uh, I guess some of that makes sense."

"Y-yes, I can't say it's entirely wrong..."

——*Hah?!*

Ainz swung around, gaping at the twins. This didn't look like a scheme to curry favor.

What part of that crap had made any sense? How could it not be entirely wrong?

O-or am I the one who's wrong? Maybe that's how kings are supposed to think? Jircniv was a bit like that, I suppose... What about the kuagoa king? He was super servile.

"Hmm. You *are* my grandchildren. You may be unlearned, but you have the minds to comprehend truth."

"——Ugh, I'm wasting time. I should use...Magic Ward: Fire."

"But you've made one fatal error," Aura said. "Only the Supreme Beings are worthy of tribute, not some lowly elf like you. But I guess if you wanna make the elves around here serve you, knock yourself out."

No, no...that's so many kinds of wrong. But nothing I say can change it. I guess I get how Aura and Mare feel. If we could make friends outside of Naza-rick...I suppose I'll have to place my hopes on Shizu and the girl with the scary eyes. My attempts didn't work out this time...or, given how she acted when we left, Shizu wasn't... Perhaps Sebas...? Argh, I'm getting distracted again!

"What? The Supreme Beings? Is that what the dark elves believe?" Decem considered it, then shook his head. "So be it. I can always hear more later."

"Do you have that kind of time? Like I said, the humans are busy sacking your country."

He'd wasted a moment, so Ainz hastily cast his next spell.

"False Data: Life."

Then a vibration shook the room from below. The Theocracy must have finally broken out the siege weapons.

Decem and the twins both glanced at the floor, falling silent. Ainz kept casting.

"False Data: Mana."

"Tch. These humans are a nuisance. I could go in person and wipe them out, but…I'm not in the mood. Come."

"…Where to?"

"Penetrate Up."

"Haven't really thought about it, but with my power, anywhere."

"No plan at all, huh? Worthless. And what'll happen if we go with you?"

"Earth… Hmm, that's a waste if I've read it wrong but…" Ainz hesitated, then took out a scroll and used it to cast Earth Master.

"Oh." Decem's eyes raked Aura's body. "You *are* still a child. It will take time before you're grown, but oh well. I've waited this long. A few decades is certainly not short, but I'll have to convince myself it is. You asked what would happen? The answer is simple. You'll make children with me."

"——Huh? What?"

"——Hah? Greater Luck."

"You as well," Decem said, looking at Mare. "Once a female is impregnated, you have to wait a while before trying again. In that sense, I might pin my hopes on you, boy. The two of us can sire a great number of children in no time at all. I feared that might thin the blood, but if grandchildren can awaken, great-grandchildren might as well. Worth experimenting with, at least. In any case—it's a bother, but I should bring some citizens with us for you to use. Still…why is a boy dressed as a girl? Is this a dark elf thing? Honestly, I'm displeased enough you're not pure elves, but it's far better than expanding my criteria to include all humanoid races."

Aura and Mare were just staring up at him, mouths hanging open.

"_____"

"Doesn't make sense yet? No matter. Come on."

Seeing the children just standing there, Decem reached for them—for Aura.

——Ainz batted his hand away. This registered as an attack, and Perfect Unknowable was instantly broken.

Shocked, Decem tried to turn—but before that happened, Ainz buried his fist in the man's face.

Decem went flying, rolling across the floor.

"You pedo motherfucker. That girl's in my care. How dare you lay your creepy eyes on her. Drop dead!"

Even as he hurled insults, the calm part of his mind was furious at himself for ruining his own plan.

Perfect Unknowable was a huge advantage and not worth losing in a fit of anger. Such a waste!

When Ainz's emotions crossed a certain threshold, they were forcibly reset. If that had kicked in, he could've handled this rationally—perhaps casting an instant death spell instead of punching him. He'd been less angry and more disgusted—and that didn't trigger the reset.

"Wha—wha—?"

Decem got up, reeling. Blood poured from both nostrils. Clearly not major damage. Life Essence showed no real loss of health.

Ainz's full swing had landed a clean hit—and that was it.

There'd been a small chance he was using a spell like False Data: Life or an item to disguise his HP, but it didn't seem like it was substantially inaccurate.

Ainz turned a palm to the twins, telling them not to budge.

Estimating Decem's total strength from his HP and MP, he was over level 70 but probably not level 80.

But there was one thing to watch out for—albeit a very low possibility.

Namely, there might be classes not from *Yggdrasil* exclusive to this world—that didn't raise HP and MP. In other words, he might be level 100, but his combined HP and MP made him look level 70.

This was extremely unlikely. But not impossible.

We could gang up on him and go for a quick kill, but that's a bad idea. I at least want to work out how he pulled off that teleport...

As Ainz figured out his strategy, Decem began yelling.

"A-an undead?! Why here...out of thin air?!" His gaze turned to the twins. "Is one of you a necromancer?"

"Indeed," Ainz said, answering before they could respond. "These two are necromancers beyond compare. And I am a guardian created by them and their parents, their four powers combined. I shall never allow anyone lacking to lay a finger on them. Should you be able to best me, you may take them with you—" Here he smirked, projecting contempt. "Not that you *can*."

"Hmm..." Decem let go of his nose. The bleeding had stopped. "I'm almost impressed. I haven't bled in...decades? Perhaps a century! You certainly have the strength to back your arrogance. Hardly how one addresses a king, but you are lucky. Rejoice, for I shall personally demonstrate the discrepancy in our power. You will bow!"

He was looking at Aura and Mare the whole time, like he'd fully bought Ainz's total fabrication.

Huh, Ainz thought.

Why not doubt his story? Why act like he took it at face value?

Perhaps he had no means of turning invisible. Otherwise, he'd have assumed Ainz had been lurking all along, under cover of Invisibility—and was not actually a summon.

In which case, he was like Mare—a specialized druid.

Or is this a performance for my benefit? But what would be the point of bluffing here?

He tried to place himself in this man's shoes, but stopping to think things over would arouse his suspicions.

"Then let us duel one-on-one! How better to prove who is stronger, my masters or you?"

Decem's eyes went wide; then he laughed, like that was inherently hilarious.

Ainz used Silent Magic to send a Message to Mare.

Mare, that was a lie. If I'm at a disadvantage, step in and make sure this man dies. Quietly pass this on to Aura.

Obviously. No way was he giving the twins to this creep. Only a fool would insist on fighting one-on-one when your life was on the line. True, there were fights you could afford to lose, but those did not include any battles to the death.

Still...

Ainz definitely blew it this time.

He would've preferred to spend more time buffing himself. Yet, he couldn't abide the thought of this deviant touching Aura. And he might have skills Ainz was unaware of—a forced teleport, for instance.

"A moment ago—when I saw you commanding this undead—I knew for a fact you are my grandchildren."

The ground began to move.

Like waves retreating down the beach to the bay—the dirt on the floor headed Decem's way.

Ainz ignored this, making a show of taking out a scroll—like he'd had it hidden under his robe—and activating its magic.

This was a real waste. But the situation left him with no choice. With no clear indication how knowledgeable his foe was, he couldn't afford to make him cautious.

The spell used was an eighth-tier magic, Dimensional Lock.

Demons and angels—residents of other worlds—had this as a special skill, and this spell replicated that with magic. It negated attempts to move outside the area of affect with any instant-movement spells—Teleportation chief among them.

By this time, Decem's dirt mound had formed a giant.

Clearly an elemental.

Mare let out a surprised noise, and Ainz was right there with him.

A primal earth elemental?!

No ordinary means could summon *this* type of elemental, and it made Ainz all the more cautious.

Unlike Mare, Ainz managed to stifle his shock—he made not a sound. Rule one of Player Killing for Dummies was not revealing what you knew.

Against a child like Mare, he might assume this was a reaction to the sheer power of the summon, but with Ainz, he would likely take it as a sign he knew what this was.

So Ainz shrugged instead.

"Hmm, is that it? Earth elementals are just huge piles of dirt. You don't want to soil your hands, so you're having this thing fight me instead? You must think I'm entirely feeble."

"Aha! You know what this is?" Decem smirked.

Cool.

"Of course. There's no mistaking an earth elemental. I've summoned and defeated them myself. Mine was not quite this large—at this size, I'll acknowledge it must take some strength to command. Size is an indicator of power. But bigger is not always better."

"True! I agree. Dragonlords have a clear advantage in bulk yet are helpless before elves. Still, I'm impressed. Your knowledge is accurate. This is, indeed, an earth elemental. Ha-ha-ha! You are well-informed—or at least have a good memory. Very respectable." Decem's sarcasm levels were off the charts. "The perfect opportunity! Why not try taking a hit from it? A blow from this elemental you scoff at?"

The primal earth elemental slowly raised a fist.

It oughtta be able to move way faster than that. He's doing this deliberately—but that works for me.

If Decem was going to toy with him like a cat with its prey, Ainz was on board.

Perfect.

Hiding his grin—not that his face moved—Ainz mentally reviewed what he knew about primal earth elementals.

They started at level 80 and were definitely the tanks of the primal class. Well, that was basically true for *all* earth elementals.

Their attacks were supposedly imbued with all the metal attributes—at level or below—the earth contained. So if you had a weakness to silver, like Lupusregina, their attacks would take advantage of that.

There was also a minor stat boost provided if both the elemental and their opponent were in contact with soil. However, since all the dirt in the room had already gathered at Decem's side, leaving only wooden floors, that didn't apply here. Elementals could dive into the soil—similarly useless indoors. In conclusion, this wasn't a great location for a primal earth elemental to fight.

The main means of attack was swinging those arms around. Simple but quite powerful. Speed and accuracy weren't that high, but it would still be hard for a rear-line fighter like Ainz to dodge. And they did battering damage, which was effective against Ainz.

They could extend their arms like whips for sweep attacks, but that lessened the damage done.

Like their attacks, their defense was believed to have a variety of metal attributes, and it was treated as having Weapon Resistance V to all types. And that stacked with Reduce Physical Damage. For those reasons, it made an ideal tank and was quite a tricky foe if you were only going at it with physical attacks.

Naturally, it had its weaknesses.

It had no real tricks to play—no special abilities. In other words, nothing that could really shake up a fight.

And anything that exploited metallic weaknesses worked just fine.

HeroHero would have made short work of it.

In other words, it was weak to acid, et al.—and one more attribute.

Ainz got ready to draw a staff from his item box. It wasn't time for that just yet. This foe thought he was a standard-issue undead. Best not to reveal any abilities that would make him cautious.

The question was—could he withstand this blow?

He did fancy the idea of acting like he only realized this was no ordinary earth elemental after taking the hit. The downside was that if that didn't kill him, his foe might start taking this fight seriously.

Yeah, he's definitely specialized in summons. And that means the elemental's blow will be pretty destructive. Taking unnecessary damage could work against me later. I should—

"Wall of Skeletons."

The elemental's fist came crashing down, and Ainz summoned a massive wall made entirely of bones. It crumbled as soon as it appeared.

I thought so… He lost mana.

"——Wh-wh-what?!" Ainz said, loud enough that the man could hear him. "How can it destroy my wall in a single blow?!"

"Ha-ha-ha! Your walls must be fragile indeed, unable to withstand a hit from a mere earth elemental!"

Decem seemed to be in a very good mood, so Ainz tossed a spell at him. "Lopsided Duel."

This was a third-tier spell. If his opponent tried to teleport away, this spell would ensure Ainz was automatically taken to the same place. Even if someone was protected by Delay Teleportation, this allowed him to ignore that and move at the same time.

That could be a two-edged sword. If they teleported right into the middle of their friends, you'd be dragged along with them and get the snot beat out of you. That was why it was so low tier despite the obvious benefits. Before it got patched, you'd been able to cast it on a friend and move them with you, but they soon issued a fix that made the spell work only on enemies.

Naturally, if Decem fled somewhere with an opponent as strong as he was, Ainz would need to run for it, but that wasn't actually hard—like the name implied, if Ainz teleported away, it would not pull Decem along with him.

"——What did you do?"

"……An instant-death spell. I take it you've got countermeasures in place?"

"……Hmm, that's at least mildly intelligent. After realizing it can't beat Behemoth, it attacks me. Did you think I was somehow weaker than the elemental?"

By Yggdrasil *rules, the summoner would never be weaker than the summon, but I bet you are actually lower level. You've deemed me weaker than you but ignored my question because you have no strategy against instant-death spells? Also, why "Behemoth"?*

Decem jerked his chin, and the primal earth elemental raised its fist. Moving faster now. He heard Decem cast a spell at the same time.

"Mercy of Shorea Robusta."

Tch. I figured he could use tenth tier, but that one's obnoxious. Gotta double the spell on my finishing blow.

Mercy of Shorea Robusta was indeed a tenth-tier spell, and it came with one of the highest mana costs around—on the same level as Reality Slash.

It had three effects.

First, for a period of time, it would steadily restore your health. But this was not an impressive heal, and at Decem's level, it was hard to call that useful.

Second, it completely protected against instant death. If you just wanted this protection, there were lower-level spells for that, but there was a good reason many druids acquired this skill anyway.

That main appeal was the third effect, which allowed you to come back to life if your HP hit 0. In this case, the resurrection carried no level-down penalty. Zero HP was a required condition—deaths caused by things that didn't deal combat damage, like drowning, were not affected. Still, it was a pretty good spell. Priests had revival spells that could avoid the level-down penalty if cast right after a death, and druids had Phoenix Breath, but this spell was widely used to prevent accidental deaths. It didn't give you much health after a revival, so combo hits would still kill you outright—but still, people had been saved by it…on occasion.

And since this was classified as resurrection magic, it could negate fatalities caused by Ainz's ultimate move, the Goal of All Life Is Death. But that would make this spell dissipate, even if it would normally still have active time left. This was because all spell effects were lost at the moment of resurrection.

My bluff about casting an instant-death spell made him cautious—bad move on my part. I should have mentioned something I can't use. Will do in the future.

"Triplet Magic: Wall of Skeletons."

As expected, the first blow smashed a wall, and the next blow smashed the second. That left one standing—and while Decem's line of sight was blocked, Ainz moved a bit away, took out a scroll, and used the spell.

"Piercing Cacophony."

This was a buff and might not be necessary, but just in case.

The primal earth elemental attacked again.

Shattering the bone wall—

"Triplet Magic: Wall of Skeletons."

As the first of these new walls went down, he heard Decem cast.

"Aspect of Elemental."

An eighth-tier druid spell, this granted you an elemental's resistances. This negated a lot of status effects—poison and sickness included. It also negated the effects of critical hits and any effects that depended on them.

The ninth-tier Elemental Form was similar.

This was rough—he was swiftly eliminating a lot of Ainz's strengths.

Still—

How far can I diminish his MP pool?

Triplet Silent Magic: Greater Magic Seal.

Ainz moved a few more steps. This put him a ninety-degree turn away from his original position (assuming Decem as the center). He was closer to the stairs now.

The primal earth elemental's attack broke through the bones. Sadly, he could not make more.

Triplet Maximize Boosted Silent Magic: Magic Arrow.

This took a huge chunk of MP.

Even a low-level spell would do a lot strengthened four times.

If the primary earth elemental had been a standard summon, he could have simply used Greater Rejection and had no need to use spells like this. But if Decem's class build was a specialized summoner, there was a solid chance Ainz would be unable to dismiss the summon even with his level advantage.

And Greater Rejection could only cancel summons—it couldn't do anything to creatures made with a Create skill.

Elemental Adjutant, etc. If he sacrificed experience to create it, it can stick around for basically ever. Given that it's costing MP to maintain it, I don't think that's this…but I don't wanna gamble.

Better to prepare just in case.

"Oh—" Decem saw where Ainz was standing relative to the twins and frowned. "Why would you move there? You claim to be their guardian, yet prepare to flee?"

"Tch!"

"Ha-ha-ha! I'd be glad to assist!"

Ainz made a run for the door, his back wide open and the primary earth elemental took a swing at it. The sheer bulk had a knock-back effect that sent Ainz flying.

"Oh? One blow isn't enough to finish you. I see you're not all talk. Yet, resistance is futile."

Ainz used Fly to land at the top of the stairs without losing his balance.

"But if you're running, I assume you're abandoning your masters here?"

"Of course not."

Ainz made another Wall of Skeletons.

"This again?" Decem said, sounding appalled. "Not even trying to harm my elemental? Your strategy is laughable."

"Ha-ha-ha!" Ainz chortled. "I know the humans are invading your country! Elf king, time is on *my* side."

"…Ah. That explains it. Aren't you clever? But that, too, is futile. Impossible."

"Mm? You think so?"

"Did you really think mere humans could defeat *me*, commander of the highest-tier elemental?"

I scoffed at that man who summoned an angel, but in this case, a primal earth elemental is more or less the highest tier around. Do the Theocracy really know how strong he is? Or do they have a way to defeat him? This guy sure doesn't think so. Who is in the dark here, Decem or the Theocracy? Would the latter really call that the highest-level angel if they were aware of Decem's abilities?

Ainz had gone quiet, thinking.

"It should be obvious, really," a scornful voice said. "What a shallow fool you are. I suppose you are undead. You've got air where your brain should be."

I can't tell. If they're serious about this war, they have to have someone on his level in their camp. In which case, time isn't on my side. I don't want to fight two in a row...

What would be the best way to tire out his opponent?

As he considered this, he threw up another Wall of Skeletons.

Like his Message to Mare, if you really wanted to win, fighting one-on-one was stupid. But this time, he was forced to do so—unless he was on the verge of losing. That was why this fight was such a headache.

This way of fighting tied his hands.

He knew Decem was unable to see through Perfect Unknowable. Using that would give him an overwhelming advantage.

But he couldn't use it.

Why not?

If he cast Perfect Unknowable and started unilaterally attacking, what then?

Or if he did anything else that made Decem realize his true strength—using high-level spells like Stop Time, for instance?

If Decem realized he could not win, he would likely retreat. Fortunately, his attacks were unlikely to target the twins—it might happen, but the odds were low. The man's goal here was to capture Aura—and Mare, if possible. He was unlikely to do anything that might prove fatal.

But before they figured out how Decem had arrived so suddenly, they didn't want him fleeing.

Someone who appeared out of thin air might well disappear. They had to prepare for the worst and act as if he had a skill for that.

And if they let him get away, this degenerate might continue to come after the twins.

That had to be avoided.

Without knowing the full extent of Decem's powers, that would be akin to dangling them off the edge of a cliff.

Thus, the plan.

———Keep him here and make sure he dies.

That meant he couldn't easily ask the twins to help.

Numbers were a major factor in ensuring victory. If Ainz had run into foes of unknown strength who outnumbered him, retreat would be his first consideration. Decem should have done the same.

His best plan was to keep Decem in the dark about the mounting danger until Ainz knew for sure he could kill him. For that reason, he sidelined the twins and avoided summoning any undead.

This was also why he'd dangled them as bait.

He would limit his foe's options and guide his thoughts, making it so he wouldn't—couldn't leave the battle.

It's the whatchamacallit—the sunk-in cost fallacy. How long this actually keeps him here is… Well, let's hope he doesn't figure it out. Let's hope he doesn't have much combat experience. I've got to at least break his spirit.

•

"*H-he's so scary…*"

Aura could hear Mare's voice quiver, even through the necklace.

"*Yup. He is.*"

"*I didn't know Lord Ainz could be this scary.*"

Aura and Mare knew exactly why their master—the absolute ruler—was fighting this way.

To figure out what his foe could do? That was possibly a part of it. But that wasn't the main goal.

He was after one thing.

Drag that elf into the muck, don't let him escape, and make sure he was dead.

If you didn't know how strong a foe was, then during a fight, you had to think about when to cut your losses and run.

There were many signs that should happen, but barring an outright inability to harm them, a good indicator was when your own health dropped below a certain threshold.

But what if you had plenty of health but were running low on MP?

And had used a lot of magic to get to that point?

If it felt like you'd probably win if you held out a little longer?

It was hard to cut your losses even if you knew you should. Most people took stock of their foes, learned from bad experiences, and made rules for themselves.

But if you had no real combat experience and knew little about your opponent, that made it harder to figure out when to cut and run.

And their master knew that applied here.

Their opponent was a king and extremely arrogant. He'd never fought anyone anywhere close to his level. Which meant it was easy to back him into a corner where he couldn't run.

"*All these cheap lines are bluffs. Lord Ainz really does think like a monster. I know that's rude, but…*"

Aura shivered.

"*I can see why Demiurge said Lord Ainz was worse than he could ever be.*"

Mare shuddered.

"*The way he showed off the scroll usage is really something.*"

"*All while not revealing what he's actually capable of.*"

An approach this thorough was downright terrifying. And highly educational.

Both agreed they were incredibly fortunate to be serving someone like him.

•

Walls went up as soon as he smashed them.

The sight of this brought a rising irritation beneath Decem's smile. So much time wasted.

How many times had it been now? He hadn't bothered counting, but it had to be dozens.

Each wall was fragile enough to take out with a single blow, but this undead was generating several at once and moving around so Behemoth could not reach him.

Weaklings must compensate with schemes. Or perhaps this is the best spell it has, and it's just desperate.

This undead might not be entirely weak, but it was clearly not as strong as himself or Behemoth. Everything he'd seen so far had reinforced that impression.

If this undead were stronger than Behemoth, it would have attacked it aggressively. Yet, all it did was squirm around pathetically, using defensive spells. Like it was waiting for help to arrive. Behemoth took damage with each wall it smashed, but this was inconsequential. No one would be foolish enough to think they could win like this.

Just a sad, futile hope that if it chips away enough of Behemoth's health, it'll be easier for the humans to defeat. But Behemoth has far more stamina than you imagine. You'll be out of magic first.

A wall down, another behind.

Decem sighed.

The thought of fighting this foe any longer wearied him.

Perhaps that's its goal. Hoping I get fed up and leave. But how do I wrap this up quickly?

He knew well enough it was smarter to ignore the walls. But Decem's Behemoth was sorely lacking in other skills. Ignoring the walls meant lumbering all the way around, and if it did that, the undead would just make more.

A game of tag.

Decem could control and command elementals stronger than himself. Normally, you could control only those weaker than you, but the class he had mastered let him escape those constraints. But the downside to it was that sustained combat gradually used up his magic.

He didn't have to stay focused on controlling Behemoth, so he could cast other spells himself. But that reduced the time he could keep Behemoth in the fight.

Fine. I'll have to use an attack spell. Behemoth and me: If we're both attacking, he won't have time to make walls.

Decem could use spells up to the tenth tier.

This was a realm the run-of-the-mill casters of the world would never achieve, no matter how hard they worked. Only the chosen few were allowed access to it.

But he had managed to get there only by specializing in summoning. It was not his forte. Even so, if he used a tenth-tier spell, he ought to be able to eliminate a mere undead. But was it worth wasting precious magic on this? Should he not keep it in reserve to allow Behemoth to fight more? That thought made him hesitate.

I must convince this undead and the humans that they can never defeat Behemoth or me. That way, they won't futilely buy time.

He had informed them of the facts but convinced no one.

Nor had he expected to.

Why would anyone believe what an enemy said? Yet, Decem had simply told the truth. Nothing had ever been able to defeat Behemoth. Even an ancient dragon had been no match for it. It had buffed itself with second-tier magic, and the Behemoth's fists had squished it flat.

Decem himself would perish if the Behemoth turned on him.

His father was likely the only one who could ever have defeated it. But his father was long dead. In other words—nothing alive could win.

Perhaps it thinks it can prevail if I run out of magic, but that's hardly true.

A caster with no magic left could be easily defeated. That was true for an undead caster and likely the basis for this farce.

And it certainly was a plan with some merit to it.

Decem had specialized in elemental control, and if his magic ran out—and he could no longer keep Behemoth going—his combat abilities would be greatly diminished. But that did not make him weak. He was a top-ranking druid, and his flesh boasted prowess matched by few creatures. A swing of his fist could cut a fragile human in two. A kick could leave a footprint in steel armor and pulp the organs of whoever wore it.

He was certain he could kill a thousand—ten thousand—soldiers with his bare hands.

Then was there no concern here? He couldn't quite say for sure.

He had let Behemoth handle all his fights for so long. Killing a few thousand soldiers meant swinging his fists that many times, and he couldn't be sure his stamina would last that long without making the attempt. Worse—

If I personally wade into the fray, I'll get human blood on me. How savage!

Decem was proud of his elementalist skills. Taking up arms to personally kill someone was positively barbaric. That had to be avoided at all costs.

So what should he do?

The magic loss is getting hard to ignore. I can still fight...but not for long. I can't keep Behemoth moving forever. I'll need to kill the humans outside while keeping my grandchildren immobilized with magic so they cannot resist. Which means I've got little to spare.

In which case, he could ill afford to waste more magic on this undead.

Should I ignore the undead and grab my grandchildren? But they'll likely just summon it again...

That would force him to restart this insipid battle.

And resorting to that itself was unbecoming.

Fighting to win would demonstrate his strength, break their wills, prove his superiority. Failing that would mean they continued to resist him endlessly.

He had to destroy this undead here.

I'm back to that, but how do I do it?

All previous enemies had snapped like twigs under the Behemoth's blows. He'd never even imagined fighting someone who flitted around, scrabbling for time.

Hmph. Good experience. Allows me to master the art of swatting flies. Let's try— Yes.

Decem glared at the wall before Behemoth. No—the undead who ought to be behind it.

I suppose I must. Killing it quick will be worth the magic. An elementalist resorting to attack skills is gauche, entirely bereft of aesthetic appeal...but it must be done. If it's any consolation, it is at least superior to engaging in fisticuffs.

His mind made up, Decem selected a spell and cast it.

"Shining Burst."

A seventh-tier attack spell that called a veritable sun into being and detonated it. A half sphere of blinding light vaporized the vexing wall—but the wall behind it remained unscathed.

Interesting. Wide-ranging spells aren't able to down multiple walls, either.

He would much rather have taken them all out in one fell swoop, but learning one more function of his foe's spell would have to suffice. He need merely pick a different spell next time.

Even with area-of-effect spells, there were those that spread out, those that exploded, and those that fired beams—each distinct and unique.

The Behemoth's massive right fist smashed through another wall, and a breath later, the left came down on the final one. At long last, a glimpse of the undead reeling beyond.

You're just going to make more walls, aren't you?

Then he need merely pick a spell based on that outcome.

But his prediction proved unfounded.

Walking away from Behemoth, the undead took an item out from beneath its robe. Likely a scroll.

Elves used the bark of a particular tree in place of scrolls and weren't able to infuse them with anything above druid-accessible third-tier spells. The undead was not using druid magic, so Decem assumed the branch of magic it did use explained the use of scrolls.

Low-level spells? It mocks me. As if those could accomplish anything. Or can its scrolls contain higher-level magic? But where would it have obtained them? A quirk of the summon?

The scroll vanished, and the spell activated.

"Wha—?!"

A dense mist spread out around the undead, blanketing the area. Visibility had dropped to mere yards. It was thick as spilled milk. He could make out nothing farther than five yards out.

Another infuriating spell choice.

He wanted to cast an attack spell, but that wouldn't do much if he couldn't see. Even with an area spell. And the undead had been walking around when it used that scroll; it had likely moved away the moment it activated. Even if he aimed a spell at the undead's last known location, there was no guarantee he'd hit.

He had Behemoth move around, searching for the undead—but it was acting sluggish.

The Behemoth relied on sight for detection. It had nothing that could see through this mist and had lost track of its target.

Decem used the fourth-tier spell Tremor Sense.

This was a detection skill that could pick up even the slightest vibrations, letting him know exactly where his foe was. It worked best on the ground but was functional on floors, too. However—

——*What? He's not here?*

It might be impossible to see through the mist, but Tremor Sense easily located his grandchildren—they weren't moving, so it was detecting subtle weight shifts. That suggested the undead hadn't teleported away—and the twins canceling their summon was even less likely. What could this mean? It didn't take Decem long.

It's not touching the floor! It's floating!

The undead had *looked* like it was running around but had actually been flying somehow.

Tremor Sense relied on tiny vibrations transmitted from below and couldn't detect anything in the air.

This undead really knew how to get up his left nostril.

"More silly time wasting! A demented nuisance!"

Most vexing. It might even be faster and easier to call the humans in here and take them all out at once.

And it's so weak! If we were outside, I'd have killed it by now!

But no means of dragging this undead or his grandchildren outdoors sprang to mind. He could punch through the castle walls and throw them out, but that was easier said than done.

Decem told Behemoth to stop wandering and wait close at hand.

He had no clue what this thing was doing in the mist, but it might be trying to sneak up on him. He was hardly going to die from a single hit, so this was no real concern, but he was vehemently opposed to letting a lesser being draw blood again.

The clock kept ticking as he waited for his foe to make a move. The length of time was not itself significant, but he could feel his magic slowly draining away, and that made the wait agonizing.

——*I can't afford to waste any more time on this!*

He had to clear the mist. He racked his brain, trying to recollect some spells he'd long left unused. Behemoth had so effectively defeated all his enemies that he'd never even bothered to cast half the spells he acquired,. But he *did* know a wind spell capable of blowing this away.

He went with a ninth-tier spell—Tempest.

Gale-force winds raged, and the mist instantly vanished. But Tempest brought with it torrential rain that also blocked his line of sight. Such was the force of the storm that even Decem could barely stand upright. Moving through it was not an option.

Behemoth alone stood fast—it might not be fleet of foot, but mere wind could not slow it down.

This wind should pin that undead down, at least.

He couldn't see through the rain. Behemoth likely couldn't locate the undead. But Decem could. Tremor Sense was picking up every drop that hit the floor, and these vibrations were indistinguishable from footsteps—if someone was walking through the storm, he couldn't tell. What he could identify was areas where the rains *weren't* hitting. His mental map of the room soon found two objects blocking the rainfall. One was likely his grandchildren, so the other must be the undead.

——*It's on the move?*

The rain was coming down too hard to see through. Winds only the

Behemoth's bulk could withstand blew through the room. How was that undead moving in this? Even if it was flying, the wind would still buffet it.

Decem thought for one second—and then canceled Tempest.

The magic storm vanished as if it had never existed. Proof it had been real lay in the wet floor and his soaked clothes.

Decem swept his wet hair off his face, turning his eyes toward the wall between him and the undead's location. It must have gone up even as his spell vanished.

"Will you stop that?!" Decem roared. "Come out and fight me! Sneaking around behind your flimsy walls like a lily-livered cur!"

"——Not much of a fight without a strategy or two. Don't make me state the obvious. That said, mind if I ask you a few questions?"

The undead's voice carried over the wall.

Given the steady drain on his magic, he should ignore that—but he was curious. This undead's words likely reflected the thoughts of these twins—and by extension, their parents. Worth learning.

"...........Go on?"

"Should you not face these humans? The battle outside has raged for quite some time. They may be slaughtering the elves down below."

Not the question he'd expected but one easily answered.

Decem considered dismissing Behemoth's combat form, but it would take time to bring it back. And this undead was *crafty*. It would likely attack at the slightest opening, even in the middle of a discussion. That attack would not be remotely fatal, but that was no reason to stand here and let it happen. He decided to keep the Behemoth active despite the magic drain.

"Perhaps there is an argument for saving them—my blood might awaken in future generations, after all. But there are elves elsewhere. And those who manage to escape from this crisis with their lives have potential. Essentially, I fail to see the benefit of saving anyone weak enough to be killed by mere humans."

"Then my next question. I've heard there is an elf treasure."

"A treasure? Meaning myself? Or perhaps this?"

"...By *this*, you mean that primal earth elemental?"

"Primal…?"

"That puzzles you? You have summoned a primal earth elemental, yes? Or is it a different race—or is there a separate elven name? Do you call it something else?"

This imbecile still believed this to be an ordinary elemental or variant thereof. Infuriating. He had to correct this at once, for the benefit of his grandchildren's education.

"That is Behemoth. The earthen guardian elemental Behemoth."

"So I didn't mishear that. An earthen guardian elemental…and not a great beast that strides the land? Is it a raid boss? It looks nothing like the behemoth I know. Who first gave it that name? You?"

"No—"

"——Then who?"

Very eager. Why insist upon that? What great beast? He vaguely remembered hearing the term *raid boss* before, but…did this undead, or rather his grandchildren, know something he didn't? Perhaps best he offer no further answers.

"If you want to know, remove those walls. Show your face when you speak—basic manners."

"Then I don't need to know. I merely asked out of intellectual curiosity."

Decem looked at the twins.

Was it the summoned undead that wanted this information or had his grandchildren learned something somewhere? They were soaking wet, but their faces were impassive—he could glean nothing from them.

"Not to change the subject—"

"Enough. There is no use speaking with you further."

Feeling antsy, he glared at the twins. He couldn't afford further magic loss. These questions had been nothing like what he'd expected and were not worth engaging with.

"Then enough talk."

The walls vanished.

He'd been about to cast Green Chain on the twins, so this shook him. He wasn't sure which way to aim.

"——Good enough, I suppose. You've lost enough mana."

"……What?"

The undead's tone had grown awfully still.

Why did it suddenly seem so sure of itself?

This useless summon, capable only of biding time—

He ordered Behemoth to flatten it—

Then Decem's eyes flitted to the stairs behind it. He'd wondered if the human forces were almost here, if the change in attitude was because its goal had been achieved. There was no one there. He listened close and heard no footsteps, let alone a human's.

"I said you'd lost enough mana. That club—your Behemoth will likely not last much longer. I doubt you can maintain it more than a few more minutes."

"Oh, I see. You believe you can beat me if I'm out of magic. True, I was unable to dodge your swing. But that was because you were summoned abruptly. If I'd known it was coming, I could have handled that easily."

"——I know."

So quiet. Decem found himself swallowing.

Why was it acting like this?

It felt wrong.

Why was he unnerved by a mere undead?

He was the strongest of the elves, descended from the elf who'd conquered the very world.

Grinding his back teeth, he squished the shameful emotions.

"So?" he bellowed. "Your fist made me bleed, and in your arrogance, you believe you have a chance. Though that blow did but paltry damage."

"I'm aware."

The louder Decem got, the softer the undead's voice grew. This was downright uncanny.

Was it—?

A moment of weakness, a possibility too remote.

But then…why?

Why fight like that?

Deception.

This confidence was all for show.

No other explanation existed.

"Behemoth!" Was this a roar or a shriek? Even he couldn't tell. "Smash!!"

"Let's begin." An instant later, the meaning of these words grew clear. "Triplet Maximize Magic: Cacophonous Burst. Release."

First, an explosion of sound. Then came an angel's wings.

Behemoth was between Decem and the undead. A storm of sound waves struck it; then its bulk was buffeted by a rain of light every bit as powerful as Tempest. The earthen guardian elemental's health visibly dropped. Unlike living organisms, it shed no blood and lost no pieces, but Decem controlled it—he knew it was barely alive.

Consternation.

No other word for it.

Behemoth was the most powerful elemental. A being that could dominate anyone. Even the most draining of their previous fights had never substantially dented its prodigious health.

And yet—

Here—

Never had he seen it take this much damage, teeter on death's door.

"H-how…?!"

"Impressive. I struck the weakness, yet six blows were not enough. If I were specced further into offensive magic, could I have managed it?"

Still the voice was flat, betraying no emotion. It was like he was facing a completely different undead.

Wh-what is even happening?

The wave of confusion began to ebb—replaced with fear.

His earlier notion returned.

Was this undead actually *stronger* than him?

"Behemoth! Protect me!"

The elemental did as it was told. It moved to block the undead's line of sight and began swinging its fist.

I have you now! Huh? What?!

Behemoth swung its other fist. This could only mean the first blow had not finished the undead off!

Two blows landed, yet he could see the undead standing there behind Behemoth.

Intact.

Those fists had crushed all foes yet could not budge this undead.

"Triplet Maximize Magic: Cacophonous Burst."

And before his very eyes, the invincible great elemental—was reduced to so much soil.

An immense sense of loss.

Like something had been torn right out of his heart. Leaving a gaping hole behind.

"A tad overkill... I thought you might have a skill, so I don't regret the choice. What do you say?"

"——Eep!"

Impossible.

That elemental was all-powerful, his other half. It could never be defeated.

But it was no longer there.

What now?

What was he supposed to do?

What was this undead—?

"Don't be so scared. Reality Slash."

Incredible pain.

Pain the likes of which he'd never felt before.

"Ah...ahhh!" He looked down and saw blood gushing from his chest, staining clothes still wet from the rain. "Ow...owww!"

Ow.

Ow.

Ow.

That singular thought pounded at the inside of his skull.

"I get that. Were I not in this body, the pain from that blow would have driven me mad. I suggest you surrender. I guarantee I will hurt you no more. Surrender and you will be saved."

"Ah...ahhh...ahhhh...owww... Y-you mean that?"

Tears welling up from the sheer agony, Decem directed his question at his grandchildren.

They jumped, and the girl said, "Yes!"

"See? My mistress granted permission. Surrender your arms. Never fear—we'll return them once we're sure they're not a threat. I promise. I tell no lies. I swear on my masters' bond. Trust me."

The undead's voice was earnest, sincere. He almost believed it.

Ow.

Mercy of Shorea Robusta was likely healing his wounds a little, but the cut ran deep, and it did nothing for the pain.

For a moment, Decem considered surrender might be worth escaping this. But he had his pride.

He'd been king a long time, ruled this country. He could not beg younger dark elves for his life, even if they were his grandchildren.

Ow.

No magic left. Well, some, but using that to fight this undead? He could not imagine winning.

Should he try to close in?

No, he had no reason to be confident there. If that undead used a spell like that again, he'd be dead.

Ow.

Decem's eyes turned to the stairs behind it.

No one there.

Then—

He ran. That was all.

It hurt.

He was scared.

In pain.

Shaking.

And yet, Decem ran.

The still-flowing blood was a sign his life was ebbing away.

Fear of death overwhelmed his mind. He had a magic item that resisted fear, but it did nothing for the emotions generated from within.

And so—the fear lent wind to his sails. His body did what his mind demanded. He ran faster than he ever had before.

The world sped past him. He was right on top of the undead.

"Stop! I *will* kill you!"

He ignored the warning. As he passed the undead, it cast a spell.

"Stop Time!"

No pain. No, perhaps there was—but running kept aggravating the deep gouge in his chest, and the torment of that overwhelmed him so much, he could feel nothing else.

So Decem ran on. The stairs were right before him.

The pain in his chest was astounding, but his feet never wavered.

"Aura!"

Had the undead cast something? If there was a spell, it did not affect Decem.

He kept running.

Once he reached the stairs—the ground below his feet exploded. Three times.

The shock lifted him, and he strained every muscle he had to keep himself upright, to avoid slowing down. His feet didn't hurt much—or rather, the pain in his chest and the fear left him numb to anything else.

He heard the undead speaking behind him but could not care.

Decem leaped down the stairs.

No sounds of pursuit. As he started to relax, the pain in his feet caught up with him.

He almost shrieked but bit it back. Loud noises would be bad.

He glanced down and found his legs shredded. These fresh injuries had been caused by those explosions.

The sight of these injuries added to the pain.

Decem looked over his shoulder. He spotted a trail of blood in his wake. Even with no tracking abilities, they could easily follow him.

Ow.

He didn't want to run.

But he had to. Else even more pain awaited him.

And—he did not want to die.

That alone forced his legs through the pain.

Why is this happening to me? Why did my grandchildren not help?

It made no sense.

Why would they not help the elf race?

Damn it!

He swore inside—saying anything aloud might give away his position—and ran off, shedding tears as he went.

•

Ainz had used his nicest voice with Decem, urging surrender. Perhaps the conditions weren't right for the mystery teleport; perhaps he was just too cornered to think straight—but he looked ready to raise the flag.

Finally. Ainz grinned inside.

The offer was a lie, of course. He guaranteed nothing at all. He would kill the man the moment he cast off his gear.

If his mind was sufficiently broken, perhaps he would not target the twins again, but death was the only way to be sure.

But an instant later, the fire was back in Decem's eyes.

Mm?

Decem broke into a run. Right at Ainz.

Tch, closing in for a fight? Then—so be it!

Doing his best not to let his smile show, he acted surprised and alarmed.

Certainly, arcane casters like Ainz loathed close combat—it might even be called their weakness. But if Decem wanted a fight, Ainz was all for it. He might lose a little HP, but it ensured Decem's death. Except—an instant later, his surprise was genuine. Not that it showed on his expressionless visage.

Decem's path led slightly to one side, not slowing at all.

Ainz realized he'd guessed wrong.

Shit, he's bolting!

It pained him to admit, but his opinion of Decem went up—not quite a full notch but a smidgen at least.

Full-on flight was the option Ainz was least prepared to handle. In Decem's shoes, Ainz would have done the same—admittedly, much earlier.

But because he knew that, Ainz had assumed Decem would use magic to escape and prepared for that eventuality. He didn't have anything prepared for this guy just making a break for it on foot. Lack of time was a factor, and there'd been only so much he could do while hiding his own skill.

"Stop! I will kill you!"

He shouted a warning but knew it would not work. And even if he did stop, Ainz was still going to kill him. Even as he spoke, he was already considering his next option.

A wall—he'd just jump over, and then Ainz would lose sight of him, leaving him unable to handle his next means of flight.

If he could land a mind-control spell, that would end things. But Decem was supposed to be over level 70, and odds were the spell would fail. Items and means of countering mind-control magic were widely available in *Yggdrasil*. It was reasonably difficult to block *all* of them, but he likely had a few measures in place.

Emperor Jircniv, for instance, had carried magic items to resist mind control. Gambling that Decem might not would be simpleminded. Ainz would have loved to use an instant-death spell, but with Mercy of Shorea Robusta active, there was no point.

"Stop Time!"

He didn't stop.

Decem kept going.

Ainz didn't bother swearing. He'd known this was a possible outcome. He'd just have to get help.

He barked the order.

"Aura!"

"Okay!"

She drew her bow—

"Shadow Stitch Shot!"

——and fired at Decem's shadow. Still Decem did not break stride. He was at the stairs now. At least there was *a* countermeasure in place—set down while Ainz had been skulking beneath Wall of Skeletons.

Explode Mine went off beneath Decem's feet.

"You can't run. Your feet—"

Decem paid him no heed. His footsteps retreated down the stairs, the sound growing faint.

"——Did he know it was a bluff? Or was he just not listening anymore? The man didn't even know to use piercing damage against wall spells, so I expected less."

He'd hoped that bluff would slow him down, but nope.

Decem was a druid. Different branch but still a caster. It was entirely possible he'd figured out the nature of Ainz's magical trap. Generally, you couldn't have multiple of the same spell active—which was also the principle that prevented you repeatedly casting summon spells to get an army of the same monster.

"Sorry," Aura said. "I let him escape."

Ainz turned from the stairs to face her.

"No...... Yes, I suppose that you did. That skill was the wrong choice, Aura. During combat, we saw the man had countermeasures against instant-death and time effects. A safe assumption that he'd have measures against movement obstruction as well."

Aura made to apologize again, but he waved her off.

"But I did not warn you of that, so I am equally complicit. Honestly, it hadn't occurred to me that he could break through that. The biggest question is...what now?"

"We should pursue and kill."

"Wait!"

Aura was ready to run off after him, but Ainz stopped her.

Decem was at least a level-70 druid, so at Ainz's movement speed, he likely wouldn't catch up. Aura and Mare could manage it, but that would leave Ainz isolated—and he'd used up a fair amount of mana.

Could use a Gate, fetch forces from Nazarick— No time. Gotta decide if I let him go or make sure he's dead.

Decem had lost a lot of mana, but his physical attributes were still rather high. Ainz stood no chance against him in a regular brawl with no magic. *Assuming he wasn't just using Perfect Unknowable.*

Aura has no beasts with her, so if he's got another trick up his sleeve, she might not be able to handle it. I could summon an undead… No, what if he can summon that primal earth elemental again? No, no, there's no way he can.

Repeat summoning an elemental more powerful than the caster was a real balance breaker. Even with the mana drain. Ainz was heavily specced toward Ghost Magic and couldn't pull that off. Still, what he considered impossible was all based on *Yggdrasil* rules and might not apply to this world.

So far, his game knowledge had served him well, but that same game knowledge said Decem shouldn't have been able to summon that elemental at all. In which case—

"——Mare!"

"Y-yes?"

"It's a risk, but go alone and slay Decem. You're in alt gear, but take every precaution. If you deem the fight unwinnable, conserve magic and buy time." He would rather issue a whole heap more instructions, but time was critical. "Go!"

"Okay!" Mare answered with an uncharacteristically enthusiastic response.

He ran off down the stairs at an impressive speed. His footsteps were soon out of earshot.

Ainz considered summoning an undead to follow, but given the peculiar situation they were in, he'd rather keep them around to use as a shield. Lopsided Duel was still active; Ainz himself might wind up in combat with that king once more before this was over. And he would have to end it quick, then.

"——Aura, you're guarding me. Let's quickly loot this treasury. Take it all! Then we'll go after Mare."

"Got it!"

3

Military headquarters were chaotic on any front line, but they were especially busy when a war neared its conclusion. Even after the fighting was all said and done, a flood of bureaucrats would sweep in to assist with the occupation.

Currently, the strategists were collating information brought by messengers from all directions, examining each piece, inserting it where it belonged, and endeavoring to maintain a current map of the battlefield. Beyond that, they would need to tabulate the casualties and arrange transport for the prisoners. Menial tasks like corpse disposal tended to fall by the wayside during war.

Either way, information that came to Marshal Valerian Ein Aubigne was confirmed and accurate.

So when the news he'd been waiting for arrived, he looked genuinely relieved.

"Sir, we've definitely broken through the elven defenses. Enemy resistance is down seventy percent. That seems slightly high, but the lack of strong fighters on their side seems to have had a significant impact. We believe the remaining forces are in hiding throughout the city. How shall we proceed?"

"Avoid unnecessary casualties. Holed up guerrillas are no real threat, but those moving freely about the city using disruptive tactics could hurt us. Expand our occupied territory, apply pressure, flush the elves into the open—and into our nets. Avoid fighting indoors. Make sure stronger individuals are placed in each squad sent into the city itself."

"Yes, sir. I'll send word."

"Any elves who break through the perimeter are undoubtedly on suicide runs. Keep reminding all posts to remain vigilant."

"Understood."

"——We've cleared a path, but is there any response from the castle?"

"None. Silent as ever."

Normally, Valerian's expression would have darkened here.

It was hard to believe the castle was completely abandoned. Odds were the elf elite were defending it. And officers from all corners would have retreated there. And there was the elf king himself.

The elemental that king commanded had just recently eliminated the Firestorm Scripture's subleader. Though not quite a hero, he had stood on the threshold—and died easily.

And the Theocracy had records from a century ago showing that a Black Scripture team composed entirely of hero-class members had been demolished by the elf king's raw power. The strategy they'd employed was lost to time, but it appeared to have worked—so this foe was hardly invulnerable. But the armies Valerian commanded would be little use against him—arguably, the war with the elves had yet to clear its greatest obstacle.

But—their ace had arrived.

"Keep me updated. We're ready to carry out an assault?"

"Yes, they're awaiting orders."

With that word, Valerian rose from his seat.

"Then we've done our part. Good work, men. Have them remain on standby a good distance from the castle and focus on your other tasks. I'll report to our guest."

He left the tent, headed for another. The owner of that tent was not big on visitors and not someone you could afford to annoy.

Valerian spoke from outside the tent flap.

"Pardon me. May I come in?"

"Go ahead."

A ready response.

Valerian took a deep breath before stepping in.

Not because their guest was a threat. They'd met upon her arrival and he found her altogether rational. But he always had to brace himself before facing any of the Black Scripture's heroes—individuals who far surpassed the realm of mortal man. He knew she would not harm him, but he had to act as if stepping into the cage of a carnivorous beast.

And that wasn't the only reason.

The guest within was not only a powerful hero, they were exceptional even by Theocracy standards.

It was possible for races to crossbreed, but within the Theocracy, this was taboo.

Their country existed to ensure a bright future for humans alone, and all other races—even humanoid ones—were their enemies.

But that stance had begun a mere century ago. Before that, the Theocracy had been mindful of the welfare of other humanoid races and explored the idea of fighting alongside them.

That had all changed one day—and this guest of theirs was a big part of the reason why.

She was the Theocracy's strongest warrior and possessed a lengthy life span. She had been trained by one reputed to be their divine protector—about whom little was known beyond their existence. That was the sum of what Valerian had been told about her.

But in that sea of uncertainty lay a few convictions.

For one thing, when he had been promoted to marshal, he had been specifically told to never cross her. Not that he was foolish enough to try and act superior around the king of the jungle.

He peeled back the tent flap and found a basic chair and bed, a shelf and a table with a helmet on top. From the outside, it looked like any other tent, but the furnishings within were rather high quality. All brought from the Theocracy via Teleportation, their quality far beyond what lay in the marshal's own tent.

She was in the center, armor gleaming—hopping up and down.

"May I ask what you're doing?" he asked, baffled. Some unique ritual, perhaps?

"Mm? Nothing in particular. I just felt the need to stay in motion."

"I see."

She hopped for another few seconds, then stopped.

"No need to stand on formalities," she said. "Technically, you outrank me."

Despite what her words, she was not exactly acting like she was speaking to a superior officer.

"I'm afraid that is unacceptable. You are the Theocracy's finest and disciple of the divine protector."

"So stiff! But suit yourself. I take it seeing you here means what I think it means?"

"Indeed. Only the castle remains. We assume surviving forces are gathering there..."

"I'll handle 'em. But I'm only targeting the one man, so don't expect me to make a clean sweep."

"Understood. We'll leave him in your hands."

The girl they called No Death–No Life smiled.

Valerian felt compelled to avert his eyes.

That bloodlust was not for him. He knew that. But he could not suppress the fear.

"Oh, sorry. Can I ask one thing?"

"Certainly. If I can answer..."

"Good. If I'm being honest, I don't have a personal grudge against the son of a bitch. He didn't do nothing to me directly, you know? Maybe you could argue he was never much of a father, but from his perspective, that ain't exactly a fair accusation. Odds are he doesn't even know I exist. It's my mother who's got it in for him. The way I feel here is all stuff she drilled into me."

He had no idea how to respond to this. Was she looking for agreement or not? And she was the elf king's daughter?! Then who was her mother? So many questions.

Valerian was too lost to provide any answers, but she just kept talking.

Ah.

This was a monologue. She wasn't expecting any reply.

"Then should I turn this rage back on her? On the one who stuck me with it? Alas, she is dead, and I cannot do so. Perhaps I merely loathe my father in her stead. But to rid myself of this grudge, my best option might be to go after something my mother loved."

The tone had changed.

Valerian stole a look at her face.

Still, she smiled. No change there.

But—was this *really* a smile?

He gulped.

Fearing that one false word from him would cause the Theocracy's doom.

She caught his tension, and her smile turned sheepish.

"…Ah, this again. I do apologize. Did I spook you? I'm not trying to take out my grudge on the Theocracy, I promise. I mean, when everything's said and done, I do like the place."

"D-do you? Good to hear."

He barely managed to get the words out, but his relief was palpable.

"It's just… I dunno. I wonder if I'll actually be free once I resolve the grudge my mother branded me with. The more I talk about it, the more awkward I feel. It's an emotional time for me."

"That's understandable."

"If we knew each other better, you could totally ask, *How old* are *you?*"

"I'm afraid the thought did not occur to me."

Valerian bowed his head, but she didn't seem concerned.

"I wonder what my mother thought."

"Mm?"

"……The weak are trampled. So be strong. There's nothing wrong with that idea. Part of me thinks no child needs training that intense, but it's not like I'm the only child forced to train at death's door from an early age. There could be people out there who've trained harder than I ever have in pursuit of power. Which means these thoughts are my weakness."

"That's…certainly difficult to say for sure, I suppose."

Did she want a yes or no? How could he respond without vexing her? That was the one thought on his mind, and thus his answer was entirely meaningless.

Perhaps that came through loud and clear. Her smile was genuine this time.

"Once this is done, maybe I should go through our old records. Things lost on me back in the day might become clear in someone else's eyes. I'm sure…there's something left. Some clue to tell me how she felt about me… But it's high time I got moving."

.

"Hee-hahhh-hee-hahhh-hee-hahhh—"

Given Decem's physical abilities, he should not be gasping for air after this short of a run, even at top speed. But he was badly out of breath. The cause: abject fear. And the emotional disruption was affecting his physical performance.

As he ran, he perked up his ears, trying to detect anyone following.

Nothing.

No one following him.

Had he gotten away?

No—Decem mentally shook that off.

He couldn't get comfortable.

His pride as the strongest elf no longer mattered. He just had to get away.

Defeat was not the end. He knew there were elves outside the forest. He could go far from here, found a new kingdom. He had that kind of power—should still have it.

I won't make the same mistake.

Grandchildren, great-grandchildren—he now had proof blood could awaken not just in his children's generation. He had to be smarter this time.

Yes. This is neither failure nor my defeat. Merely a good experience. I will not waste it. I am no fool. Only a fool repeats the same mistakes!

Exactly.

First, he should have his children mate with dark elves. Or perhaps make children with dark elves himself?

No time right now. Need to get out via the most direct route. Or…perhaps I should grab food, at least.

He considered this as he ran.

Decem could normally teleport to the location of the elemental linked to him, but now that Behemoth was down, that wasn't an option. Thus, he had to get away on his own two feet. That said, he could use magic to fly, so *on foot* wasn't his only option.

Yes, Decem had magic.

Even if he grabbed no further supplies, with the magic items on his person right now, he could manage. At least until he reached civilization and could appropriate what he needed. With Decem's strength, no one could possibly resist.

Certainly, he had just incurred a loss—a painful thing to admit—but those grandchildren's strength was irregular. Achievable only because they had his blood, and the odds of anyone that strong living at his eventual destination were extremely low. But throwing his strength around would attract attention. If word of Decem's presence spread, the undead his grandchildren controlled might come after him again.

But what did they want? Were they on that floor to access the treasury? If they're just looters, they may not care if I live or die...

Perhaps a vain hope. He found it hard to believe what they'd said—or had their undead say—was true.

Perhaps my life was their primary goal.

He had to fear the worst. His life depended on it.

In which case, I really must go as far as I can and try not to stick out like a sore thumb. Avoiding all use of magic. In which case...food.

Druid spells could make fruit. The treasury contained a staff that could cast that six times every four hours. But Decem himself had not learned the spell. And he had not learned to survive in the forest. He knew he could defend himself against attacking beasts but as for acquiring anything edible—and properly cooking his kills—he'd be at a total loss.

I had basic provisions in my room. Fruit and spirits. I should grab those and then get through the woods without using magic, as fast as I can. Then rob anyone I meet, killing them so word does not reach my grandchildren's ears. After that, I just get as far as I can. Oh, I should bring something of value. I've heard jewels or precious metals can be useful?

Panting, he at last made it to his chambers.

There should be several women within, but bringing them along would attract attention, and they would slow him down. He decided to just leave them behind.

Or perhaps just bring one or two?

He was a king, and while it displeased him to even consider it, he could carry them without much trouble.

A woman who can prepare food might be worth bringing. And there's no telling when I'll next meet an elf once I leave the forest. It would be a good idea to bring someone to make children with.

The pain had left him sweaty, so he wiped his brow and caught his breath. He did not wish to appear any less regal before the women.

There was still no sign of that undead on his heels, and he was still looking that way as he opened the door.

"Welcome home."

A cheery woman's voice.

Decem was instantly furious.

Women always abased themselves before him. Yet, she dared speak in such a tone? It felt like she was sneering at him for losing to his grandchildren. Yet, when he turned to the room, his anger dissipated.

It was *red*.

His entire chambers had been painted a new color.

Blood.

The stench of it was far beyond what that word implied alone. How had he not noticed from outside? The smell of his own blood must have bamboozled his nose.

The corpses of the women he'd left here were strewn around, and a new woman was seated on a chair in the center—she must have brought it herself.

He did not recognize her. She wore magnificent armor, her helm in one hand, a bizarre staff in the other. At the tip were three bloodstained blades, each curved. It was impossible for him to imagine what purpose it had been designed for just by looking at it.

He got the impression she was no elf. But she bore signs of the elven race, so perhaps she was one? And those eyes—

"Nice to meet you, Dad."

She grinned.

That explained it.

"Ah. Ah. You're those children's mother."

Her expression stiffened, but then she grinned again.

"Yep, I'm...their mom! Those wounds—they beat you, huh? They're that good? How'd they do it? Fill me in, Dad."

Decem opened his mouth and closed it again. She was trying to buy time, and he didn't have any.

He turned on his heel to leave.

"——Get back here!"

"Gah!"

A sharp pain on his legs and he hit the floor.

One of the blades from her bizarre staff had caught his feet, tripping him—and dragged him back into the room.

Fresh wounds, more blood. But nothing as bad as the gouge the undead had opened on his chest or the injuries to his feet as he fled.

Yet—he could not comprehend it.

They'd been a fair distance apart. Yet, this woman had been on him in a flash, snaring his legs. Like she—his child—was far faster than he.

He felt a weight on his back.

She'd put her foot on him.

"Kahhh!"

Decem couldn't budge.

Was she really that much stronger than he was? Or was this some skill?

"That chest wound come from a blade? What's with the legs? I heard you use an earth elemental, but where is it?"

A flurry of questions. Clearly confident.

Certainly, Decem was badly hurt. And he'd lost Behemoth. But that didn't make him weak. His physical prowess was alive and well, and he could instantly kill most run-of-the-mill creatures with a single blow. He'd put all that strength into his flight, and though the pain slowed him a bit—she should not have been able to catch up.

He was forced to admit it.

This woman had more brute strength than he did.

But that begged the question.

He had no memory of any child this powerful. He turned his head, looking up at her.

"Wh-what do you want? Why do this to me?"

All he wanted to know. She laughed out loud.

"The strong can do whatever they want to the weak. Right?"

"Gah...hngg."

This was true.

That was how Decem had lived.

"The morals of a wild beast. But they fit a savage dwelling in these uncivilized woods."

"D-did the women here tell you?"

"............Hahh."

She let out a long sigh, like she was venting heat.

And then the pressure on his back started to build.

"Gugh...gah..."

It forced the air from his lungs.

"Are you gonna answer my question? Or did you forget them already? Are you going senile?"

"Garghhh..."

Decem could not endure the force she was using. His whole body creaked, and his lips flapped, desperate for air but unable to draw any.

She clicked her tongue and eased off, but not enough that he could scramble away. It was all he could do to gasp for air.

"What hurt you like this?"

Why...is this happening to me? Since my grandchildren...it's all gone wrong! But why is she asking about the wounds? Does she not know what her kids did? Do those necromancers have more than one type of undead...? No, is this... something else?

One child, two grandchildren, all his equal—no, superior. Three all at once. Perhaps there was some other reason for this?

Oh! Those grand— I thought they were mine, but the bloodline could mean— Did my father? No! They're my cousins?!

That seemed the most likely.

His father had been an elf hero, the finest sword fighter he had ever seen.

He'd been one of the Eight Kings of Avarice—an epithet that sounded more like an insult than an honorific, to be sure. The most likely explanation was that weaklings had tried to sully his deeds with that moniker.

Decem had inherited that exalted blood, though not his talent for fencing. Perhaps this woman had taken up the mantle.

"C'mon, I need you to start talking. If you don't, I'll just kill you!"

"Ahhh…ah…*hurk!*"

He couldn't even insist he would talk if only she'd take her foot off him. He heard another crack inside and felt a sharp pain on his chest. Like he was being disemboweled. He stiffened up, his nails scrabbling at the floor involuntarily.

"……I thought I stopped feeling any pity for my mother long ago, but the thought of having trash like this rape a baby into her…how can I not sympathize?"

This was a whisper to herself—and her foot pressed down harder. *Snap. Pop.* Each horrid sound made the agony worse.

He felt blood rising up from his throat. He spit it out, and it trickled down the sides of his mouth.

Everything hurt.

Agony and pain.

Why was this happening to him?

He hadn't done anything wrong.

Decem used his last bit of strength, struggling. Fighting for any air. But he could not get away. All his efforts were useless before her power.

Death.

He was going to die.

He'd felt that not long before, but this was even worse.

He was scared.

Terrified.

He couldn't bear this.

It was too much.

Why was this—?

"…You really piss me off. A piece of shit like you and I… Mother…"

Darkness—

Why—?

Tears fell.

Why is she being so cruel?

"You really, really!"

He couldn't breathe.

He didn't want to die—

Help—

Save—

———

——His consciousness returned, but the pain was not gone, and he still could not breathe.

What?

What had happened?

"……The body's inflating? Just give it up!"

——*Crack-crack-crack-crack.*

The sound of bones breaking.

Ow—

What is—?

Happ—

And Decem was plunged into darkness once more.

•

"That's your philosophy, right? You brought it on yourself. Still, it's a real shame. I would've enjoyed dragging your death out…"

He was her father in blood alone, but now he lay still. No Death's gaze moved to the elf corpses strewn around.

Perhaps there hadn't been any need to do that to them. She had a lot of pent-up rage when it came to her mother, and she'd taken it out on them. But more than that, she hadn't wanted the country she loved doing the same things as this man. A man whose very existence made her want to vomit. They were better off dead, she'd thought—and thus, they'd been turned into a sea of blood.

Optimists held that where there was life, there was hope. They would never have understood what drove her to do this. But No Death could not understand how anyone could think positively about life.

Her eyes snapped to the door.

There was a dark elf...girl standing in the open entrance.

Clearly one of the children pursuing the elf king.

Her eyes were different colors—proof of royalty. No Death let out a soft sigh.

They'd never met before, but the king had assumed she was their mother. That meant this girl must be his granddaughter, No Death's niece.

Surprised to find a part of herself against the idea of killing this girl, No Death kicked the dead king and his caved-in chest as hard as she could, right at the little girl.

It flew at speeds no ordinary mortal—or even an extraordinary one— could possibly dodge, but the girl managed it easily.

The body hit the wall beyond the door with a splat, transforming into a red bloom.

If she can dodge that, she's physically impressive. His injuries look like they were inflicted with blades, but...

Her niece was carrying a black staff—crushing damage. Clearly, the king's injuries had been inflicted by someone else. He had mentioned there were multiple, so there must be at least one more. But there were spells that cast magic blades and magic items that could change shape.

It was always possible this girl had done the deed.

Or did the other hit the chest and she hit the legs? With that staff or a spell?

Why had this dark elf attacked the king at all?

There was no shortage of reasons to loathe the bastard. The most likely explanation was the same thing that had brought No Death here—a grudge passed down from mother to child. But this girl looked too young for that grudge to have settled in, to be motivated to mess him up that badly.

There was a slight chance she didn't know her own strength, had been play fighting and accidentally mangled him...but the circumstantial evidence suggested otherwise. Dead or not, she hadn't tried to catch the king—just dodged.

"Er, um...r-right. Who might you be?"

She was acting all timid. Like some man's fantasy of cute. Clearly, she'd lived in a world No Death had no part of.

Yet, there was a clear disconnect between her outward appearance and whatever was going on inside. She never even glanced at the king's corpse behind her, showed no signs of alarm at the gory spectacle in the room around them—even though it was clearly No Death's handiwork.

She dodged my attack and still behaves like this? Wooow. Odds are this timid thing is an act. I'd better be real careful here. How do I play this?

How should she answer the girl's question? She'd prefer to avoid combat, supply false information, and slowly pry info out of the kid.

But that wasn't happening.

From what the elf king said, the kid had backup. If this kid had been the one who beat him up, why was there no blood on her? Even if she healed her wounds, the stains should've remained. That suggested she was *way* stronger than he'd been.

Even if this girl hadn't been the one fighting, she was the one who'd wound up chasing after him—so clearly she and her companions were all major threats. She couldn't begin to tell just *how* bad, but if they regrouped, the risk to No Death would be far too great.

Right now, there was no sign of anyone else—this was her chance to strike. She should probably forget about learning anything, strike first, and try and take this girl out quick.

The enemy of my enemy is my friend—that's pure wishful thinking. I'm better off assuming she's trouble.

Quickly going over this in her mind, she smiled—hoping to lower the girl's guard. And finally answered the question.

"Hey there. I'm...from the Nation of Darkness. What about you? You all alone?"

That made the girl twitch. She still seemed to have no confidence at all but frowned like she was thinking.

Can't get a read. Did I blow it? Should have picked an answer that narrowed down her responses. Right now, I can't tell if she's never heard of the Nation, is from there herself, or...considers them her enemy. She didn't immediately attack, so that last one is a lesser possibility, but she might just be doing what I am and trying to glean some intel first. Maybe I should have said the Council State. That might have worked better.

She'd gone with the Nation of Darkness because she knew their king had a dark elf girl among his retainers.

That information hadn't come from a spy infiltrating the Nation's government.

Star Reader–Second Sight had confirmed her presence at the King of Darkness's side on the Katze Plains during the war with the Re-Estize Kingdom.

She'd re-created what she saw in an illusion, a detailed depiction of the King of Darkness and his forces. That included his sole retainer—a dark elf. But her appearance was on the blurry side, and they hadn't quite been able to make out her face.

That was expected. Star Reader–Second Sight had been asked to monitor the entire battlefield and lacked the memory capacity to devote space to any individual's features—plus, what happened after that had left far too strong an impression and quite a lot of other information had been lost in its wake.

But from that vague impression, this girl didn't seem much like the one who'd accompanied the King of Darkness that day. Both had carried a black staff, but the armor this girl wore was totally different. Still...the illusion's quality had been so poor, they'd had only a vague idea what that retainer wore.

If this girl was from the Nation of Darkness, what would she wear here? Her optimal gear, just as No Death was. This was a battlefield. There was no telling what could happen; nobody would show up dressed in street clothes. Even Kaire and Star Reader–Second Sight ignored appearances, wearing armor based purely on function.

But that was true for the Katze Plain as well. The truly strong never had multiple sets of "best equipment." Reaching those heights required superlative gear, and it was natural to hone your combat techniques to match that gear. She knew someone who'd been a master of the club but, after joining the Black Scripture, had been given an ax and forced to dedicate years of his life to mastering it.

By that logic, the Nation's dark elf and this girl had to be different people, but they had too much in common to entirely rule it out.

That's why No Death tried to bait a response only to come up empty.

It was so much simpler to just hook someone with a scythe, she thought, tightening her grip on it.

And there was the problem of facial recognition with other races.

Most humanoid races did all right identifying one another, but it was hardly perfect. Unless it was your own race, there were markers you could miss on top of a pervading sense they all looked the same.

"Um, er, y-yes, it's just me here."

"Okay. Well, I bet everyone's worried about you."

Fah. Acting all cutesy, lying with a straight face. Definitely can't trust appearances here. That means anything I do learn talking may be bullshit. I knew from the get-go that she's got backup coming, so no point wasting time chatting. Gotta overpower her and get to safety. Then pry the truth out of her using magic…or just old-fashioned pain.

Acting all anxious, the girl moved her free hand to the necklace round her neck.

A natural gesture. Like a nervous tick, her hand moving unconsciously. It fit in perfectly with the whole timid-kid vibe—but No Death knew damn well that was an act and figured this had to be significant.

"Tch!"

Before the sound of her tongue click even faded, she closed the gap. Slamming her helmet on, her weapon—Charon's Guidance—skimmed across the floor, sweeping directly at the girl's legs.

If it cut them off, great.

No Death held nothing back, going all out. Even the strongest man among her colleagues would have struggled to avoid this attack.

And—

The girl deflected it purely by placing her staff in its path.

A weapon that could shred steel bounced off—and she was not surprised. She'd been well aware this could happen. What got her—the hand holding the staff hadn't even budged. Against her full strength.

——So she is a warrior class.

This was a clear indicator of the dark elf girl's build.

……Or wait…a warrior in light armor? Does that mean…? But we were sure the elf king was his only kid. But look at her…!

Dark elves and elves had similar life spans and aged at equal speeds.

"Th-that was sudd——"

Could be another branch of the bloodline. Or am I overthinking it?

The dark elf girl was muttering something, but even as her brain raced, No Death's hands kept moving. They were enemies. The only value talking had was if you were buying time or had already won.

The girl jumped back, and she followed her into the hall.

She got a good swing with plenty of momentum behind it and slammed her scythe into the girl's wrist.

Given the sheer size of the weapon, she couldn't avoid hitting the walls and floor—but that posed no obstacle. This was a weapon once wielded by Sulshana, the god who'd saved the Theocracy—no, all humanity. It could easily cut through wood and stone. It might catch a bit, but it barely slowed the speed of her swings.

Yet, the blow bounced off.

So did the next.

And the next.

Three strikes in a row, each like a lightning bolt and every one deflected by the girl's staff. Not the most spectacular staff technique, but the reaction speed was tremendous. Those moves made it clear she was every bit as powerful as No Death.

Pretty good. A warrior on my level? That's bad news. If I'm forced on the defensive, I'll be in trouble.

Even this brief exchange told her that much.

The elf king had said she had allies. If they were as good as this girl, No Death would be forced to run. But she couldn't assume they'd let her, just because the elf king had managed it. Him getting away made it more likely they'd have a scheme to stop her from doing the same. Assuming they weren't idiots.

Which meant—

——*Force her down in a quick fight. Kill her…? Like I have a choice. Might just have to bring the body back and see if we can revive her.*

She felt her eyes going to the girl's belly and forced them not to.

Her armor was like a dress made of metal, and it left her soft-looking belly exposed—not a shred of visible muscle there. Boldly revealing a weak point right where all sorts of vital organs lay. Still, it wasn't safe to assume aiming there would do much damage.

Most armor's defense was determined by the mana poured in, the metal used, and whatever special skills were involved in the forging. That slim waist likely had defensive properties derived from the strength of the armor's magic. But it did mean there was no defense provided by the materials used in the armor's creation. It was definitely the least defended point.

So why wear something like this?

Displaying a clear weakness would bait an enemy's attack. There was likely some sort of trap.

She knew that but couldn't help but hope a clean hit there might finish this girl off. That's why she wouldn't let herself even look.

"Power of Gaea."

Out of nowhere, the girl cast a spell. No Death's eyes nearly popped out of her head.

Huh?! Magic?! She's not a warrior?! No, no, there are warrior classes that learn a few spells, but… Huh?

No Death herself could use faith magic, but she'd never heard of the spell this girl used. It hadn't affected her, so she could safely assume it was some kind of self-buff.

If the girl was a warrior main and dabbled in magic on the side, then she didn't need to be that worried. But if she was primarily a caster, that was another story.

Magic had a whole range of options, making casters much less predictable than a warrior. For all she knew, a really nasty spell could instantly turn the tables.

That qualifier was because No Death was not well briefed on pure caster builds. She would have to be that much more cautious here. Even if this girl could just match what No Death could, those minor healing spells could really draw this fight out.

She had to assume the worst. Assume this girl wasn't a warrior but some kind of caster.

Hard to be sure of anything, but their initial exchange suggested she wasn't an arcane caster. That type was usually quite poor at close-up fighting. That meant she was a class that had options there—a druid or a priest? Some type of faith magic.

There was always a chance she was an exception to that arcane caster rule or even specialized in psychic or wild magic. But No Death knew even less about those. No use thinking about it. It'd be better to just make a mental note to be ready for anything.

And—since she was a dark elf, druid was far more likely.

Especially if she was related to the elf king.

Problem was—No Death didn't really have anything good against druids. Instead, she activated one of two special abilities she'd acquired while mastering Inquisitor. This was in case the girl was a faith caster capable of using spells higher tier than anything No Death knew about.

"Denounce Heretic."

This ability mildly increased the mana cost of spells used in No Death's vicinity, if the priest worshipped a different god than she did. The effect would not be immediately transparent, but over a lengthy battle, the extra mana cost could add up.

She wasn't planning on drawing this fight out, but this would help if her opponent started with high-tier spells. Using a targeted ability like this before knowing what her foe could do might mean it was a wasted move, but tricks like this really mattered only if you used them early on.

"Elemental Form: Earth."

Another spell she'd never heard. The girl's skin turned brown.

She could assume the visual was not the main effect. She wondered if this was her true form—if this girl had never actually been a dark elf—but there seemed no point in speculating.

In a battle to the death, questions without answers were worth caution, but not getting hung up on.

Same with magic.

She didn't know what that spell did, so should spend minimal time thinking on it. No Death moved on to her next ability.

"Condemn Heretic."

This was her other Inquisitor skill. It had a similar effect, the difference being that it increased the rate of spell failures. Naturally, if a spell failed, the mana used to cast it was still lost.

Since she'd activated both, she couldn't use any other Inquisitor abilities until the effective period ran out, but that's how it worked. It wasn't like she lost the physical enhancements or magic-related strengths the class had given her, so that was a fair price.

No Death was going for a quick kill, so this might seem a little roundabout. She was not hoping for a lengthy battle. To her mind, there were roughly two ways a fight could go. A beatdown that just pressed your own advantage and never let a foe fight back or whittling down an opponent, watching their moves while never letting them gain an advantage.

She'd planned on going all in, but since this girl was blocking each of her attacks, that forced them into a fight where they took turns playing their cards. Frustratingly, that meant it was the girl in control of the battle flow. No Death's only option was to go alone with that plot and try and turn the tables on her eventually.

"Er, um…I am sorry."

Were those two spells enough, or was that all she could use? The girl offered words of apology while swinging the staff high—then it shot down with bloodcurdling speed.

No Death shuddered.

Not because of the uncanny attack speed.

This girl hadn't meant that apology in the slightest. Neither voice nor expression betrayed any remorse. It was like she'd just been ordered to apologize. Like some kind of puppet——

——*Don't think!*

That wasn't what mattered here. Only the incoming attack did.

By a warrior's standard, the attack did not pass muster. No feints, just a very basic swing.

The speed was intense, but it was easy enough to dodge or block.

No Death chose the latter. She'd see how this foe dodged and blocked, so she wanted to compare their raw physical strength.

As she thought, her scythe easily blocked the blow—

——*Damn!!*

She thought she'd blocked it well, but it made both knees and elbows buckle. The staff forced her back and bore down on her brow.

She gritted her teeth and grunted, pushing against the dark elf. It wasn't enough to throw this girl off balance, but her weapon did lift away.

An opening.

Keeping her eyes off the exposed waist, No Death use her martial arts.

Super Stride of Wind! Sturdy Arm, Strong Blow! Super Pierce! Greater Ability Boost! Greater Possibility Perception!

She'd specifically avoided using any earlier, saving them for this moment.

Boosting her movement speed and dexterity, enhancing all damage done, boosting pierce damage, strengthening her flesh, and honing her sixth sense.

It was all aimed at a single point.

That visibly exposed belly.

It might be a trap, but she was sure she could endure it. And she couldn't resist the allure of maybe doing enough damage to break the deadlock and instantly change the balance of power in her favor. No Death had good reason for trying to end this quickly.

Conquering the distance between them like a bolt from the blue, leaving the sound of the wind itself behind, she rocketed toward the girl's tender-looking navel.

Surprised by the sudden boost in speed and strength, the girl failed to block No Death's charge in time.

She forced through unexpected resistance—this was far harder than skin—stabbing her scythe blade home.

Nice!

She couldn't help but grin.

No Death had maxed the Executioner class. This increased the damage of any critical hits and opened up the possibility of killing foes with a single attack. She also had an ability that could deepen the wound when doing over a set amount of damage with a cutting weapon; unfortunately, this time she hadn't used the crescent blades that spread like wings on either side but the stabbing blade at the end of the central rod, which meant that ability didn't apply. But this attack should still have done substantial damage to the girl.

But the look of jubilation proved fleeting.

The impact made its way up the weapon to her hands…and it felt odd.

There was no familiar squish of organs slicing.

And before she learned the reason, out of the corner of her eye—she saw a shadow coming toward her head.

"——Instant Reflex!"

Too late. Far too late.

For just a moment, she'd been distracted by that odd sensation. A huge blunder.

There was a hard *clang.*

A swing of that staff connected with her head.

She quickly used Dull Pain and then Super Stride of Wind to bound away. She jerked her scythe back out of the girl, doing more damage.

That blunt strike had broken her skin, and blood was flowing down her face. Her martial art was diminishing the pain, but even the slightest shift of her expression was agonizing. Her vision blurred.

No Death wore armor that had belonged to the wind god. Yet, she'd still taken enough damage to leave her reeling. She hadn't taken a blow like that in recent memory.

"——Heavy Recovery."

Staying a step out of range, No Death used the highest-tier healing spell she knew. It wouldn't fully fix her, but it should work for now. Even as she cast the spell, she looked to the girl, wary of further attacks.

And her eyes went wide.

Not only were the girl's guts not spilling out, she wasn't even bleeding. Proof she had hurt her was on her face—her expression twisted with pain. There *was* a split open in that earth-colored skin.

"Owww...," she said, taking out a scroll and activating the spell on it. "Heal."

A higher-tier spell than the one No Death had used.

——Sixth tier! How does she have that scroll? Shit! That'll recover all the damage I just did! I dunno how much stamina she has, but it's pretty damn clear I came out of that exchange worse off! And the way her belly felt...far too hard. I knew it was a trap!

There must have been a spell on the belly that negated critical hits. But apparently, the thrust to the navel *had* left the girl in pain. It had done the trick and baited her attack but was clearly not a pleasant experience for the dark elf.

What kind of asshole designed this armor? No Death spat. *If you knew it would be targeted, you oughtta include some pain resistance. This equipment was basically cursed.*

Infuriated, No Death fought off the urge to muss up her hair. Didn't want to do anything that stimulated the pain and couldn't afford the opening.

She couldn't take pleasure in forcing her to use a sixth-tier scroll. No guarantee it was her only one. She might have several more. In which case, she stood no chance of winning with standard tactics. Still—no matter how many Heal scrolls this girl had, she had an ace that could kill her.

She couldn't use it yet, though. She had few things to try first.

For one, nobody used Heal on a scratch. She'd done plenty of damage, so what she should do now is attack so relentlessly, the girl couldn't use another scroll.

Her plan set, No Death raised her scythe. She used her martial arts and lunged back into range.

This time, she was aiming for the wrist.

What?!

The girl didn't even try and dodge.

A moment ago, she'd merely seemed unable to match No Death's speed, but not now. She didn't even show signs of trying to defend herself. No Death remembered how this had gone last time—but if she was this close, she had to attack.

As she entered lethal range, she spun herself like a top, maximizing centrifugal force and slamming the scythe on the girl's forearm.

She sped past. Did blood spray as the girl's hand and armor flew away? Nope. That move had typically sliced through lesser armors, but this girl's wrist remained intact.

——It was insanely hard.

Nothing like that belly.

Those wrists were covered in armor, so that might go without saying, but it was even harder than expected. Was the armor itself a match for what the Six Gods had worn, or was she using some sort of defensive martial art?

Worst of all was how she'd blocked No Death's mightiest blow with her arm alone, not even staggering.

But No Death didn't have time to think.

As she blocked the blow to her right wrist, the girl shifted the staff to her left hand only and was already swinging it down.

Wanting to avoid a painful repeat, No Death used Instant Reflex and Evasion, desperately twisting away.

But even with this, she couldn't fully avoid it.

Instant Reflex ensured she was positioned right, and she had activated a martial art as the attack came in but it was still too late to evade.

The blow dug into No Death's shoulder. She was mentally ready for this one, so she timed a martial art at the same instant she expected the hit to land.

Super Defense Boost.

This upped her defenses. Not as powerful as Reinforce Outer Skin, but No Death was a half elf; she had no outer skin.

Even with the martial art, the blow hurt like it had gone halfway through her. Super Defense Boost barely did a thing. The outcome was only slightly better than last time.

She managed to stifle a groan. No need to tell her foe how hurt she was. But—

Not good.

The exchange had made it clear this was the girl's true strategy.

Just like it had the first time.

When No Death attacked, she struck back. The girl's approach was simply let her opponent land a blow and then hit back harder.

Possibly because she couldn't score a clean hit fighting any other way, but No Death doubted that. The girl had chosen this approach for a reason.

She knows she's got the defenses for it…is she a tank, like Cedran? Is that why the belly's exposed? What damage she takes, Heal can handle.

If her offense was a bit lacking and her build focused on defense—a tank who could cast and as strong as No Death herself—then the girl's estimated abilities made sense. Though the battering damage seemed a bit too brutal for that.

Maybe the staff was a magic item, with power of its own. It was strong enough that even a weapon used by the Six Gods could not cut through it, so that seemed likely.

No Death was growing more and more certain this *was* the girl who'd been at the King of Darkness's side. Given his powerful spells and terrifying armies, it made sense he'd have a store of incredible equipment for his minions.

She stepped back a bit, bracing her scythe, watching the girl's movements carefully.

The dark elf was standing rock steady while No Death kept throwing herself at her.

Like a rookie going at a veteran.

I really am screwed here.

The girl had the advantage.

She could fully block No Death's blows, while unleashing attacks No Death couldn't dodge. Did the source of the girl's confidence lie in her physical skills, her defense, her offense, or her healing? It was hard to say, but if this girl had decided on the simple formula of taking a hit, hitting back, and then healing up, then she must have decided she could win that way. Maybe she was intentionally choosing a less efficient fighting style to see what tricks No Death had to offer.

Given that this girl seemed to have no intention of closing the distance and attacking herself, she might be trying to buy time until her backup arrived. She wasn't sure how strong they were, but their arrival would definitely tip the balance to the girl's side. That would explain why she'd be going for a battle of attrition, slowly but surely racking up damage.

No Death had few options here. Ideally, she wanted to play her foe's game and come out ahead. Landing her own hits, while preventing the girl from landing any more. But that was clearly not working out.

The girl's armor was absurdly impenetrable, and to stand any chance of harming her, No Death had to fully commit to the attack. And that meant she would inevitably be exposed, which the girl could use against her. So what now?

I'm at an impasse. Do I use this?

No Death's gaze flicked down to her grip, to the scythe in her hand.

Charon's Guidance, the scythe once used by the god Sulshana. It was made of a rare metal the Theocracy had yet to discover, giving it durability and lethality that matched its previous owner.

It allowed the use of Death twice every eight hours.

It also had an extensive spell list; every four hours, it allowed five casts from it.

Undead Flames, which applied negative energy to her attacks.

Undeath Avoidance, protection against intelligent undead.

Create Undead, which allowed her to make undead monsters.

Disease, which could inflict sickness.

Sleep to the Undead, which had a shot at instantly destroying undead with no Repel resistance.

Evileye, which allowed her choice of a range of sight-based effects.

Death Mask, which defended against sight-based effects while boosting Fear.

And Hand of Glory, which could be used two ways.

That wasn't all, either—every twenty-four hours it could summon thirty spartiates—a special undead equivalent to the fifth-tier summonable heavy skeleton warrior. Spartiates came with better equipment, but since they couldn't be buffed with special skills, they were weaker overall. Still, this was a genuinely impressive magic item.

No Death thought it felt too early to pull a card from her sleeve.

She still had options in basic combat and showing her hand while still having no clue what her foe had in store felt like she was losing the mind games.

"Er, um…a-are you not coming?" the girl stammered.

No Death swore under her breath.

She wants me to attack?! I'll show this little shit!

She leaped backward, activating a few martial arts.

Dual Air Slash. Sturdy Arm, Strong Blow. Flow Acceleration. She swung her scythe, and two blades formed in the path of the swing, shooting toward the girl.

Who stepped forward.

Forward.

Projectile-based martial arts—like Air Slash—had less force than a direct hit. But with a blade bearing down on you, paying that no heed and advancing right into it? That was madness.

No, I did the same thing to her. This sure does rattle you.

When the aura blades hit the girl, she winced—though this also seemed kinda phony—but that was all. As she stepped within range, she grunted, swinging that black staff with a highly telegraphed motion.

No Death managed to evade this one.

The girl's attacks still didn't pass muster. But they were clearly getting more polished. At first, they'd been something No Death could manage, but now even if she was ready for them, a moment's hesitation would mean she wouldn't land a clean hit.

Keep grinning! Laugh! Make her think you can read every move!

No Death forced a smile onto her lips and laughed loud enough that the girl could hear.

Was that stiff smile convincing? The girl was swinging again.

I've gotta leave myself enough room to pop Greater Evasion or I'm done.

She tried backing off to get some range, but the girl just closed on in.

The gap wasn't widening.

"Spartiates!"

Five undead rose up like a wall between them.

The girl swung, and one went down.

Five spartiates wouldn't block more than five of this girl's blows, but that was plenty.

No Death kicked off the wall into a vault, skimming the ceiling and trying to get behind the girl.

But the girl's knees bent, and then she leaped back like the ground had exploded. Really didn't want to get surrounded? The spartiates weren't a threat, but maybe she thought they'd get in her way, act as a distraction?

She clearly wasn't taking any damage from their blows.

The girl launched herself backward, and as her feet touched down, she stabbed the staff into the floor, scraping a groove to bring herself to a quick stop. A ridiculous action. Too much momentum forcibly controlled by ludicrous arm strength.

Such a…weird choice. Is she not used to going all out? Or just not that experienced in combat?

No Death sent a mental order to her spartiates to advance. Undead knew no fear, so they obeyed, all throwing themselves at the girl. No Death followed in their wake.

The girl pulled out another scroll.

"Fire Storm."

A torrent of flames blanketed the area. The raging inferno burned No Death but vanished in an instant, as if it had been but an illusion. The blistering burns left behind proved it had been real. The only saving grace was that since she'd used a scroll, the spell hadn't done that much damage.

The spartiates were still technically mobile, too. But that just meant they hadn't taken fatal damage. If another spell hit, they'd be gone for sure.

No Death spun the scythe around her body, sideswiping the girl with the butt end. She hit armor, so it was hard to be sure, but it didn't seem like the blunt strike did any extra damage. The spartiates each thrust their spear, but all were parried with a single sweep of the staff, which moved so fast that it kicked up a gale. Only No Death's blows were even capable of making contact.

But she took advantage of the opening, spinning like a dancer and dropping low like a scuttling spider, skimming a slash at the girl's ankles.

This went right through the nearby spartiate, and it vanished. That was a summon's lot in life.

Moving like she was aiming for the girl's Achilles tendon, the scythe's blade sliced her armor. Sparks flew.

It was just as impenetrable down here as it was up there.

Even with Sturdy Arm, Strong Blow, and Greater Cutting and her class effects in play, it didn't feel like she was slicing through that.

But that wasn't the only reason she'd gone for the ankles.

She braced her legs front and back, gritted her teeth, and, with the scythe still hooked on the girl's feet, yanked back on it. Intending to pull her feet out from under her and knock her down. But—

"——Too heavy!"

She didn't budge.

Like a tree trunk.

Impossible.

But still somehow true.

No Death had taken her foe's strength into account and put her full force into it, but she was the one who wound up nearly stumbling forward. The sheer weight her arms felt clashed with this little girl's appearance.

Perhaps this was a special ability or magic-item effect, but it made No Death feel like she was trying to fight a towering tree. The way that yank felt, no matter how hard she pulled, this girl wasn't going down.

A shudder ran through her.

The girl must have seen her off balance. She fully extended her staff hand, reaching through the spartiates and swinging it down toward No Death.

Full advantage of reach and swing, making for a spine-chilling attack.

She was in no position to dodge. Even if a spartiate jumped in the way, that would hardly slow this swing down.

But No Death sent them an order anyway.

The moment she did, the nearest spartiate tackled No Death, shoving her out of range. The girl's staff dropped like a black meteor, shattering the spartiate in her stead.

No Death rolled across the floor, deftly unhooking the scythe from the girl's ankles as she did. She used the momentum to scramble to her feet and thrust the scythe forward to keep the girl back.

But the girl wasn't trying to follow her. Instead, her tiny body flashed, and black gusts burst out, shattering the remaining spartiates.

The rain of bone fragments soon dissipated into thin air, and the girl raised her staff again, no emotion in her eyes at all. Then she started fidgeting, as if she'd just remembered to.

Do I summon more? There's one thing I wanna confirm first.

No Death starting spinning the scythe above her head. *Vnn, vnn.* The sound of it slicing the wind broke through the silence, echoing. The girl was patiently waiting, watching to see what this led to.

Slowly, bit by bit, No Death's toes crept toward the girl.

She closed the gap until—

The blade had built enough speed, and with a sharp breath, No Death made it shoot out toward the girl's left wrist.

Even with a blade coming at her so fast it cleaved the air itself, the girl didn't seem concerned. She just mechanically placed her body in the blade's path, clearly aiming to hit back with another counter. She was getting used to No Death's speed; she moved without a hitch.

But—as the blade shot through the air toward the girl's arm, its path leaped upward.

Changing up the patten she'd twice demonstrated.

It was going right for that scrawny throat.

Would this hit prove fatal? From the way things were going, she wasn't too sure. But like the belly, the throat was exposed. Probably a trap, but still—if she scored a direct hit, like the belly, odds were she could lay down some real hurt. A number of her classes would kick in, and she might do enough damage to turn this losing fight around.

The exchanges thus far had proven No Death was the more accomplished fighter. That was why she'd avoided using any feints, going entirely for basic attacks. The girl had grown used to that simplicity, and for that reason, like her martial-art-enhanced charge earlier, she was unable to dodge the swing at her neck

The scythe's blade sliced that slender throat, and—

"Gah!"

——the staff hit her.

She'd held it in so far, but this time, the impact forced a grunt out of her.

No Death leaped back, eyes wide.

"......Again?"

Not a drop of blood fell from the girl's throat. But there was a faint mark showing she had sliced the skin. That must have done damage. Did she have some ability active that negated attacks on weak points? That would invalidate a number of the skills No Death had acquired.

Is she even alive? Is she...an undead the King of Darkness made?

She must have looked rattled, because the girl stammered, "Er, um…d-do you want to surrender? Er, well…I won't hurt you anymore, and I can guarantee your safety…after."

What did No Death think about that offer?

Creepy.

From the get-go, this girl's attacks had contained absolutely no hostility, no bloodlust. Some people might call that a kind heart or ascribe some other emotion to it—but if you weren't trying to hurt or kill and still repeatedly dropped skull-crushing blows, could that really be called kindness?

To No Death's point of view, this girl was deeply unsettling. Even if she was her niece, she felt no connection to this strange dark elf.

If this offer was made for reasons she could understand—pity or even superiority—she might have been insulted, but not repulsed. But this girl had no such emotions.

…It would make more sense if I treat her like an emotionless undead acting the part.

It was all kinds of messed up, but to her, it felt like every action and mannerism was pure performance. Still, that wasn't what mattered here. No Death's personal opinion was irrelevant.

She had to focus on how she could get out of this mess and turn things to her advantage. If suggesting she might surrender would help, then it was worth exploring the dead.

"I could do that…," she began and then trailed off.

Right.

Talking was what you did if you were buying time or had already won.

Was the girl winning?

——No. There was no clear victor yet. The girl did have a bit of an advantage. But if she'd started talking here, she was most likely just trying to buy time.

"——Tch!"

With her loudest click yet, No Death once more closed the gap. She could try hurling martial arts from a distance, but this girl had those scrolls at her disposal. No clue how many or where she was keeping them, but it was safe to assume there were more where those came from, and chipping away at each other would not end well for her.

On the plus side, it seemed safe to assume this girl had no other ranged attacks. If she did, she wouldn't have needed to use a scroll.

Did she raise a thief class? Is that how she's using scrolls? No, she did use those self-buff-looking spells, so that's not likely.

But No Death also had no effective ranged attacks; at a distance, she didn't see a way to win.

But what about up close?

Less awful. So that's where she'd have to take her chances.

This time, she took a swing right at the kid's face. Maybe the girl didn't want to get cut there, because she slapped the scythe away with her staff.

This stung No Death's hands.

The staff swung round into a counter. Greater Evasion and Instant Reflex were enough for her to dodge it.

They were either evenly matched or her warrior know-how—predicting her opponent's moves, adjusting her read—was starting to show and tipping the scales her way. But no matter how much damage she racked up, a single Heal would undo it all and lead to a loss.

Then I should go for it...

No Death had two aces up her sleeve.

The first guaranteed a kill.

The second was extremely versatile.

She could use the second to defeat a foe or cover her escape, so she didn't want to waste it.

Was it time to pop the first one?

When she'd attacked, the girl acted like it hurt. But was that real? Doubting it wasn't getting her anywhere.

Every thought she'd had about this girl was pure conjecture. Every bit of it could be wrong. Maybe she was just as cute as she looked. Maybe she really didn't like fighting at all.

But No Death couldn't shake that fishy feeling.

What do I do? If…let's say there are others as powerful as her. In that case, I might find myself in a situation where I wish I hadn't used it too early. I'd rather kill this girl without using that move…but can I?

The answer was, *I don't know.*

If that was her only Heal scroll, maybe? But getting it done quickly probably wasn't possible.

Naturally, these thoughts didn't slow her hands. She was slashing away with her scythe but drawing no blood and getting hit by those brutal counters.

The girl could stand still and take aim, but No Death had to dart in and out of range, swinging her blade all over. She had to keep her feet moving to control the distance and she had to keep her weapon moving to attack. If she didn't devote a chunk of those resources to evasion and defense, it was tough to avoid getting hit by those counters—and the girl didn't seem to mind that she got hit first.

The only place the girl did actively block was her face. And when she aimed for the stomach, the girl's counter was extra nasty.

That was the sum of what she knew.

I guess…I gotta? It will end this.

Use it now or would she need it later? That was the question.

She was looping through it.

The girl's flesh split open, but in return, she landed a clean hit on No Death's side.

She felt bones creak and imagined her innards shaking; she was flung backward. The pain was so great, she almost threw up, and her boost went skidding across the floor as she tried to regain her footing.

That was the hardest blow yet. It affected her breathing. The pain had her diaphragm twitching. Acting confident, she thumped the floor with the butt of her weapon, leaning against the staff, her legs crossed. She slowly pulled her helmet off, flashing a mask—a smile—like it hadn't hurt at all.

A pose allowed by her foe's lack of aggression.

"Well, fine," she muttered breezily. Her mind made up. Time to make sure this girl died.

The girl didn't come after her.

And that would cost her life.

"Hey, you suggested I surrender, yeah? One thing I gotta know…are you undead? Did the King of Darkness make you?"

"Huh? Er, um…why that question? And not like…terms?"

"Answer me."

"……………………I-I'm not undead. I'm what I look like!"

"Cool," No Death said, thinking.

Had the girl delayed her answer because she didn't get why it was asked or—because she wanted time to think?

I mean, I asked 'cause just looking didn't tell me anything…and why'd she just brush off the mention of the King of Darkness? Fine, whatever. Undead or not, this'll kill her.

She put the helmet back on and used the talent she was born with.

Aiming this talent at the divine weapon allowed her to use the ultimate power of the god of death, Sulshana. Thus—

"——The Goal of All Life Is Death."

A clock appeared behind her.

This was her ace, one she could only use when wielding the scythe.

It guaranteed death.

Absolute death, which could not be resisted.

Not once had anyone escaped the move.

"Huh?!"

The girl sounded surprised. It was a genuine burst of emotion that No Death assumed was actual shock.

Huh? So she isn't undead? Well, I'd react like that, too. If you don't know what this is, it's downright uncanny, a mystery move at work. But the clock itself doesn't do anything. It just buffs what comes next. So—it's too soon to be surprised.

Next, No Death used a skill contained within the scythe itself.

Naturally, she chose—

"——Death."

As she cast the spell, there was a tick. The clock behind her advanced.

——She'd won.

Victory was hers.

"Phoenix Flame."

A bird of fire spread its wings behind the girl.

Another spell! But…heh-heh, no use. I don't know what that does, but nothing can survive this power. Your only shot is to kill me before I use it!

Death was normally a spell that activated instantly, but if she used this ability, it took a full twelve seconds to activate. She had no clue what would happen if she died during that interval, so she was on the defensive.

The girl must have assumed the spell had no effect, because she swung her staff up and charged forward.

So far, she'd been just receiving, only using counters—if she was on the offensive, she must have sensed something amiss. Against the unknown, she could have turtled up, gone to wait-and-see mode. The fact that she hadn't showed she had good instincts.

But No Death had the advantage on technique and experience. If she wasn't attacking and just deflecting and evading, she could handle this. Naturally, she couldn't escape taking a hit forever, but she had to last only a handful of seconds.

——*Six.*

She dodged the girl's combo. One blink would spell death, a flurry hard to see even for someone in the realm beyond the heroes. Clearly an onslaught from someone at No Death's level. But playing pure defense, watching close—she could tell the girl's physical specs were high, but she wasn't taking full advantage of them. She wasn't used to this kind of exertion.

——*Eight.*

Common in those born with strength.

Her physical talents were too good—she could win by sheer overwhelming force, so she'd never needed to use tricky techniques, never had to guess another's moves. Refused to go to the effort of learning those things—and wound up eating dirt when they met someone better. Never realizing the cause was their own arrogance.

Like this girl soon would.

——*Eleven. It's over. Good-bye.*

Easily dodging a blow that would cause a concussion just grazing anyone else, No Death bade the dark elf farewell.

This girl had been sinister in a way that defied words, but now that she'd won, she had to admit—the kid was cute. She was too young to really know much of anything. The sin lay not with her but with the parents who'd raised her.

She deflected the staff, ignored a chance to strike—and was faced with an enigma.

The girl wasn't dead.

......Huh?

For a moment, No Death's mind went blank.

That move meant certain death and yet, she hadn't died. She must've counted the time wrong. That was the most logical answer.

Outside of training, she'd never fought anyone this strong. She didn't think she was stressing it, but she must have been. In that state, it was difficult to gauge time accurately. She was just a little off.

...Two more.

She gave it two more seconds, nice long ones.

But the girl didn't die.

She still wasn't dead.

The girl was making energetic little noises, "Hyah!" or "Hoo!" that were totally at odds with her terrifying attacks.

"H-how?!"

It was unfathomable.

That move killed *everything.* Even the undead, who were already dead. Even golems who had no life at all. No Death herself could not comprehend the move's power, so how had this girl survived?

The girl's attacks were hurting, so she was no illusion. What else could she be? Did that move just not work on dark elves? Or her bloodline? Or— had the spell she cast thwarted it?

In which case, how had she known what the move did? Even No Death had access to it only through her talent and didn't know everything about it. Nor did the handful of Theocracy people who knew she could use it. If anyone did know the full details, that would be Sulshana—the scythe's true owner.

Was that god backing this girl? Given the girl's apparent immortality, that felt weirdly convincing. But then—

"——Unh!"

Confusion and panic had made her stiffen up, and a blow she could have dodged landed cleanly.

"Argh!"

No Death swung through the pain. A desperate flail that sank into the girl's flesh and before she could tell if it had done anything, that staff pummeled her. The pain left her seeing stars, and her body tipped—but before it toppled over, she got her legs under her.

Her mind was in overdrive.

Her plan had gone awry.

What now?

What was her best option?

She'd taken a beating but still had strength left. She wasn't done for yet. But given her foe's potential reinforcements, it was time to pick fight or flight.

But if she tried flight, was she even fast enough to get away? She couldn't say for sure. In which case—

——*I've gotta use my other ace?*

Not the worst idea. But No Death was still hesitant. She'd *just* watched her other ace get thwarted like it was nothing.

It was hard to imagine this one would be, too. But—did this girl have some crazy move that could cancel it out?

——*How many scrolls does she have? How many spells does she know? I don't have anything like enough information!*

And when you didn't have a clue what your opponent could do, it was tough to be sure it was worth playing your own card. But like she kept saying—time was against No Death but helped this girl.

She could push through it, but the pain from these staff hits was definitely making it harder to think.

No Death's grin grew broader.

The smile hid her emotions, her thoughts, her feelings from everyone—especially her enemies.

That's why she grinned. She had made her choice.

——*No more thinking! I don't know enough for thinking to matter!*

All she really knew was that she'd showed off one ace and let this girl know whatever countermeasure she'd used was effective against it. That fact alone was a far greater loss than the total damage No Death had taken.

She used her last ace ability, and a burst of white light formed—another No Death.

No Death had two ultimate moves.

The first left no life behind—slightly more accurately, her talent allowed her access to the move that slept in this weapon, the ace of its former owner.

Her second ultimate came from her class—Lesser Walküre/Almighty. This created a copy of her.

Einherjar.

Its combat performance was no match for the real No Death, but it *was* based on her strengths—so the copy still possessed overwhelming power.

The girl's eyes went wide, and she made another shocked noise. It was just like the last time, which No Death felt didn't bode well.

Before No Death even had a chance to send a mental directive to her Einherjar, the girl pulled out an orb.

An instant later, she'd summoned a giant that barely fit because of the hallway. It was an earth elemental.

Utterly baffling.

She'd figured there was a solid chance this girl was a druid. So summoning an elemental made sense—but she'd used an item, not a spell.

All for an elemental—one that didn't really seem that powerful.

Can't summon elementals, can't use attack spells...a druid who can only buff herself? Or am I just overlooking something, jumping to the wrong conclusion? I heard the elf king used a giant earth elemental, but is this it? But...this isn't...all that big...

What she'd heard about the elf king's elemental made it sound overwhelming, so powerful that even the exceptional stood no chance against it.

That suggested this was a different kind. But it might seem unimpressive only compared to No Death's own strengths; to anyone weaker, it would probably be more than big enough.

Still, this elemental posed no threat to her.

She could leave it to the Einherjar and focus on the girl. It should finish off the elemental soon enough, and then it would be two-on-one.

No, we should team up and eliminate this elemental together.

"C'mon!"

No Death charged in, her scythe striking the elemental. The Einherjar matched her.

Earth elementals resisted physical attacks, but their advantage was a steep one. They easily cut deep into that tough hide. But sturdiness was this foe's calling card; a couple of hits would hardly be fatal.

But the earth elemental vanished.

"——Ha?"

She was so lost. She definitely hadn't defeated it—

Because an instant later, there was an earth elemental right in front of her. This one was even bigger.

What was going on here?

This couldn't be the same one.

"A sacrificial summon?"

She'd never heard of any skills or spells that worked like that. But the name itself fit the circumstances so well, it popped right out of her mouth.

This new—if that was the right word—earth elemental was clearly stronger than the last. Even the exceptional few would not stand a chance. Still—

I can beat it. But...is that the right choice?

If she damaged or defeated it, would it just be replaced with one even stronger?

She found that hard to believe but couldn't entirely rule out the possibility.

No Death put the Einherjar on standby while she took a good look at the girl.

She was just fidgeting around behind the elemental, watching her. It didn't seem like she'd order the earth elemental to attack.

Who the hell is this girl? If she was undead, I could safely assume the King of Darkness made her, but if she's just a regular dark elf... How would you go about keeping a kid this strong secret? With her power, you'd think word would get around. Or did the country keep her hidden, like mine did me?

The Nation of Darkness had been founded a few years prior.

The Empire had trumpeted the notion that those lands had originally belonged to the Nation, but the Theocracy had been around long enough to know that was a bald-faced lie.

The Nation and its king had not previously existed.

If the King of Darkness did appear out of nowhere, then he might be the same thing as the gods of yore—but that's not confirmed. It's hard...to believe... but what if...this girl is the same? No, her eyes bear the mark of royalty; it's more likely she's related to the elf king. Maybe the King of Darkness got his hands on this girl somehow and that's what inspired him to come here and found a multi-racial nation?

She didn't know. There was no proof of anything. Even the connection between this girl and the King of Darkness was pure speculation.

But that would be the worst-case scenario, and she should be prepared for it.

If this girl really is from the Nation, then they've got at least two on my level, her and the king himself. Shit, is he here, too?

That brought a hint of panic.

How dumb was she? Assuming this girl was from the Nation, then that had always been in the cards.

Anywhere else, the very idea would be absurd.

No other king would waltz into the middle of a war between two other countries; it wasn't worth the risk. But the King of Darkness had popped up in the Sacred Kingdom and thrown his weight around. Proving to the rest of the world that a caster capable of wiping out entire armies might just show up *anywhere*.

There were also hard-to-believe reports that he'd shown up in the arena in the Empire before they became a vassal state.

No Death was cursing herself now.

If she was right about this and the King of Darkness was here in person, what could be worse? This girl alone was bad enough, but if that undead showed up, No Death was doomed. The Theocracy hadn't exactly fully analyzed the undead king's combat potential, but they knew he'd wiped out an army over ten thousand strong, so it was hard to believe he was weaker than this girl.

Right now, I'm just piling speculation on speculation, but…it adds up. It does. I dunno why they're here, but…if the king does show up, do I negotiate?

If he could steal the elf king's elemental, then he could steal the country.

The girl bore proof of the king's blood—there in her eyes.

With proof of royal blood and the king's earth elemental in her command, the elves would likely bow to her.

And if he drives us off, he'll earn accolades. Flawless timing. Flawless… timing?

A new wave of panic swept over her.

The Nation of Darkness was invading the Re-Estize Kingdom, hell-bent on wiping it out. That's why the Theocracy rushed to end our war with the elves. But what if that was actually the Nation's true goal all along?

It was like the sides of a rubik q suddenly aligned. No Death had experienced no fear, no matter the fight she was in, but now it felt like her core had turned to ice, and her whole body shivered. If this was the Nation's scheme from the very beginning, it all made sense.

The Re-Estize Kingdom was never their primary purpose. Their goal was to put the elves under their domain and strike back at the Theocracy. In which case…the defeat at E-Naeurl exposed their invasion. Was that done not to strike fear in the hearts of the kingdom's people but timed to spur the Theocracy into action? Or maybe both?! Does he plan to put us all under his power in rapid succession? That can't be true! It's not possible we've been dancing to the Nation's tune all along! That's absurd!

She was loath to admit it, but like a moment before—she had to account for the worst.

The supreme executive agency had said the King of Darkness deserved the utmost caution. As uncanny as his schemes were, it was his raw power that posed the greatest threat.

And yet—

Yes and yet—if this was the king's own scheme, then spells that slew ten thousand soldiers in the blink of an eye were not nearly as frightening. Nor were the powerful minions that could massacre a kingdom nine million strong. His true horror lay in the mind that could see a hundred moves ahead and tug at invisible strings that let him control even his adversaries.

A formidable threat in his own right and a strategic mastermind—how could you fight that? That crushed the one weapon the weak had against the strong.

......Or are the plots the work of that demon prime minister Albedo? Either way... No, wait... What if it's not just these two countries but the Theocracy, too? Come here, wipe out these troops, then declare war?

True, there were people out there who could insist it didn't matter how many weak soldiers were slain. Those in the realm of heroes had power the equivalent of ten thousand average infantry. Such thoughts might seem rational to the powerful—but what about your average citizen?

The Theocracy had made human supremacy their motto and galvanized the country around it. The flip side of that idea was that unless weak humans came together to act first against the other races, they risked being wiped out themselves. Just as the Dragon Kingdom was threatened by the beastmen.

But even if they knew an overwhelmingly powerful foe wanted to wipe them out, did the masses have the fortitude to endure two back-to-back wars? Especially if they heard their armies had been massacred without toppling their old enemies in the elf kingdom?

No Death's lips curled in her usual smile—the one she used to hide her true feelings.

No joy here, no humor to be found—quite the opposite.

This smile was born from despair. At the scheme woven round, at the trap they'd stepped right into.

What do I do? Try and urge the soldiers to flee? Or run so that I might live?

She was the Theocracy's strongest fighter, and her death would be a terrible blow. Running was probably wise.

No Death was too busy trying to figure out her best option to do much of anything else, and the girl must have read something into that.

"Er, um, you know?" she said. "Like I said, you can surrender. I-it's not too late! I'd rather not kill you."

That would let her bring back intel on their foes, so it wasn't the worst idea. But—

"——Can't run, I can't run!!"

"Huh?"

The girl looked baffled. As well she would. The girl had asked a question and—from the girl's perspective—No Death's answer was unrelated. But in her mind, it made perfect sense.

Yes. This was the only way.

If this was genuinely a Nation ploy, then there was only one way out of the trap.

Become the cornered beast, tear into this girl, and crush the Nation's ploy right here.

The loss of a fighter this powerful would undoubtedly disrupt their plans.

Perhaps a horrible trap awaited them, but this was her chance to break them free of it. Only she had that opportunity.

Yeah, only I can save my country!

Did she owe them enough to risk her life? That was hard to answer. But every now and then, she'd met someone she liked. She'd lived long enough to lose most of them, but they'd loved this country, and that was worth betting her life on once.

Maybe it'll be the death of me, but I'm gonna go for the kill. Nothing more, nothing less.

Her mind was made up.

She'd kept retreat in mind. But only because she'd wanted to move with the confidence that escape was always a viable option—not a narrow escape at the last second. The other part of it was that so far, she hadn't seriously wanted this to end in death. Not because she had any hesitation about killing someone who might be her niece. She wouldn't hesitate to clip arms and legs, hog-tie, or even kill a child this age if the need arose. But it *was* true she'd made her own survival her top priority.

No longer.

If she didn't throw the dice now, when would she?

Tomorrow, things were only going to be worse.

"Go!" she yelled.

The Einherjar obeyed, lunging forward.

She did not need to speak aloud. She could order it around with her mind alone. Arguably, verbal commands were a mistake, warning her enemy. No Death knew that. She'd yelled anyway because she wanted to rouse her spirits and force herself to commit to this path of action.

She had the Einherjar take the elemental while she lunged at the girl.

But the elemental spread its arms, blocking the passage.

Fine, then.

She and her double would team up on this elemental and kill the girl afterward.

If this elemental had been stolen from the elf king, then defeating it would rob her of a symbol of royalty. That might at least slow the Nation's plans.

Two scythes sliced away at the elemental.

Honestly, a bad foe for her—no blood, no critical points to hit.

Higher elementals heavily resisted physical attacks. Even the scythe No Death wielded could not one-shot them.

Not the sort of foe she wanted to go up against, but she didn't exactly have time to grumble.

Since the elemental was blocking the hall, the girl's attacks couldn't reach her. Even if she used one of those scrolls, it would be hard for the spell to get through. What she had to worry about here was the girl casting that buff spell on the elemental.

With two of me, I've got the advantage. But nothing's guaranteed. If I can't get around it, I can't stop her buffing it. Still...

Did the girl not know this would happen?

Something seemed off about it. But she couldn't quite put a finger on what.

The elemental swung an arm like a brick mountain. She'd have loved to jump back but couldn't afford the drop in DPS that hit-and-away tactics would bring. She hooked the incoming arm with her scythe, deflecting it. The earth elemental's power was prodigious, but it wasn't hard to adjust the course by applying force along the side. Still, this weapon wasn't built for deflections; this was purely achievable by the core difference in their strength.

Out of the corner of her eye, she saw the Einherjar pull off the same trick.

It was weaker than her, so if it could do that, then this earth elemental was definitely not all that strong—like she'd thought.

But that didn't make it weak.

A mere hero would likely be unable to dodge it and wind up crushed by its fists. Whether that proved fatal was another question, but they'd definitely be badly hurt.

The attack dealt with, No Death glanced past it, one eye on the girl. Right up against the elemental like this, any glance away was risky, but missing what the girl did was even worse.

She couldn't believe her eyes.

——*Huh?*

The girl had turned her back and was running off.

An adorable little trot but extremely fast.

She'd made a run for it.

"————!!"

No Death worked it out.

She hadn't summoned this earth elemental to counter the Einherjar.

She'd just wanted time to escape.

The girl's act had obfuscated it, but she must have been on her last legs.

The girl had never intended to get in a fight to the death. That explained several of her choices.

Like when No Death had tried to get behind her, and she'd reacted impulsively—not because she was scared of being surrounded but because she wanted to keep her escape route open.

Her words and actions spoke to that.

"Shi—"

She had to choose the best of three options right now.

Chase the girl?

Fell this elemental?

Or run herself?

The third would be easy enough.

Outside the summoner's field of view, the elemental could not receive any situational orders.

If it had been told to stand in this passage and kill anyone who tried to get through, then if No Death tried to run, it wouldn't give chase. If it was told to kill the woman in front of it, then even if No Death ran for it, it would obediently follow after, attacking mindlessly.

But it would simply pursue relentlessly, not smart enough to try and get ahead of her.

And No Death was faster and nimbler. She'd win that race.

If she turned and ran off at top speed, the earth elemental would be left grasping in the dark for her.

But that was unacceptable. She had to reject the idea.

She could not afford to take her eyes off the greater potential threat— the Nation of Darkness's plan.

So what about options one and two?

Following the girl was easier said than done. Even if they got this wall out of the way quickly, at the speed that girl was going, catching up would require a lot of luck. And she was likely headed straight for her reinforcements. The outcome of that fight was anyone's guess.

In which case, option two might be best.

This threw her earlier commitment into the wind, and if this *wasn't* the same elemental the elf king commanded, it would be a complete waste of time.

But given the risk and reward involved, it was her only real option.

The fish that got away was always bigger, but she had to be satisfied with what she'd caught.

No Death fixed her glare on the earth elemental—and, down the hall, saw the girl swing round to face them.

One last one-liner? She watched, keeping her eyes on the elemental—and the girl's lips moved.

"Good, I saved enough mana."

At this distance, she should never have heard it, but she had elf blood in her veins and high stats overall—she wasn't sure if that helped, but she caught the hint of relief in the girl's voice. But before she worked out what it meant, the girl raised the staff high.

Mare had mastered the disciple of disaster class, earning its ace move.

A weaker version of the world disaster's ultimate move.

Its name: Micro-catastrophe.

It required a vast reserve of mana, but the raw destructive force outperformed Ainz's super-tier spells. Naturally, this paled in comparison to the Macro-catastrophe. But the resulting pure energy blast blew away everything around and was more than strong enough.

In that instant, No Death was hit by a tremendous impact.

Shit, I'm dead, her instincts cried.

The raging force vaporized the elemental.

At last, she got it. The elemental was neither there to fight the Einherjar nor to allow the girl's escape. It was bait, forcing her to stand in the path of this emission of pure violence.

A moment after the elemental went down, her double did as well.

And then—

——*Not yet! I'm not dying here! I refuse!*

In that vortex of destruction, giving up might have been easier. But No Death clung to life with everything she had. Yet—her mind faded. A moment ago, she'd felt as if her body was being torn apart—but that pain was gone. She couldn't tell where she was or which way was up.

Is this what death feels like?

What the fuck?

Those were No Death's thoughts on the matter.

Had she not been about to put her life on the line?

Throw every last bit of strength she had into a battle against a villainous state's horrific plot, all to protect her homeland?

Cowards.

Sure, that was her selfish take on it. Even as her mind faded out, she knew the truth of the matter. But what else could she call it?

The death of the elemental was no comfort. That had never been anything but a pawn to sacrifice. At best, it had been deemed a worthy loss to take out the Theocracy's finest warrior.

Who was that girl?

If she was from the Nation of Darkness, how much of this was the evil king's scheme?

This was defeat.

Not because she'd fallen to her enemy's spell. She had not even been allowed to risk her life, and the humiliation of that could never be overcome.

Horrid.

She didn't want this.

She didn't want defeat.

She'd never wanted to learn what it was like to lose.

She'd simply wanted to reject her own strength. Or—perhaps her mother.

The blood in her own veins. What going unloved had given her.

But if that cursed strength let her protect what mattered…

Then perhaps, her mother might relent.

She was finally motivated.

Only for it to crumble.

I just have to hope…the Nation…isn't involved…

And then it all went black.

•

Ainz and Aura emerged from the elf treasury.

The upshot—he wasn't entirely sure it was a disappointment. There had been mystery fruits, coconuts larger than Aura was tall, and there was no way to appraise their value at the moment.

But nothing made of particularly rare metals turned up. The materials were all things easily found in nature—a tad disappointing, but at least they could still hope for some unusual effects or previously unseen abilities.

So Ainz wasn't upset. Perhaps the needle even tipped toward pleased.

The haul was already gone.

He'd used a Gate to toss it all near the log house above Nazarick.

This might have come as a shock to whichever member of the Pleiades was on duty, but since he'd sent Mare out on his own, he didn't want to stop and explain. He simply barked an order to take care of the items—given the risk entailed—within the log house for now.

When that was done, he assumed a grave expression—his bony features never changed—and turned to Aura.

"Well then, Aura, let's do this."

"Yes, Lord Ainz!!"

She sounded enthusiastic and bent down with her back to him.

To be clear, her movement speed was far greater than his own. If she took off, she'd leave him in the dust. Naturally, since she had to track the elf king's blood trails, she wouldn't hit her top speed. But even then, Ainz would likely not keep up. He did have equipment that could improve his speed, but changing gear meant more than simply swapping that slot for something else.

Ainz's default loadout was a resistance puzzle, min-maxed to the extreme limits of his equipment weight capacity. If anything changed that balance, he'd have to consider the cumulative effects—which took time. He had little trouble using scrolls or consumables, but this brought out his finicky side.

And even if he did use it, he wasn't sure he could keep up with Aura.

So his best option—was to have Aura carry him.

Naturally, an adult man riding a little girl around was an extremely—*extremely*—uncomfortable visual. Ainz would much rather not. The emotion wasn't strong enough to be repressed, which meant it stuck like a thorn in his side.

But Mare's life might depend on this decision.

Certainly, Mare should have no issues defeating the elf king. Ainz was pretty sure they'd seen the end of what he could do, and he was exhausted and injured—he had no path to victory. But nothing was ever guaranteed.

He could send a Message asking for an update, but mid-combat, that could prove distracting. His best option was simply to catch up as soon as possible.

So Ainz had to swallow his pride. Make this choice not as Satoru Suzuki but as Ainz Ooal Gown.

That left one concern.

How should she carry him?

Given Aura's strength, she could probably manage the princess carry. Others might well go for the standard piggyback. Yet, Ainz had chosen to treat her like a mount—or more accurately, this had been Aura's own choice.

At first, he'd suggested she heft him onto her shoulder like so much baggage. That was less inherently mortifying, and the self-deprecating joke contained within that metaphor amused him.

But Aura insisted she could never treat him like baggage, and attempting to argue the point seemed like it would take a while.

Ainz himself had ruled out the princess carry—that would simply lead to emotional resets.

Which left the mount.

His mind made up, he steeled himself and stepped aboard the little girl's back. He also took a dagger out of his item box. It was not clear if he would need it, but better safe than sorry.

Floating next to them was an Elemental Skull, called here via Summon Tenth-Tier Undead.

Some might suggest he bring out some other undead and ride them instead of Aura. But he hadn't for one simple reason.

Which would be sacrificed first?

Faced with an unexpected threat, his summons would act as a shield, giving Aura and Ainz time to retreat. For that reason, he could not use an undead as a mount.

Certainly, he could simply dismount if they encountered an enemy, but that delay might prove fatal. Ainz knew this was overcautious. But they were in the middle of a war zone, and the odds of something unexpected were that much higher—best to consider safety first and be prepared— using an undead as a shield, for instance.

Elemental Skulls were more about magical DPS than tanking, but he'd gone with it anyway because tanks weren't always the best choice to cover a retreat. In *Yggdrasil*, DPS units trying to tank was not advisable. Only absolutely freaks like Touch Me had ever managed to play both at once and just proved how inadvisable it was. No one else could copy him. But you were certainly welcome to try.

Aura took off.

Following the faint traces of blood on the floor, she bounded down the stairs—and then drew to a halt.

Taking her eyes off the trail, she looked ahead. Ainz followed her gaze but saw no one.

He considered asking, but if something had gone wrong, best he stand ready to give the Elemental Skull an order—and wait for Aura's word. And he had a hunch what this might be.

His hunch proved correct.

"Lord Ainz, message from Mare."

"——Ah," he intoned. It was hard to act dignified while seated on her back, but he could at least maintain a master's tone of voice. "From your

attitude, I surmise Mare is not asking for help. Can I assume he's successfully captured the elf king?"

"Well...the king has already been killed."

"What?"

Without the primal earth elemental, the elf king would certainly have
been rather weak. But not weak enough to be slain by just anyone from this
world—he should have been able to escape any such threat.

"......There was another powerful figure in play here? Did Mare
engage?"

"Yes and he defeated them, but they're still alive. What should we do?
Mare suggests they might possess valuable intel. They might have been
monitoring the fight between you and Shalltear."

"What? They saw that? Did they have a World Item? Let's catch up
with him and secure this person. Then we'll return to Nazarick. Time's
a-wasting! Aura, sorry about this—it won't be much longer."

The report hadn't used a plural, so evidently there'd only been the
one real threat. Still, it was possible they had a number of weaker fighters
accompanying them. Without knowledge of the specifics, beating a hasty
retreat was the ideal move.

"I'm not put out at all—but let's hurry. Lord Ainz, hold on tight."

The words barely left her mouth and Aura shot off like a bullet. Far
faster than before, didn't even slow on corners—running up the walls
instead. Ainz had never been on a roller coaster, but he imagined it felt like
this. This body felt no fear, yet it was still rather frightening. Perhaps even
scarier with his gaze this low.

When acting as a warrior, he could run at similar speeds, but there was
a big difference between running on your own power and putting yourself at
the mercy of someone else's full-throttle cornering.

In what felt like mere seconds, Mare came within view.

He had an unfamiliar human on his shoulder, his other hand holding
his own staff and a new sinister-looking scythe.

Ainz had a ton of questions. *I heard the elf king was slain, but where's the body? What happened to the magic items he had on him?* But they were on enemy ground. Withdrawing safely was the priority.

Looking grave, he stepped down from Aura's back acting confident, like riding her had been absolutely necessary and totally normal. Then he stuck the dagger in the floor.

It was difficult to quickly remember a featureless corridor, but if a recognizable dagger was left sticking out of it, that would make things easier. This dagger was long since embedded in his memory, so he could use it as a spell target.

Ainz opened a Gate.

"Go on in."

Mare stammered in reply and then carried the human on through.

Ainz dismissed the Elemental Skull, and then he and Aura went through the Gate.

Once through, he found the pile of items from the treasury. To one side, he found Entoma bowing her head—she must have come out to collect the pile. And she probably realized the new Gate likely signified Ainz's return.

Some death knights stood awkwardly around them, likely here to help her.

"Welcome home, Lord Ainz."

"Hmm, keep working on these, Entoma. You have a ring?"

"I do."

"Then loan it to Aura. Aura, this is a valuable source of information. Do not let it die. Take it swiftly to the Ice Prison. I'm sure Neuronist can handle it, but make sure all gear is removed."

"L-Lord Ainz, a moment…?"

"What, Mare? You look concerned."

"Y-yes, this human…is really strong. I've used Sandman's Sand on her, but if something wakes her up, I don't think Neuronist could win."

"…Ah, in that case… Aura, remain close to this woman until I return. Stay on guard."

Aura slipped on the ring, took the human from Mare, and teleported away. Ainz turned back to Mare.

"So...why is it you think this human was watching the Shalltear battle?"

That was the question of the hour.

"R-right, this human used both your the Goal of All Life Is Death and Shalltear's Einherjar. I can't imagine that's unrelated!"

"She *what*?!"

Ordinarily, nobody had more than one move powerful enough to call an ace. Having two available boggled his mind. Perhaps Mare's idea was on the money. Did she have a means of copying skills?

"I'm shocked you left her alive."

"Y-yes, I thought Micro-catastrophe would kill her, but she's got incredible life force. And luckily didn't die."

"You used Micro-catastrophe on her?! And she survived... That woman really is powerful. You may have been the lucky one. What about the elf king?"

Mare described his end, and Ainz furrowed his nonexistent brow. The king had likely had a magic item capable of thwarting Stop Time, and he'd like to go collect that but also wanted to learn more about this new human.

He should probably prioritize the item. The human would not easily escape Nazarick.

Well, I can send Pandora's Actor. He can search the place. Or should I have him investigate the human? No, better I do that myself. In which case...

Ainz turned to Entoma.

"Entoma, please wait here. I'm going to call in Pandora's Actor."

As she answered, he activated Message.

Epilogue

When her master returned from the elf country, Albedo greeted him at the Ice Prison, then returned to his office to resume her duties.

Toppling the Re-Estize Kingdom had dramatically expanded their domains and her workload. Albedo's abilities were specialized in domestic affairs, so nothing here really gave her much trouble. Since they'd burned most cities to the ground, really thorny issues like occupational politics had largely gone up in flames.

For that reason, Albedo was devoting a considerable portion of her mental faculties to the creation of internal resources detailing occupational strategies for use in the many countries that would eventually come under their control.

What had worked in E-Rantel might be applicable even when expanded to a national level, but it was not hard to imagine that would come with some growing pains. Cities and countries each had their own requirements, and approaching them as separate beasts would avoid further problems down the line.

Naturally, what she drew up here might not apply universally to every country. Different races and cultures made all the difference. But the barebones outline of it should remain useful.

Once it's written up, I'll run it by Demiurge and Pandora's Actor, then get Lord Ainz's approval.

Their minds should ensure her work was even finer.

I could ask that girl, too...

Her master was the wisest of them all, so having him look first might be the fastest approach—he could certainly find things the other two would miss—but as head of the floor guardians, it would never do for her to offer documents that contained obvious problems.

These thoughts on her mind, she made her way through the pile on her desk when—

"Albedo! Come to the Ice Prison."

This Message made her jump. She sensed a towering rage behind her master's thoughts.

Once you hit a certain level, resistance to mind control was vital. Charm or Dominate could be instantly fatal otherwise. Every floor guardian had measures in place.

Despite that, Albedo felt a twinge of fear. She might have been able to null the side effects, but it was impossible to ignore the raw emotion behind them.

He knew.

Albedo was working on something behind her master's back. Had he found out?

Had Demiurge sniffed it out and informed him?

It was still at the experimental phase. She had not fully deployed it yet. Would that engender this much fury?

She could think of no other reason why such anger would be directed her way.

What was this?

Albedo hastily used the ring's power, moving to the Ice Prison.

Her master stood before the cage housing the half elf they'd captured. Behind him stood the domain guardian, Neuronist, with Aura and Mare.

His expression was unchanged, but she could still sense the towering fury.

Albedo immediately prostrated herself before him.

"I cannot apologize enough!"

"......F-for what?"

He sounded genuinely confused. She swiftly concluded the cause of his fury was not what she'd imagined. This kowtow was a poor choice.

But she'd thought of an excuse on her way here. Her master might be vastly more intelligent that her, but given enough time, she could form plans as good as his.

Or at least I hope so.

"——If anything in Nazarick has displeased you and incurred your wrath, Lord Ainz, then that is the fault of the captain of the guardians—myself. I besmirch Lord Tabula Smaragdina's reputation. Thus, the only possible response is to bow my head and profess my sorrow."

"............No, Albedo, that's not right at all. First, let me correct a misunderstanding. This fury is not directed at Nazarick at all."

Albedo breathed a sigh of relief. Not performative—from the heart.

"Th-then what is the cause?"

"Raise your head and stand before me. I do not enjoy having those who are faultless bow before me."

"Thank you, Lord Ainz."

Albedo rose to her feet.

The twins momentarily looked dubious, which concerned her, but that was not important now.

"Then can I assume the prisoner had provided you with unpleasant information?"

He had been using Control Amnesia to gather just that.

Her master had practiced this quite a bit, but even for him, it took weeks just to skim the surface of memories lasting any length of time. Sorting carefully through the memories to find critical information could theoretically take years. And if he was adjusting those memories as he went, decades.

Many might assume examining memories would prevent false information, but what they learned was only what the individual believed to be true. It was quite possible for people to have simply been deceived.

Achieving any degree of certainty required searching the memories of multiple subjects, and nobody had time for that. Ultimately, her master said simpler means of gathering information were far more practical.

Same for memory manipulation.

For example, say he burned a village down and a surviving villager had the nerve to bear a grudge against him and sought the power to harm him— this was not possible, but for the sake of argument, assume they achieved it.

If they removed the villager's memories of who had burned the village, did that solve the problem and turn the villager into a useful tool? No. While on his quest for power, he had likely told someone he was out for revenge—and unless all such moments were eliminated, the villager would notice the inconsistencies.

In other words, the villager might not remember his village burning down, but he would remember saying, "An undead named Ainz burned my village down," over drinks.

Here, the prisoner was unconscious, and this was merely a useful way to gather some information ahead of time.

"——Shalltear."

That word was enough for Albedo.

"......Who is the prisoner with?"

"......Albedo."

"Lord Ainz." She bent a knee.

"Everyone not required for Nazarick defense can put aside their current line of work. We will invade and destroy the Theocracy at once. They started the fight; we'll finish it. Agreed?"

His tone was gentle. But the emotions behind it were the polar opposite. She could not remember the last time he'd been so angry.

"——Indeed. As you say. I'll send word to all floor guardians and have them prepare."

"Good. Get to it, Albedo. Now."

His kind tone made her shiver. Albedo bowed low.

OVERLORD
Character Profiles

Character 64

Antilene Heran Fouche

Humanoid

The Black Scripture's Additional Seat
No Death–No Life

Residence	Within the Sanctuary in the Theocracy capital, Silksuntechs
Birthday	Would rather not say
Hobby	Throwing coin around, buying new things (food or fashion) to see what they're like

Class Levels	
Fighter	10 lv
Berserker	10 lv
Master Fighter	10 lv
Lesser Walküre/Almighty	5 lv
Weapon Master	7 lv
Rogue	1 lv
Assassin	5 lv
Executioner	10 lv
Cleric	10 lv
High Cleric	10 lv
Inquisitor	10 lv

[Race levels] + [Class levels] ——————— 88 levels
● Race levels   Class levels ●

0 acquired total   88 acquired total

Ordinarily, you can't acquire Walküre without meeting the prerequisite, but she makes that possible. However, that makes it a lesser class, less powerful than pure Walküre, and the ace move Einherjar is weaker, too.

At great sacrifice and a great deal of data, it might be possible for natives of this world to ignore the prereqs and acquire Walküre proper. Just as some characters have Ninja despite not having the necessary levels.

But practically speaking, it's not really doable. Walküre is just that much harder to acquire than Ninja; even those beyond heroes can't readily obtain the lesser version, so obtaining the necessary sample pool is unreasonable.

Even with the support of someone well versed in *Yggdrasil* knowledge, it's unlikely anyone local will ever obtain the class.

In fact, over the centuries, the only native to obtain Walküre—albeit the lesser version—is No Death–No Life.

Upon acquiring your first level in Walküre, you pick a weapon specialty. But subsequent levels allow you to pick weapons of other attribute types—bludgeoning, cutting, stabbing—and master them. A Walküre who picked Lance at level 1 might pick cutting weapons at level 2, allowing them to use all weapons with the cutting attribute and lances. However, this also weakens their Einherjar.

No Death–No Life accepted this drawback, prioritizing mastery of all types of weapons—especially those wielded by the other Six Gods.

This is because the talent she was born with is a type of psychometry, and even with the diversification's downside, the upside of being able to use all those weapons outweighed it.

She can also use faith spells up to the third tier but hasn't relied on them much. Her main focus is healing wounds and curing status ailments, not making herself stronger. She was so strong that her prior fights never required it, and it never occurred to her that lack of experience there could be a weakness. A fatal error.

If she had used faith spells to buff herself, her close-quarters fight with Mare would not have been nearly as lopsided.

Character *65*

DECEM HOUGAN

HUMANOID

The Elf King

Occupation	Elf king
Residence	Elf Palace
Class Levels	Druid —————————— **?** lv
	High Druid —————————— **?** lv
	Summoner —————————— **?** lv
	Elementalist (Earth) —————————— **?** lv
Birthday	Rabbit 14
Hobby	Strengthening elves

{ personal character }

Royal blood is exalted, and gifting it should be a source of joy and gratitude. But he will not acknowledge the weak as his blood and frequently
sends his children off to die, so he had no surviving heirs. This did not go
down well with the elves, but they knew they could not win, so none dared
to openly confront him.

OVERLORD
Character Profiles

THE
FORTY-ONE
SUPREME
BEINGS

COMPILATION

13/41

DEATH SUZAKU

GROTESQUE

The Monster Professor

personal character

The guild's eldest member, he was a professor at a college managed by a megacorp in real life. He made little attempt to influence the guild's direction, preferring to let the others lead. This was because he was sick and tired of campus politics and needing to court the favor of businessmen and students alike. That being said, he did not always act the part of a calm and rational adult—he absolutely loved PvP. Had acquired the faith casting class Onmyouji. While he had a wide variety of spells, he was primarily an offensive caster.

Afterword

It's been far too long! I'm Maruyama.
Thank you for picking up this book and reading through it.

At the end of Volume 14, I wrote that 15 would be out in early spring, 2021, but that proved off by more than a year. But don't worry: 16 is right behind, so I hope that makes up for it.
Does it?
One volume a year…if I was a reader, I'd think that was a bit too slow, but hard to say what people feel unless you're them. I've become a lot more forgiving of other authors. I'm sure they're just busy! It happens.

Still, there was a *lot* going on. Everyone likes it when good things happen, but it feels like only bad things are. That said! There is a fourth season of the anime, which should be airing by the time this book comes out.
Honestly, I feel like that's about the only piece of good news I've had lately, but the fact that I have any might mean I'm lucky. If I had lots of upbeat things to share, that would be ideal, but sadly, that's about it.
But hooray for the fourth season!
This is all thanks to your support.

*   *   *

Overlord will be complete in two more volumes. Just stick with me a little longer. I'm afraid even I don't know how many years that will take.

But if I can manage it, I'm hoping the gaps between them will be a little smaller than this one. Still, preparing them will take some time. At the very least, I can promise that I'm trying to get them out faster.

Finally, I'd like to express my deepest gratitude to everyone who helped get *Overlord* Volume 15 and Volume 16 out.

Later!

June 2022

KUGANE MARUYAMA

Afterword by so-bin

THE SCHEDULE DEMANDS I DO THIS AFTERWORD NOW, BUT THE ILLUSTRATIONS TOOK ALL THE BEST MOMENTS. I CAN'T THINK OF WHAT TO DRAW HERE! THE VOLUME 16 COVER WAS ABSOLUTELY BRUTAL, BUT I THINK IT TURNED OUT OKAY? NORMALLY, CENTERING IT AROUND A CUTE KID WOULD BE FUN, BUT WITH OVERLORD, MONSTER COVERS ARE ALWAYS EASIER. BUT THIS WAS THE REQUEST, SO I HAD NO CHOICE!

FIN

So-bin

HAVE YOU BEEN TURNED ON TO LIGHT NOVELS YET?

86—EIGHTY-SIX, VOL. 1–11

In truth, there is no such thing as a bloodless war. Beyond the fortified walls protecting the eighty-five Republic Sectors lies the "nonexistent" Eighty-Sixth Sector. The young men and women of this forsaken land are branded the Eighty-Six and, stripped of their humanity, pilot "unmanned" weapons into battle...

Manga adaptation available now!

WOLF & PARCHMENT, VOL. 1–6

The young man Col dreams of one day joining the holy clergy and departs on a journey from the bathhouse, Spice and Wolf. Winfiel Kingdom's prince has invited him to help correct the sins of the Church. But as his travels begin, Col discovers in his luggage a young girl with a wolf's ears and tail named Myuri, who stowed away for the ride!

Manga adaptation available now!

SOLO LEVELING, VOL. 1–8

E-rank hunter Jinwoo Sung has no money, no talent, and no prospects to speak of—and apparently, no luck, either! When he enters a hidden double dungeon one fateful day, he's abandoned by his party and left to die at the hands of some of the most horrific monsters he's ever encountered.

Comic adaptation available now!

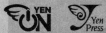